EVIDENCE

BOOKS BY NEIL RAVIN

M.D.
Informed Consent
Seven North

EVIDENCE

NEIL RAVIN

CHARLES SCRIBNER'S SONS

NEW YORK

This is a work of fiction. Names, characters, places and
incidents are either the product of the author's imagination or are
used fictitiously. Any resemblance to actual persons, living or
dead, or to actual events or locales is entirely coincidental.

Library of Congress Cataloging-in-Publication Data

Ravin, Neil.
Evidence.

I. Title.
PS3568.A84E9   1987   813'.54   87-4912
ISBN 0-684-18768-X

Published simultaneously in Canada by Collier Macmillan Canada, Inc.
Composition by Westchester Book Composition, Yorktown Heights, N.Y.
Manufactured by Fairfield Graphics, Fairfield, Pennsylvania
Designed by Christine Kettner
First Edition

FOR ARTHUR ZIMAN
and
FOR LOUIS RAVIN

"How godlike, how immortal is he? . . .
But the slave and prisoner of his own opinion of himself,
a fame won by his own deeds.
Public opinion is a weak tyrant
compared with our own private opinion.
What a man thinks of himself,
that it is which determines,
or rather indicates, his fate."

Henry David Thoreau

EVIDENCE

AUTHOR'S NOTE

No matter what I say, my stories are simply not taken as fiction in some quarters. William Borroughs named my novel *M.D.* as one of his favorite nonfiction pieces. Letters have arrived from doctors in hospitals I never knew existed complaining or congratulating me for my depiction of their institutions. Editors assure me I ought to take all this as high praise.

And in a sense, I've asked for it. Certain stories deserve to be told straight, served neat and unencumbered. They carry enough weight on their own, without my adding to the load.

So if it "rings true," I take my editors' advice and feel satisfied.

I placed this story in Washington, D.C., and environs because this is where I live. There is no St. George's Hospital in Washington, D.C., and to my knowledge no department of surgery in Washington, D.C., has ever had the particular problem depicted here, although the problem of what to do with a faltering surgeon is not an uncommon one. Every couple of years I hear of a case that sounds in some respects like that of Dr. Thomas McIlheny (who is, let me hasten to add, a fictional character, a product of my own rambling imagination). The ways in which the Dr. McIlhenys of the world are dealt with vary within institutions, and it is never easy. But the story told here is not meant to recount a specific case. I have no inclina-

3

tion to discuss real-life cases. Real-life cases are always embedded in circumstances beyond my control.

The difficulties doctors have policing their profession continue and will always be with us, and the solutions do not often make headlines.

It's usually a case of a very imperfect system righting itself and ultimately getting the job done.

CHAPTER

1

What a lovely instrument, the retrospectroscope. Also known as hindsight is twenty-twenty. Through it diagnoses can almost always be seen clearly—or at least they appear in better focus. It's highly regarded for its accuracy, although questions have been raised about its usefulness.

Looking through one now, I can see that the first signs and symptoms of what was pullulating in St. George's in the autumn of that year were evident that third week of September, the night I was writing my note on a patient in the surgical intensive care unit, locally called the SICU, listening to Bill Ryan's opinions about womanhood and the department of surgery.

It was late, past midnight anyway, and the air in the SICU was crisp from the laminar flow system, and there was the racy feel you sometimes get those hours in a hospital when people are too busy to be tired, when they are excited to be cogs in something spinning.

Patients were rolled right out of the operating rooms to the SICU and kept there until they were stable. If they got into trouble on any of the surgical wards with postoperative complications, they wound up in the SICU.

The nurses who worked there saw all the mistakes of surgeon and nature coming at them, and, man and nature being what they are, most nights there was plenty coming at them.

This particular night Ryan was supposed to be writing a note about some bacteria or another found growing in the blood and spinal fluid of some surgical Great Case. But he was more engrossed in elucidating for me the finer points of a brown-eyed, red-haired nurse with skin tanned copper who was looking very good in her blue scrub dress.

I was trying to concentrate, but I was not inspired by the note I was writing and I was being distracted by Ryan and by the redhead he was currently appreciating. Her name was Maureen. I couldn't see the last name on her nameplate.

Finally I put my chart down and looked at Ryan's redhead. Then I tried to read some more, but I kept drifting back to her.

What had me watching her was the way she was going over her patient in the stall across from us.

Her patient had tubes coming out of every orifice, and out of a few other places besides, the way post-op patients often do. He had monitors beeping and flashing lights were going off on his console. Nurse Maureen was jumping around checking all the tubes and bags, and she was looking at his hemovac, with the thoracotomy tube from his lung draining into it, when the tube went from white to bloodred and the hemovac filled with blood before you could gulp hard.

Hemovac tubes drain the chest cavity and they do not fill with blood unless the chest is filling with blood. Suddenly, and without invitation.

The nurse said, "Aw, give me a break," as if she'd just run her stocking. Then she called to the nurse at the next stall, "Call a code. He's blowing open." There was more alarm in that, but she wasn't shaken. She was too busy.

I got up and walked over to see what I could do. Ryan was

6

behind me, saying, "Jesus, Abrams, what are you going to do, open his chest?"

I didn't have a chance. Residents and anesthesiologists came flying from everywhere. I remember wondering where all those people came from at that hour. Hospitals function at night, but with skeleton staff, and the room was full of people, all looking more than just awake—pumped up, frenetic, downright panicked, some of them. And I wondered, Why are all these people working so hard? He hasn't got a snowball's chance in hell.

Then Ann Payson materialized. Ann had the capacity to do that, to just appear out of nowhere. The nurse, Maureen, said something to her I didn't catch, but I saw Ann point to the door to the operating room suite. Amid all the residents calling for IVs and Ambou bags and things, she said not very loudly but with perfect clarity and poise, "Let's go. Now."

And they had the patient roaring out of there, launched.

I went back to my note on my own patient, who was nowhere nearly as exciting. I sat down and waited for my pulse and respiratory rate to drop to only twice normal, and watched Ryan.

Ryan was staring dreamily off at the door Ann had flown through, along with the patient. He said, "Oh, she doth teach torches to burn bright. Does she not?"

My chair was about four feet from the sink and coffee niche, where the redheaded nurse Maureen and her friend who had called the code had retreated to collect themselves. The friend handed Maureen a cup of coffee and lit her a cigarette. Maureen's face was tight now. She waved off the offerings. She sat on her metal stool crossing her legs, shifting her weight, hugging herself with her own arms, holding herself together. She had functioned so smoothly and calmly during the action—now it all seemed to be hitting her and she was trying hard not to come unhinged.

Maureen said, "That fucking asshole. Who told him he was a surgeon?"

I remember those words exactly, because Maureen had a very

7

sweet face and she didn't look like she had that kind of stuff in her. Ryan was listening to her now with a sort of rapt appreciation, and me with him.

"Watch your mouth, Maureen," said her friend, looking around as if the Thought Police might arrive at any moment. "He's the boss now."

"He's not *my* boss. They didn't make him chief of nursing."

"Just keep your voice down." Her friend's voice was an urgent whisper. "Just keep it down."

"He's an asshole," Maureen reasserted. "And he's a piss poor surgeon."

The other nurse said, "He'll be all right. Ann Payson was right here."

The redhead said, "Know what fat chance means, lady? Did you see that hemovac? He must've had a liter of blood in there. He had a chest full of blood in no time. Suture must have slipped off something big. What's Ann going to be able to do? He fucked up good this time and where was he? Nobody'll be able to pull him out now. Not even Ann."

"She'll do it."

Maureen said, "We gotta do something. This just isn't right."

Now, looking back, that exchange probably should have caught my attention. A doctor ought to pick up on things, even if he is preoccupied.

Being preoccupied is a bad habit of mine. Not that that's any excuse, I realize. I spent a lot of that month and the next one preoccupied, missing connections, things that through the clarity of the retrospectroscope seem unmistakable now.

8

CHAPTER

2

There were no more surprises that night. All the routines of the SICU settled back into place. Ryan settled into his routines on women. I went on writing my note and trying to ignore him.

Ryan was very taken with the women who worked on the SICU. Ryan was very taken with women in general and tended to follow them around like a puppy, which did his social life no great harm. I had known him from Johns Hopkins, where he was doing his fellowship in Infectious Diseases and I was doing mine in Endocrine. He had cut a wide swath there, but his romantic life didn't distract him from his academic obligations, and he had published some work on infections seen in homosexuals that paved the way for the elucidation of AIDS as a distinct syndrome.

It was work a professor would have parlayed into tenure at most places. Ryan had done it all as a postgraduate Fellow. Between dates and drinks. A few too many drinks.

He and I had drifted separately downstream and each of us implanted in Washington, D.C., Ryan as a member of the division of infectious diseases, St. George's University Hospital, which is to say full-time faculty, and me into private practice.

Ryan, watching the women gliding around the SICU, looked very much as Moses must have looked when he first gazed upon the promised land.

I was glad he was now focused on the redhead. It got him off the topic of Ann Payson. He was concerned I didn't appreciate Ann as a woman because she was a surgeon and she was bright and didn't try to hide it, which in a department full of Southern males did her no good at all.

"Ann can take care of herself," I said. "Besides, the department's changing now, with the new chief."

"Would have changed a whole lot quicker and better if they'd made her chief."

I couldn't argue with that.

Ryan was sure that Ann was languishing, which disturbed Ryan because she was kind and she was smart and she was damn good-looking.

"It's not her fault she's smarter than your typical surgical asshole —which is probably why they didn't make her chief," said Ryan. "She needs someone to grab her occasionally."

"Then ask her out," I said. "Do her a favor."

"Oh, no," he said. "I'm not her type. But somebody will eventually," he said. "If you don't. Maybe this new chief."

He was right about Ann, of course, but I didn't want to listen to it. Ryan felt I didn't appreciate the finer things in life. And Ann Payson was definitely one of the finer things. Before the patient who blew apart and got launched, Ann had been into the SICU briefly to look at another patient whose heart she had just repaired.

We sat there watching her. She felt the pulses, listened to the heart, and adjusted some things on the monitors, and we followed every move. She was tall and strong for a woman but undersized as thoracic surgeons go. Her scrub mask dangled from her neck and she had removed her scrub hat, so you could see her hair.

I liked her hair. It was chestnut colored with gray streaks that were very becoming, and she wore it up in a twist on top of her head. Her skin still had a summer tan, which made her eyes look bluer.

She looked over at us staring at her from our post near the chart rack and she smiled, and Ryan beamed back and waved and just about wagged his tail and barked.

Ann laughed at him. As I said, the ladies liked Ryan. I liked Ryan. How could you not like Ryan?

But I was glad he was talking about someone else now.

He went on in a near whisper about the redhead. She was Catholic schools straight through, which meant you had to wonder about her. Catholic women, according to Ryan, were bound to be interesting.

"They're the only people left with anything to rebel against," he said.

I was trying to decipher the chart notes against the background of these ruminations. I had a patient with a gangrenous gall bladder, diabetes, and a bad heart, but he had chugged right through surgery, amazing everyone. Now his metabolic machinery had done what everyone was expecting it to do all along. He had crashed right into diabetic ketoacidosis postoperatively. They had already started insulin, saline, potassium, and everything he needed, but I like to make myself available to surgeons, in general. When you need a surgeon, you really need one, and I always like to do little ingratiating things where surgeons are concerned. As the surgical attending in this case was Ann Payson, I made myself infinitely available.

"I'm sorry to drag you in so late," Ann had said when she woke me up with the late phone call. "But you know if anything happens, the lawyers will be crawling all over me for not having an internist in here managing his sugar and things."

"No problem," I had said.

Ann had done everything right for this guy. He was an out-and-out save, and he owed what chance he had for life to Ann. But if he didn't make it, he wouldn't be around to testify in Ann's behalf, and his wife and her lawyers might not see it that way.

* * *

11

So there I was, sharing my malpractice premiums with Ann Payson, listening to Bill Ryan, and watching the show on the SICU. The best late-night entertainment in town. But when I finally finished my note and stood up and tucked the patient's chart back into the chart rack and walked off the unit, I still felt vaguely uneasy. Usually I got a nice soothing feeling at times like that— patient seen, note written, everyone tucked in for the night, home to bed. But there was a little nagging sensation that night, and it had to do with what the nurse had said. It had insinuated itself into my nose and sinuses and settled in the back of my throat. I skipped the elevator waiting open-doored outside the unit, took the stairs two at a time, and walked out briskly into the cool night air. The stars were out and it was a lovely night. I breathed it in deeply. But I couldn't clear away that feeling.

CHAPTER
3

The next morning I saw two patients in the office: a male barber with enlarging breasts and an eighty-four-year-old lady with constipation and a worried daughter. I didn't like the belly exam on the old lady. Her daughter brought her in unannounced, and I was trying to leave to get to my downtown clinic and really didn't have time to go over her carefully. But it turned out she had more than constipation and I couldn't be sure exactly what—appendix, colon cancer, garden variety senile dwindles. I drew a blood count, sent her for a belly X ray, and told her to call me if she didn't get better.

After I finished with her, I started to leave for my clinic when Mrs. Bromley, my secretary, stepped in.

Mrs. Bromley always knows just where I am supposed to be, and she was about to remind me about the clinic, but for once I was a step ahead of her.

"I don't know why you go to that bloody clinic," she said.

That was strong language for Mrs. Bromley, who is English, indispensable, and knows more about life in general and in partic-

13

ular than I can ever hope to know. Right now she was about to launch into her pre-clinic speech about the economic indefensibility of my spending time there instead of seeing patients in the office.

"It's an outrage," Mrs. Bromley said in her most scandalized tones. "My mechanic makes more hourly in his garage than they pay you for that clinic. And it's not as if we don't have enough patients to fill the time here at the office since you've become a star."

"I am hardly a star, Mrs. Bromley."

"Full professor, star, call it what you like."

"I am no smarter now than I was a month ago."

"Ah, but the patients don't know that. And now you have important friends."

"One important friend."

"That's all you need," she said. "The rest will fall into line."

The friend, Dennis Rallston, had just been made chief of medicine at St. George's University Hospital. We had become blood brothers by suffering through internship together a dozen years before. Since his appointment I'd been asked to speak at grand rounds, to hold conferences, and for advice on all sorts of matters about which I knew nothing.

About the same time I'd had some luck stumbling into diagnoses on some patients where others had gone astray, and the patients happened to be title holders in the current administration. That is apparently all you need in Washington to establish credibility as a big-time doctor—big-name patients—as if they know any more about who the good doctors are than anyone else.

So my name was recently in lights, as Mrs. Bromley liked to say. The *Washington* magazine is hardly lights in my book, but the patients kept pouring in and the schedule book was full and there was a three-week wait for new patient appointments, so the clinic downtown looked more and more expendable to the keen and unforgiving eye of Mrs. Bromley.

The particular low-paying job about which Mrs. Bromley was so

14

exercised wasn't too taxing—physical exams on bus drivers. They also intermittently coerced me into protecting the bus-riding public of Washington, D.C., from the occasional bus driver who couldn't face his day without a morning jolt of angel dust, cocaine, or heroin.

"Why do you persist in this clinic? Tell me once a single coherent explanation, and I will never again raise the topic."

"Because they pay me so little and treat me so indifferently and it's good for a doctor to be humble. They keep me humble at this clinic."

"A lack of humility has never been your problem. A lack of money has been a problem, however, and from that standpoint the clinic doesn't make any sense whatsoever."

She was right, of course. It wasn't like my inner-city clinic. I could defend that one because there I was taking care of the poor and destitute, which doctors aren't supposed to do anymore. This was the bus company employee clinic, where I was working for the company, not for the drivers, and it would have to go. I simply hadn't had time to adjust to being in demand. And I hadn't been able to believe it would last.

The drive to the bus company clinic always depressed me. It was seven miles, no turns. Get on Massachusetts Avenue in the upscale part of town and keep going, past the embassies with their tended hedges and shiny limousines, their bright flags stretching in the September breezes, around bronzed Phil Sheridan on horseback leading a charge across from the Turkish embassy, go past Dupont Circle, teeming with young executives dressed for success mixing with the black men playing chess and homosexuals on the make; across the great divide of Seventh Street where it continues on as New York Avenue and things get trashy, bums lie on the sidewalks, and men congregate outside corner liquor stores stooping and shifting and holding bottles in paper bags, where you begin to worry about sharp objects in the road and flat tires, where even the police cars drive around with their windows rolled up and the doors locked. I always got a dull, dead feeling about the time the warehouses and railroad yards came into view, heading past them, past the run-down motels the city uses for homeless shelters and the hookers use for business premises—big-legged, tight-skirted ladies of the freeway standing by the roadside, with toddlers playing in the parking lots behind them. The part of Washington they don't show on postcards. A very nice side of town. The side to which nothing ever trickles down except AIDS and smack and bullets from Saturday night specials.

I turned left at Bladensburg Road and into the fenced-in compound surrounding the clinic.

That morning the bus company's drug program man stuck his grizzled head in the door and said, "Got a post-incident for ya, Doc."

"I need this," I said. "I really need to start off my day like this."

He shrugged, smiled his gap-tooth smile, and pulled his head out the door. He knew I hated the post-incidents. Every time a driver ran his bus into a wall or off the road, they'd drag him in for blood and urine tests for alcohol and drugs. For the drivers, it was adding insult to injury. For me, it was a complicated procedure of sealing specimens and signing evidence forms in a hundred places, and it made me feel like a cop instead of a doctor.

They had the driver in the examining room, stripped to his underpants, sitting on the exam table. His name was Lydell Brown. I had met him once a few months before when he came back to work after having twisted an ankle and needed a doctor's okay. He had twisted the ankle playing basketball, so we got talking about basketball. It turned out he was one of those people colleges hire to play for them and then discard once the TV revenues are in the bank. I had seen him play in the NCAA championship, and he was something to watch. They interviewed him after the game, and he could speak passable English, but it turned out he couldn't read so well. After the championship was secure, the university discovered that it could not put its academic seal on his diploma because he hadn't seen much point in going to class.

"I was a fucking asshole," he said. "'Scuse the language, Doc."

16

Lydell Brown had felt he had been given a golden opportunity to better himself among the elm-shaded lawns of a big-name university, and all he'd done was go to work, which is to say, he went to the gym and neglected his studies. The bus company forgave him and gave him a job.

"'Bout all I'm good for," he said. "Drivin' bus. But my coach say he got me a tryout with the Bullets, we win the City."

He played for some city league now, which I gathered was the basketball equivalent of being a club fighter.

He was a clear-skinned black man, with the blue-green eyes you see not infrequently in Washington blacks, and a big muscular build. The easy talk and engaging smile I'd seen before were gone now. He wasn't here for a chat about his twisted ankle and near-pro basketball career now. He was trying hard to look irate, mostly for the benefit of his supervisor, who sat stone-faced by the wall on a stool, staring like a dead man at the opposite wall. The supervisors hated the post-incident procedure even more than I did—they had to ride all the way into the clinic with the drivers, listening to the denials and expressions of indignation the whole way.

Lydell said, "Man, I can't believe this. What they doing this to me for?"

I said, "They do it to everyone, Mr. Brown, after any accident involving a bus."

Lydell said, "This is ridiculous, man."

He never once looked me in the eye and kept his stare pretty much on the floor, flitting a look over to his supervisor now and then.

"I got a good mind to call the union," he said.

That made about as much of an impression on his supervisor as the fly does to the horse's tail.

Lydell Brown had needle tracks, fresh and old, on both arms, and his pupils were constricted.

I asked him about the needle marks.

"Oh," he said. "Got 'em climbin' a tree."

He said that with about as much conviction as the wino who says

17

he wants the quarter for a square meal. He was just going through the motions, hoping for a break. He knew I knew, but he was hoping if he denied and denied, the union could get him off with a suspension.

I told him to go into the bathroom and fill the cup with urine.

The supervisor said, "Leave the door open."

"Whaffo?"

"So's I can see you're not putting no water in the urine," said the supervisor. "It's the rules."

Lydell Brown said, "This is degrading, you know. The company treats you like a criminal."

"Degrading" was a favorite union word for the drug-screening procedure.

The supervisor said nothing. He kept his eyes on the wall in front of him, seeing if he could bring it down by sheer intensity of concentration.

"Always on your back," said Lydell Brown, looking at the urine cup. "They use you. You understand what I'm saying?"

"I understand," I said.

I understood perfectly. He was guilty as hell and I was elected to nod through his act. Lydell Brown, ex-campus hero, soon to be ex-bus driver, caught in the rules, going down again. I'd seen this performance so many times before, but something about Lydell's interpretation of the role affected me. Maybe because I heard him hold himself responsible for bouncing out of college, I had the feeling he wasn't really capable of convincing himself any of this was anybody's fault but his own. He wasn't the type who would think that he was shooting up because of all the injustice in the world. He was just playing what cards he had, and he didn't particularly like his hand.

"I know how you feel," I said.

He walked into the bathroom adjoining the exam room and filled the cup with urine. He handed it over, and I sealed it and dumped it in the plastic bag. He sat on the exam table.

It wasn't easy finding a vein Lydell Brown hadn't already used and ruined, but I eventually felt one on the back of his hand. He

18

flinched when I hit it, but I managed to fill two blue-topped tubes with blood for drug screens.

The company drug program man was in the hallway when I came out with the plastic bag with all the specimens. He was a big chocolate man with massive arms and a weary, battered face. I asked him what had happened to Lydell Brown.

He shook his head and summoned up his raspy voice. "Ran his bus into one of those concrete dividers, Doc. Fifteen people on the bus. Didn't go off the bridge, but came damn close."

"I can see why."

"Alcohol on his breath?"

"Tracks."

"New tracks?"

"Old and new. Pupils constricted. He's on something. Heroin for starters. I don't know what else."

Lydell opened the door to the examining room, dressed in his uniform. "I'm held off, Doc?"

"'Fraid so, Mr. Brown. Until the drug tests come back."

"This is just degrading, you know," Lydell Brown said again, with as much feeling as Jimmy Hoffa pleading the Fifth.

"When the results come out?"

"One or two days."

"And I can't work until then?"

"No."

"Shit, Doc. What am I going to do? Sit home?"

I shrugged.

"It all depends on the results of the tests," growled the company man.

"I want to talk to the union. I want to call 'em," said Lydell. He didn't sound aggrieved anymore, or hostile, and there was none of his fainthearted attempt at toughness. He was pretty nearly licked. He was on the short, swift slide out the door to the unemployment line. That can sober a man, make him claw to hang on.

"Can I call from here?"

"Use the phone in the front," the company man said, nodding toward the waiting room.

19

We watched him walk down the hall to the waiting room. His head retracted down into his chest, turtlelike. He seemed to shrivel in front of us.

"He thinks the union can get him off the hook, he'll be home free," said the company man. "But sooner or later he's going to have to pay the price."

CHAPTER

4

I told Mrs. Bromley about Lydell Brown when I got back to the office at five.

"You really must stop telling me about the bus drivers," she said. "You have ruined public transportation for me. I don't even drive near buses anymore, much less ride on them."

"Most of the drivers are solid citizens. They've got kids in school, mortgages. . . ."

"Then why do they have these drug-testing programs?"

"Because this is America, Mrs. Bromley. We have to keep the riffraff under surveillance."

"At least the riffraff who drive the buses, don't you think?"

"Well, there's an argument for that," I said. "Now that you mention it, I was thinking of asking you for some urine samples, every now and then."

"I'd be honored." Mrs. Bromley laughed. "Me and the riffraff."

"Drivers aren't riffraff. They're solid citizens, most of them."

"And then there are those with needle tracks up and down their arms."

"It's like doctors—you only hear the juicy stories. Want me to tell you about the twelve drivers who were overweight?"

"I want no more bus driver stories of any sort. I want to hear about all the patients you've seen in hospital. Private patients. Private patients who pay their bills."

"People don't go to the hospital anymore. It costs too much."

"What about Mr. Crutchfield on the SICU?"

"He's okay now. They're getting ready to discharge him. I won't have to see him again."

"You just broke your own rule."

Mrs. Bromley knew all my rules. She knew them better than I did. Sometimes I think she made a few of her own, then quoted them to me to guide my thinking. The particular rule she was referring to was Abrams's fifth rule: Never to say a patient is doing well and can be expected to be going home soon. As soon as you say that you invite disaster. Doing well is a retrospective diagnosis.

"You're right," I said. "But he really is. He's just about home."

A huge heap of mail was stacked on my desk, and I began going through it. That was the signal for Mrs. Bromley to retire to her station and leave me alone. She had mercy and did just that. It had been a tough day, and on days like that I needed to sit down and do something mindless and repetitive.

Mrs. Bromley killed the joy of opening mail. She plucked out anything that looked as if it might contain a check and slit it open, entering the payment into our ledger system, which only she understood. If the envelope also contained an insurance form to be filled out, I got that. There were good and efficiency-related reasons for doing things this way—when I opened envelopes, we somehow lost checks—but I missed the sight of them.

This morning, there were only three letters addressed "Dear Doctor": one inviting me to invest in a new municipal bond, one offering a cruise to Maui masquerading as a course in plastic surgery, and one inviting me to be the first doctor in my building to own a book by Mr. Malpractice himself, Melvin Belli, promising to let me in on all the tricks malpractice lawyers use to trip up

22

doctors. There was a special bulk rate for the book, in case I wanted to send copies to all my partners in crime.

When I had enough of the mail, I answered phone calls. I had a stack of phone messages right next to the stack of letters—calls from patients who wanted antibiotic prescriptions without throat cultures, calls from patients I hadn't seen for years who wanted prescriptions renewed but who didn't want to pay for office visits. Patients who should have known better—college professors, diplomats, subcabinet officers, people who had gone to college and not on basketball scholarships, people who were supposed to be well educated. People who were trying to manipulate the system, as if the visit to the doctor's office was just another bureaucratic formality to be got around. Blood pressure management by telephone without the benefit of blood pressure measurement.

These were the people who made the rules, who knew how systems worked. Washington is all about systems that are supposed to be made to work. Federal systems, local government systems, workplace systems. Systems like the one that caught Lydell Brown at his drug habit. It was a government town. A town where people jumped through hoops for government at every level—citizens breathed into breath analyzers held by city cops at "sobriety check points," and citizens took their lie detector tests, and citizens peed into little plastic cups. If you have nothing to fear, you have nothing to hide. George Orwell couldn't have said it better.

I leaned back in my chair, put my feet up on my desk, and looked at the diplomas covering the walls of my office. A damned impressive wall. Every time you pass a test in the medical profession, they give you a diploma to frame. It's a nice little custom. I wondered if they'd start testing my urine and if they'd give me a diploma if I passed.

I swung my feet to the floor and grabbed my jacket and walked out past Mrs. Bromley on the way to the door.

She looked up. "What? Leaving? And you've only just arrived."

"I've had it," I said.

23

"Oh, come now," she said. "I thought you were having great fun being surly on the phone."

"It grows old."

"Everything grows old," said Mrs. Bromley. "Just be happy that you are in a profession where the older you get the more they trust you."

"The more who trusts you?" I asked.

"Everyone."

"Everyone trusts me now," I said. "I am a physician. If you can't trust doctors, who can you trust?"

CHAPTER

5

Of course, I was called in to see Mr. Crutchfield late that same night. He decided to slip back into ketoacidosis without my permission, just to remind everyone he could do it anytime. Getting dressed to go in to the SICU in the black night I excoriated myself for having violated the fifth rule and shook my head at my own folly the entire drive in. You don't spit into the wind, you don't tug on Superman's cape, and you don't mess around with Abrams's fifth rule.

I was planted on the SICU by 2:00 A.M.

"Well, look what the cat dragged in," said a voice from behind me.

I didn't jump more than three feet. I hadn't been aware of anyone being there, except the patients and the nurses moving in and out of the shadows.

I turned around to discover the pink face of Bill Ryan. "Did I startle you?" he said ingenuously, watching me collect myself.

"Someday you're going to do that and I'm going to arrest right in

25

front of you and you're going to have to resuscitate me. Cardiac arrest, Ryan. You're going to have to save me."

"I do not do arrests anymore. I'd call a consult," said Ryan cheerfully. "I am what you call a subspecialist."

"And all this time I thought you were a real doctor," I said.

"Real doctors save lives and make money," said Ryan. "I just write notes and publish papers."

Ryan was on the full-time faculty. He got paid his salary whether or not he rallied to see patients at dark hours. But Ryan always rallied, despite his protestations to the contrary. He always came in, never handled things over the phone, just the way he'd been taught at all the prestigious places he'd trained.

"What brings you out at this hour?" Ryan demanded. "You're supposed to be wearing three-hundred-dollar suits, driving flashy cars, and never setting foot in the hospital after five p.m." This last little bit about the fat life of private practitioners was our little routine. We had gone through a similar litany the night before on the SICU, before Ryan went into his routine on women of the SICU, and before his Ann Payson-needs-a-man speech.

"Why's that?" I said, giving him his cue.

"You're in private practice," said Ryan happily. "Golf on Wednesdays. Lunch at the Jockey Club."

"You've been reading the Washington *Post* again."

"Christ, not that. But I watch TV."

"I am here on business," I said, dredging up my best brave and dutiful tone. "I have a consult. I am delighted to be here."

Ryan laughed raucously, unseemly for anyone, especially for a physician of some repute, especially on the SICU.

He said, "No consult after midnight is a good thing."

It was one of those lines we all knew from internship. Ryan still said things like that. He was one of those people who could look back on internship with a certain amount of nostalgia. Ryan could look back on the Tet offensive with a certain amount of nostalgia.

"In private practice we are eternally grateful for any consult, at any time," I said. "You guys on salary can bitch. I smile, and say,

'Thank you, sir. Thank you so much for calling me in here at one in the morning.'"

Ryan smiled his big dimpled smile that got him whatever he wanted from the nurses. "That's what I love about academic life. I get called after midnight, I can bitch."

"But you still come in."

"But I still come in," he said, looking as if he had just tasted what he ate for dinner, and he didn't like it the first time he ate it.

"For me, it's business, big boy," I said. "It pays the rent. It pays the country club dues."

"You got country club dues now?"

"I got dreams, actually. Not country clubs."

Ryan looked over the chart I was working on to see the purple stamp with the patient's name and the name of his admitting doctor.

"Who's the surgeon?"

"Ann Payson."

Ryan's pink face brightened, eyebrows flying. "I'd come in for her, anytime. She call you herself?"

"Her resident called me."

"That doesn't sound like Ann."

"She doesn't even know yet. I told the resident not to wake her."

"You are a profoundly nice guy."

"I'll let you write the note, if you're good," I said.

"Only if I get to talk to Ann about it in the morning." Ryan stood up. "In fact, I'll go over to her place right now and discuss it in person. I'm available to discuss anything in person with her at any time. Preferably at her place after a bottle of wine."

"You're a dedicated doctor, Ryan. I knew it all along."

"Fuck you, Abrams," he said, grinning. "You got Ann Payson sending you business I won't feel sorry for you. I thought you were in here bailing out some turkey gobbler surgeon."

"What gobblers? This is the St. George's University Hospital."

"Even here, big boy. Perhaps especially here. In surgery, that is."

27

"But they hired the man who wrote the book to straighten things out."

"Yeah, the man who wrote the book."

"Well, he's got a big job. Don't expect him to turn the place into the Mass General overnight."

"He's not going to turn this place into anything, ever, except maybe the late, great St. George's. They should've made Ann Payson chief. But no, that was too obvious."

"Ann's a little young to be chief."

"How old was Halsted when they made him chief?"

I had no idea how old Halsted had been when he started the famous department of surgery at Johns Hopkins.

I said, "Maybe she was too female."

"Too good, more likely," said Ryan. "But despite all that, the word is everybody would have backed her except a couple of old farts who swing the weight around here."

"You're very well informed about politics in the department of surgery."

"I live here, big boy," said Ryan. "Not like you private turkeys. I'm on staff. I talk to people."

"Maybe Ann didn't want the job."

"Maybe Roosevelt never wanted to be president," said Ryan. "Course, she couldn't go out and campaign for it. But she was the obvious choice. Trust the morons in the dean's office to select a search committee guaranteed to bring in some overstuffed honcho from the outside."

Ryan stood up, face sour, thinking of the morons in the dean's office and the search committee who had been chosen to recommend names for chief of surgery. Then he smiled as if we'd been chatting about nothing more important than last night's Orioles' game, and walked out.

I popped into the patient's stall and went over him, and when I came back out to finish my note a surgeon was sitting nearby writing his own note on another patient.

He sat tall in the saddle, a white-haired man, lean as a rake,

28

wearing a blue scrub suit under an immaculate white lab coat. I
looked at him out of the corner of my eye. He was absorbed in his
note. I could have sat in his lap and I don't think he'd have
noticed. He really looked like a surgeon. Even in tennis shorts
and a T-shirt he would have looked like a surgeon. His father
would have been a surgeon, and all his brothers. He would have
operated on his own sick puppy at age ten. He would have pulled
the puppy through. His father would have smiled and patted him
on the head and known he had another born surgeon on his
hands. That's about all I could get from a cursory inspection.

We sat there side by side writing and I became absorbed in my
note until I heard him say, "Up this late? You're tough enough to
be a surgeon."

That was one of those things surgeons like to say. Only surgeons
get up in the middle of the night to save patients. I guess if you
have to do it as much as surgeons do, you might as well make a
virtue of it.

"I can write this note in my sleep," I said. "Surgeon's up to his
elbows in someone's belly, he has to stay awake. No, I couldn't be
a surgeon."

He laughed a dry little laugh. He liked that.

"Staying awake's not the hard part," he said. "Thinking's the
hard part." He looked me over with a pair of very pale blue eyes,
the irises made more striking by the clarity of the whites of his eyes,
whites not at all injected or red-looking, despite the hour. His skin
was tight across his face. He had a hard, ascetic look, as if he ate a
hard-boiled egg for breakfast, a carrot for lunch, and slept on
cinder blocks without a pillow.

He said, "I don't believe we've met. Tom McIlheny."

He offered me a rock-hard hand, and I told him my name.
Then I said, "You're the new chief of surgery."

"That's right."

He looked pleased I knew who he was. I didn't know much
more about him at the time, other than his name, and that he was
a thoracic surgeon and the new chief. Ever since my first open-

29

heart case as a medical student, I've always felt like genuflecting or at least bowing once or twice in the presence of thoracic surgeons. Most abdominal or general surgery is surprisingly unexciting; everything very under control and plodding. But when they buzz through that sternum and crack open a chest and you're staring right down at a beating heart wriggling in front of you, and you watch them cut into those chambers and handle those arteries, you know where that "heart of a lion, eye of an eagle" stuff comes from. Whatever those thoracic surgeons make, they earn, as far as I'm concerned, and I'm a guy who thinks that a lot of doctors make too damn much, embarrassingly much. But not they who hold the hearts in their hands—they can have what they demand, if they can get you off the table alive.

Thomas McIlheny fit the mold of the heart surgeon right down to the clear eye and steady hand. But something was stirring in the creaking recesses of my mind, an image of the redheaded SICU nurse Maureen being hushed by her friend for her disparaging remarks about a surgeon. What had she said? I realized I was staring blankly at McIlheny. I couldn't recall, and I said hastily, "I'd have thought you'd have residents to write your notes for you, at two a.m."

He liked that, too. Of course he could have had residents doing his detail work for him. But here he was at nearly 2:00 A.M., and here I was to see it.

"The idea had crossed my mind. But try to get anything intelligible on paper from a resident after eight hours in the OR. At least if I write the note, I can read it the next morning and know what I meant."

"Don't think I ever saw the chief of surgery after midnight when I was a resident."

He liked that even better. He was suppressing a smile and he raised an eyebrow, "Where was that?"

"Hopkins."

"Hopkins?" he said, rolling that around his mouth. "Most of the internists around here seem to be local talent."

30

"It's an inbred place."

"You know what they say about inbreeding?" he said, watching me closely. "It's a good way to breed idiots."

Coming from a newly hired chief, that was an interesting remark. Especially since he didn't know me. It's the kind of remark that could get you a reputation. I was trying to decide if I was supposed to agree with him or if I was supposed to rise to St. George's defense when he asked, "Are you full time or private practice?"

"Private."

"Interesting. Most of the high-powered guys here are private."

I said, "I don't know how high-powered I am."

"Hopkins qualifies as high-powered."

I didn't know what to say. I knew some pretty good docs who had come up through St. George's from medical school through residency.

"I trained at Mass General, myself," he said. "Of course, that was in the dark ages."

Now, you have to understand, Mass General is the main Harvard teaching hospital. Telling me he trained there was like telling the local tennis pro you'd played Wimbledon in '09. I wasn't on the chairmanship selection committee, and besides, he already had the job. I wondered why he had trotted that out.

Then he said, "I wonder if you'd see a patient for me on Seven South?" And I realized what was going on.

It was like a secret handshake, and I was in the club. He'd said Mass General. I'd said Hopkins. I was okay. I had proper breeding, so now I got pulled out of the chorus line and had my big chance.

I asked him if the patient needed to be seen immediately.

He laughed. "No. You can sleep on this one. You don't have to try to be more compulsive than I am."

He stood up, looking absolutely unwrinkled and unblurry, despite the hour, and he shook my hand again. I stood there examining the high prominences of his cheekbones.

31

He said, "Nice to meet you," without making a move to go. Then, "Oh, Abrams."

"Yes?"

"Your tie's all crooked," he said, looking as if a spider were crawling down my neck. I straightened it reflexively and watched him march off the unit at 2:00 A.M., looking as pressed and fresh as a midshipman at morning inspection.

CHAPTER

6

The next morning I was feeling good, which had me worried. I never trust a good euphoria after a night of less than three hours' sleep. I knew it meant I was running on adrenaline and I'd crash around noon. But I was scheduled considerably beyond noon. I had three patients scheduled for the office between eight-thirty and ten; then I had to get to McIlheny's patient on Seven South before the attending Rounds I was scheduled to do with the residents.

Being asked to be an attending for the ward residents was a very big honor. Mrs. Bromley was most impressed. I had been chosen by the interns and residents as one of the private docs they'd decided wasn't completely senile. So for one month I drove in to St. George's to go over patients with them for which I was paid nothing and for which I had to rearrange my schedule for a month.

"But what a sign of esteem," Mrs. Bromley had said.

"Oh, yes, since becoming a star I am held in very high esteem. Ever notice how poverty and esteem seem wedded at universities? The job pays nothing."

"A good name is priceless," said Mrs. Bromley. "Just be back by two. You have four patients this afternoon. All new. They probably heard you were asked to do Rounds at St. George's and rushed to the phone to make appointments."

"I have to see Ann Payson's patient in the SICU after Rounds. What's his name again?"

"You can't recall? You spent until three this morning with him."

"I'm repressing it."

"You're feeling very sorry for yourself and you brought it on yourself. Crutchfield."

"There's no way I can do all that and be back here by two. The only thing that can save me will be if McIlheny's patient has a thin chart. I've always felt that medical consults should be charged on the basis of inches: charts less than half-an-inch thick, fifty dollars; between half an inch and an inch, seventy-five; and so on."

"I thought surgeons don't write much in their charts."

"You're right. There's hope. But there'll be lab results to get. If the computer's not down, and if there's a good clerk in the X-ray file room, I've got a chance."

But I had to get through with my office patients in good time, and Abrams's third law is that whenever you are in a hurry is when you should not be, and the patients were bound to be complicated and time-consuming.

The first was an airline stewardess who'd been sent in by her supervisor. I knew what she had as soon as she walked in the room. She was sent in because she had been having troubles with her complexion—oily skin, heavy sweating. Her supervisor, an old friend of mine from my sexually frenetic youth, when I had lucked into the friendly skies of an apartment full of stewardesses, had called me to say that one of her charges was getting ugly. She couldn't elaborate, but she thought this stewardess might have a "glandular problem," and damned if she didn't. You could see it in the enlargement of the tip of her nose and chin, the spaces between her teeth when she smiled, and you could feel it in her meaty handshake. She had a tumor in her pituitary gland pump-

34

ing out growth hormone, and she'd need surgery. She'd also need quite a lot of explanation, which I didn't have time for. But fortunately, she needed to have her diagnosis confirmed first, so I was able in good conscience to tell her I had to do some blood tests to confirm my suspicions before we did anything more.

"But do you think it's anything?" she asked.

"Yes. I think we'll be able to make a diagnosis with the blood tests."

"I sure hope so. I just can't live with my skin anymore."

Your skin is the least of your problems, I thought. She hadn't been able to fit her rings on her fingers and she'd gone up two shoe sizes in two years. And she was worried about her skin.

I drew her bloods and sent her out to see Mrs. Bromley to make a return appointment.

The next patient was the barber with the enlarging breasts. His blood tests showed an increased level of estrogen, but it wasn't obvious where it was coming from. Possibilities included a variety of malignancies, and I was trying hard not to say anything until I knew something for sure.

"But what could be doing this?" he asked. He was a short man with watery eyes and, now, with big breasts.

"There's a list as long as your arm, Mr. Costello. You're only going to have one thing on that list. Let's get some more test results before we start speculating."

"But why you want this CAT scan?"

"To look at your adrenal glands. That's where the problem is sometimes."

That's where the cancer is sometimes, but I hoped he wouldn't press that too hard right then. Patients have a way of telling you how much they really want to know. Mr. Costello didn't press me on what kind of problem might be in his adrenal glands.

"I been ashamed to undress in front of my wife," Mr. Costello was saying. "I got tits like a girl."

He said that with enough feeling to make me stare at him.

"We'll find out," I said.

35

"What you guys can do nowadays. I got a guy comes in for a scalp massage with a tonic grows hair. Guy's hair was so thin you could see his scalp right through. I been rubbing the tonic, now you should see. His doctor gives it to him."

"If there was anything that could grow hair, Mr. Costello, we'd all have bought stock in the company."

"But you should see this guy. His doctor gave him."

I sent him out to have Mrs. Bromley schedule his CAT scan. It was 10:00 A.M. I was on schedule.

The next patient was the eighty-four-year-old lady with the constipation and I-didn't-know-what. She had about as much use for young doctors poking around her belly as she had for long underwear in August. Her daughter said she was worse. I examined her. I told them I didn't know what she had.

"Well, at least he's honest," croaked the old lady. "But he's not much use."

I told them they ought to make an appointment with Ann Payson for a surgical opinion.

"I don't need a surgeon," barked the old woman. "I need a good stiff drink."

They gathered themselves up and left.

At ten-thirty I was ready to go to St. George's. I would just have time to see Dr. McIlheny's patient before ward rounds with the residents.

Mrs. Bromley waltzed in with a muted smile and said, "Thinking of running off to St. George's, were you?"

I was pulling off my white coat. "Yes, if you can hold down the fort."

"Not so fast. I have a friend of yours. Found him lurking about the waiting room. Claims to have an appointment."

"Tell me you're kidding. I'll forgive you."

"Mr. Samuel Sawyer."

Samuel Sawyer was my own Professor Henry Higgins and the father of my college roommate. He was the man who had rescued me from a life of red-neck small-town Southern aimlessness, and had it not been for him, I'd probably be selling insurance or real estate, playing golf at the country club, drinking beer with the good ol' boys in Beaufort, North Carolina. Had it not been for Sam Sawyer, I might be sleeping through nights, have every weekend off, go fishing more often, and generally be leading a pleasant life unblemished by what Sam Sawyer would regard as genuine accomplishment. I owed him a lot.

Sam taught history at Beaufort High. I mean, he taught real history, not that pabulum that passes for history after it's strained through all the sifters demanded by the Daughters of the American Revolution, the Southern Baptist Christian Alliance for Decency in Public Education, and whoever else has the ear of the local school board.

When I was a sophomore, I befriended Sam's son Steve who regularly twisted me like a pipe cleaner into various exotic shapes during the afternoon activity known as varsity wrestling practice. He wrestled the weight class below me, was state champ, and could pin me with an arm and a leg tied behind his back. Out of pity, or because he saw some reason for hope in my meager academic talents, Sam Sawyer took an interest in his son's sparring partner and he soon had me reading and thinking and arguing with my father that Franklin Roosevelt might not have been an agent of the international Communist conspiracy after all. Senior year he even convinced me to apply with his son to his alma mater, which was located in that strange and sinister land north of the Mason-Dixon line, Pennsylvania. Swarthmore, Pennsylvania. Sam even came by personally to convince my father to send me, once I got the acceptance letter. My father had not been keen on the idea of Pennsylvania—which he associated with Gettysburg and heartbreak for Robert E. Lee.

I roomed with Steve, and we both wrote letters home to his father. Then I went to medical school and Steve went to Vietnam, where he was killed three days after his arrival by a defective hand grenade that blew up as soon as he pulled the plug. I heard about it in medical school and I saw his name on the black marble slab,

37

so I knew it was true. I wrote his father a letter, but there really was nothing to say.

I hadn't heard from him for years, until I finished all my training and wound up in Washington, and he called on the phone and said he lived in town, having moved up here after his wife died. We both said we'd have to get together but left it sufficiently vague to know neither of us had much real desire. I suppose we realized we'd have to talk about Steve, and neither of us was looking forward to a delayed wake.

Today he looked older, but still vigorous, barrel-chested, pink-faced, with those brilliant blue eyes Steve had had. He pumped my hand with one hand and caught me behind the elbow with the other.

He said, "How are you, you old rattlesnake?"

"Can't complain."

"I should think not. Fancy office, high-class secretary, referrals from the chief of surgery. That's some recognition for a young doctor just starting out."

"You pumped Mrs. Bromley for information. You haven't changed a bit."

"It wasn't like that. I said I'd like to pop in and say hello, and she said you had this big-deal consult from the big cheese and had to get right over to the hospital. So I said, if it's the chief of surgery I'd be keeping waiting, I'd come back another day."

"I only take referrals from the top guys. Chief of surgery, president of the United States, and anyone who walks in off the street."

"Little Benjamin Abrams, all grown up. Doctor Ben. I remember you when."

"It's still when."

"No. You're all grown up. Referrals from the big cheese."

I started getting nervous. We were running out of things to talk about and I didn't want to talk about Steve. "So how do you like life in the big city?" I said. I can be very clever and engaging in conversation.

"I like it fine. Do a little contract work for the government—archives mostly. But that's not why I'm here. I want to join a gym. But they say a man my age needs a medical clearance. Can you imagine that?"

"What are you going to do? Pump iron?"

"I thought I'd just hang around and try to charm some young sprites with my wit and learning," he said, crinkling the skin around his eyes. "For that I need a physical exam."

"At least we ought to check your heart."

His heart needed checking. He had had an aortic valve replaced around 1970.

I told him, "There was a batch of Starr Edwards valves put in around nineteen-seventy that had a problem with the ball part of the valve. You know, the thing that looks like a Ping-Pong ball."

"I've seen the pictures."

"It was called 'ball variance.' The balls absorbed cholesterol very slowly, and the deposits made the balls all lumpy, so they'd strike the metal struts eccentrically and eventually they'd break apart."

"And what happened to the patients?"

"It was like a dam gave way."

"They died?"

"Of course, if yours were going to do that, it would've happened long ago. But I'd like you to get a phonocardiogram and an ECHO. Just to be sure."

"How's it sound?"

"Fine. Great. But you can't always tell from just listening."

"And if the tests don't look good?"

"You'll need a new valve."

"Hell, I come in here for a note to my aerobics instructor and go out with cardiac surgery." He said that with a grin, standing down from the examining table, pulling his shirt on. He was smiling, but his heart wasn't in it.

"You won't need surgery," I told him.

"If I do, I want the chief."

"You'll have him. You can have anyone you want."

"I'm not kidding, Ben."

He had turned suddenly serious.

"There hasn't been a case of ball variance for years."

"My luck, to make history."

"The only history you make, you'll write yourself."

He went on getting dressed. He smiled and socked me on the arm.

"Get over to see your consult. Tell that chief of surgery you're drumming up business for him."

CHAPTER

7

By the time I arrived at the parking lot at St. George's I was already making choices. I did not have time to see Mr. Crutchfield in the SICU and to write a note on the chief of surgery's patient and still get to Rounds on time. I ordered priorities, reordered them, and finally decided to see the chief's patient first. This would probably make me late to Rounds, but I was a professor now and the residents could wait and drink coffee and eat doughnuts for a few minutes, which wouldn't upset them greatly. Mr. Crutchfield could wait until later. His doctor was Ann Payson and she wouldn't mind.

Hurrying across the brick porch connecting the parking lot to the main entrance of the hospital, I was still looking at my watch when I noticed someone at my elbow. It was Ann Payson. She was wearing a tartan skirt and a gray sweater, and she was smiling.

"My patients are keeping you up nights, I hear," she said.

"I meant to call you about that," I said. "It's been busy this morning."

"My residents tell me you wouldn't let them wake me."

"No reason both of us should lose sleep."

"You were always like that," said Ann. "Even as an intern."

"That's what friends are for," I said.

"You just try to protect me," she said. "You always have."

Ann and I went back to internship, New York City, the Manhattan Hospital. That was ages ago, and a very different place. We met at one very dim morning hour when my resident made me call a surgeon to place a subclavian line in one of our ICU patients.

The resident and I had been struggling to get a line into this patient for an hour, with escalating frustration for us and increasing pain for the patient. I was sure I could get that line in and wanted to keep trying, but the resident told me to call the blades.

I had internship pride about not having to call for help, but I called. It was five or six in the morning, and the first light of day was a magenta pink, flooding the ICU, when Ann walked in. She looked impossibly clean and fresh in her blue scrub suit, sleep still in her face, carrying a long Deseret catheter. She struck me as very beautiful and very composed.

She inspected the evidence of my unsuccessful handiwork, carefully fingering each wound on the patient's arms the way a coroner examines a corpse for clues.

She was wearing a wedding ring—she was married then. Of course, she had to be. She had to be untouchable, out of my reach. That's the way internship was.

She said, "Well, you sure did try, didn't you?"

I said, "I didn't want to haul some poor surgeon out of bed. . . ." My words squibbed off in a moronic dribble. She gestured for me to pour out some Betadine for her and, gloving herself in sterile gloves, swabbed and prepped the patient's neck as I babbled on.

Finally she cut me off. "You should have called sooner."

She was right.

The rule was: If you can't get the line in with three attempts, call for help. But I had my pride. And the patient had arms that looked like trench warfare.

42

"I'm a big girl now," Ann had said. "I can get out of bed at almost any hour and lose a little sleep without breaking into little pieces."

Ann had a line in in five minutes. I had fooled around missing veins for an hour.

She finished, and my resident and I watched her walk out of the unit.

"Nice little ass," he said. "But something of a ball buster."

He was trying to make me feel better. She was right, all the way around the course. The patient comes first. *Primum non nocere* —first, do no harm. She'd made me feel pretty small. And the worst part of it was, she had done it without a trace of self-righteousness, so I couldn't even scoff at her.

All that was left was to call her a tight ass and a ball buster. But we both knew that was just a defense. I'd blown it, and my resident should have stopped me sooner—and she'd found us out and saved us.

But that was another time and another place, as they say. Last night I had not needed Ann's help, and it would have served no real purpose to wake her.

"He's doing well today," she said referring to the patient, Mr. Crutchfield.

"I was just trying to figure out when I'd have time to see him."

"You're a busy man now that you're a professor," she said.

Ann had a very nice face. There are certain people you assume are intelligent or well-bred, or any number of things you have no right assuming, just because of the structure of their faces. Ann was one of those. Her face was smiling now, and the lines around her mouth and eyes and the fine definition of her cheekbones held me. I would have liked to spend some time admiring her facial structure, but I had to move on.

"You might see an old battle-ax with constipation and some right-sided abdominal pain," I told her. "I don't know if she'll show. I saw her this morning."

"Haven't been back to my office, but my secretary hasn't paged me," said Ann.

"She probably won't show. I don't think she had anything anyway."

We walked through the revolving glass doors and down the long main corridor toward the elevators.

"I met the new king of surgery last night," I said.

"And what did you think?"

"I reserve judgment. Seems all right. He was up writing his own note on some patient on the SICU at two a.m., anyway. That counts for something."

"While I slept. My patient's gone into ketoacidosis and my residents won't even wake me. The chief is up, and I'm in bed. Dr. Abrams is taking care of business for me."

"Next time I'll let them, you keep complaining," I said. Then, "You get along with the new boss?"

"Well, he's very impressed by the old school tie. Fortunately, I happen to wear the right tie."

"He trotted out the tie for me," I said. "About the third sentence. Trained at Mass General. Seems to be impressed by the right names on sheepskins."

"He's Harvard College, Harvard Med."

"Well, so are you. Harvard, Harvard. He should be pleased with you. He's not impressed with local talent."

"Sounds like you had quite a chat, at two a.m."

"Not really. He gets to the point in a hurry." Then I added, "He's not winning contests for surgeon of the year with the SICU nurses."

Ann's eyes narrowed and she said, "Surgery's not about popularity seeking."

The elevator came.

"Got to see a patient and do Rounds," I said. "Want to come do medicine Rounds? The folks would love to have a surgeon on Rounds."

"For comic relief," she said, stepping back as the elevator door closed between us.

44

CHAPTER
8

I was only ten minutes late for Rounds, and the residents, interns, and medical students didn't seem to mind.

There were four medical students, two interns, and the resident. The resident said the patient they wanted to present was in the medical intensive care unit, which was down the hall and around the corner. As we lumbered along the hallway, the resident, a tall, sour-looking guy, turned to me and said, "You're not going to believe this one."

I didn't have time to wonder what he meant because his beeper went off with a stat page to the MICU. We all broke into a gallop like a herd of wildebeests picking up the scent of danger.

The patient he had meant to present was waiting for us at the other end of that stat page, two nurses at her side with looks of mixed horror and stupefaction. The patient was arching in her bed, knees flexed, wrists flexed hard, chin pulled toward her right shoulder as if by some invisible iron hand.

The nurses had never seen anything like it. One of them said, "Is she seizing or what?"

45

The other said, "Never seen a seizure like this."

The nurses had been born in the age of universal vaccination and had never seen acute tetanus, which, aside from acute, profound hypocalcemia, is the only thing that could do to a patient what they were witnessing—namely, acute tetanic contracture.

I watched her, a pretty lady in her thirties, now in extremis, and was momentarily unable to rise above my own fascination and break into action. Then I realized that the resident and intern were staring at me, mouths open, awaiting instructions.

"Let's have a Bristojet of calcium carbonate," I said. A nurse rustled about the crash cart and slapped a preloaded glass syringe into my hand.

I plunged the needle into the IV receptor and slowly shoved three cc's into the line. Within seconds the patient relaxed, started breathing again, pinked up, her hands went soft and her whole body lost its rigidity. She opened her eyes and smiled faintly.

"What happened?" she said.

I said, "You had a little trouble. You're fine now."

I stepped out of her room, dragging the resident and the whole gaggle of students and interns with me. They looked like a nest full of newborn robins with their mouths open.

"You guys going to tell me how she lost her parathyroid glands?" I asked.

A very young-looking female medical student presented the case from three-by-five cards. She was very nervous.

She shouldn't have been the one to be nervous. The surgeon who cut on the patient was the one who should have been nervous.

The patient had been admitted to surgery with a papillary carcinoma of the thyroid. The surgeon had decided to do a radical neck dissection and wound up removing not just the thyroid but all four parathyroid glands, a major error. The parathyroid glands keep the blood calcium level behaving itself. This patient was left with no parathyroids and not much in the way of blood calcium, either, which is why she had slipped into tetany, calcium being of great importance to muscular contraction and relaxation. And she would keep right on slipping into tetany until the medical house

46

staff could pump enough calcium and vitamin D into her to stop it.

I pulled the resident aside and asked him about the surgeon.

"He's the new chief of surgery," said the resident, his eyes giving no indication of what he thought of the new chief.

"A radical neck for papillary CA?" I said. "They stopped doing radical necks when Eisenhower was president and people were driving Edsels."

The resident was too young to know about Edsels, but he seemed to recognize Eisenhower.

"Ours is not to reason why," he said. "Ours is just to pump in calcium and Vitamin D."

They had obviously not done quite enough of that.

"Let's go back and talk to her," I said, and we all shuffled into her room. She was sitting up now, no trace of spasm. She was a very nice lady, mother of a two-year-old and a four-year-old. She was also a lawyer who worked for the Treasury. She had green eyes and black hair and she had a fresh surgical scar running from chin to chest. Her neck must have hurt, but she smiled anyway.

"I just feel so much better now," she said.

For the benefit of the medical students, I asked her a few questions about how it felt to go into tetanic contractures, and before we left I asked her how she happened to know McIlheny. The smile faded but came back with a few corners badly bent. Dr. McIlheny was not a favorite topic for her right then.

"My internist had recommended him."

I thanked her for her time, and we all retreated to the hall outside her room. Just as we reassembled, I noticed Ann Payson glide up behind the group. She leaned against the wall with her arms folded, and listened.

One of the interns asked about the radical neck. He said he couldn't understand why the surgeon had done it. The intern said he thought the procedure of choice was supposed to be a partial or incomplete removal of the thyroid followed by a dose of radioactive iodine to burn out what was left behind by the surgeon. He said he thought the whole reason for doing the procedure partly by

47

surgery and partly by radioactive iodine was to avoid accidentally cutting out all four parathyroids, which are sometimes buried in the thyroid itself. The intern was correct all the way around the course.

I said, "Well, we have an expert surgical opinion right here," and looked at Ann.

Everyone turned around.

"No fair," she said. "I've only heard the last part of the case."

"The question is the procedure of choice for papillary CA of the thyroid," I said.

"Unless there are other considerations," she said, "a near-total or partial with follow-up RAI."

"Ever heard of anyone doing a radical?" asked one of the medical students.

Ann shot a look in my direction, shoved her hands in her lab coat pockets, and shrugged.

"I can think of a few reasons for doing a radical, even today. But I haven't heard the case."

"You're being diplomatic," said the resident.

Ann smiled and slid by us out the MICU door.

"Surgeons stick together," said the intern.

"Give her a break," I said. "You want her to comment on a case she doesn't know personally?"

"Just asked about the procedure of choice."

"She didn't feel she had all the facts," I said. "You don't go off swinging half-cocked."

"Well, you heard the case," said the intern. "Can you see any reason this lady got a radical and all her parathyroids cut out so she has to take Vitamin D and calcium the rest of her life?"

"No," I said. "I really can't."

CHAPTER

9

When Rounds broke up I paged Ann from a phone in the nursing station.

There was a dull din in the background when she answered, but I could hear her.

"Where are you?" I asked.

"In the cafeteria," she said.

"Are you on the run or can I join you?"

"You eat lunch now? I thought you never had time."

"I've got time today."

"I've got a case at one," she said.

"I'll be right down."

For once, Ann was alone at her cafeteria table. Usually, people tended to gravitate toward her table. Medical students, nurses, interns, all felt comfortable just plopping their trays down next to her. Strangely, it was the other surgeons who tended to stop awkwardly before her and ask formally if they might presume to join her.

She was wearing blue surgical scrubs under a white lab coat and above her breast pocket in blue embroidered letters was printed "Ann Payson, M.D." She looked like a Hollywood version of a doctor, too good-looking, too composed, too unharried. I slid in next to her.

"No lunch?" she said.

"What's the story on the radical neck for papillary CA?"

"Oh, this is business, then, isn't it?"

"That's not an answer."

"I don't know the answer," she said. She was angry now. Her eyes didn't show it, but her mouth gave her away—it had a tight, hard look. "Dr. McIlheny believes in getting out as much tumor as you can."

"But a radical neck?"

"Maybe he found a lot of disease in the neck. I don't know the case."

"You know all you need to know. Papillary CA. You don't go doing radical necks for that, and you know it. You get what you can and let the nuclear medicine boys clean up with RAI. There's no excuse for a radical neck."

"Why argue with me?" Ann said, forking tuna casserole into her mouth, not meeting my eyes. "Talk to the guy who did the surgery."

"I just might do that. I was just trying to get some background."

"Can't help you."

"Can't or won't?"

"Hey, what is this?" She put her fork down and met my stare. "What do I know? I've got enough to do with my own patients. I don't look over the shoulder of other guys."

"You go to the conferences."

"So?"

"So you hear the new chief talking about doing radical necks in conferences?"

"No."

"How is Dr. McIlheny shaping up?"

"I told you. We get along fine. Harvard, Harvard, don't you know?"

"Ann, this is me, Ben Abrams. We're friends."

She smiled one of those smiles I rarely saw her use in the hospital. "We are considerably more than that, good doctor."

"I know."

"You're blushing." She laughed. "How sweet. You still can blush. There's hope for you yet."

"Oh, by the way, you'll be happy to know that my four o'clock case this afternoon is that lady who you sent over this morning. The one with the sour-looking daughter."

"Mrs. What's-her-name? The eighty-four-year-old lady with the constipation?"

"That's the one."

"I can't believe they saw you so fast."

"I walked into my office and there they were in my waiting room. Daughter told my secretary you wanted her mother seen immediately."

"And you think she's got something?"

"Probably an appendix," said Ann. She looked up at me as she took another forkful. "I guess you thought so, too, when you felt that mass in the right lower quadrant."

"I would have thought so," I said, "if I had felt a mass." I could feel my face go hot.

"Missed the mass?" Ann smiled, shrugging. "Oh, well. You sent her in. That's the main thing."

I sat there looking at my tray with the chicken salad sandwich. It should have been humble pie.

Up to that moment I had been hungry, but suddenly it all evaporated. I could have just as easily sent that lady on her way. If it hadn't been for the daughter, Mother probably would have gone home and perforated and possibly died, for all the help Dr. Abrams had been.

I didn't have long to wallow in my self-castigation. Ryan arrived.

"Hello, the very animals I was hoping to see," he said. He sat down with a tray piled high and began working methodically through his food.

"You're a big spender today," said Ann.

"I'm flush today. Just got my check in the mail." He surveyed his harvest, unable to decide on what to devour next.

"We got paid today?" Ann asked.

"This was not a faculty check," Ryan replied. "This was a check from the lawyers."

"The lawyers?" Ann and I said together.

Ryan was very pleased with our interest.

"Yes, I am in the employ of the enemy."

"What are you talking about?"

"Remember that case I told you about? The one where the radiologists in that Georgia swamp hospital left that guy in pulmonary edema on the CAT scan table because they were too fucking busy making money to cover their procedure room?"

"The one where they flew you down to testify?" I asked.

"You testified against some docs?" said Ann, jaw dropping.

"Would have done it for the plane fare," said Ryan. "These guys were real skunks."

"So the jury came in?" I asked.

"Two million for the plaintiff," said Ryan.

"And what did you get?" asked Ann.

"Two thousand," said Ryan happily.

"Two thousand," repeated Ann hollowly. I couldn't tell what she was thinking. She seemed incredulous.

Then she said, "So you've been well paid for your crusade." She said that with a smile that looked pasted up, hanging on by the corners, wondering what it would hit when it fell.

"What crusade?" said Ryan. He wasn't sure how Ann meant that, but he was sure he didn't like that smile. "Hey, we don't clean up the garbage, we're all going to wind up smelling."

"Bill, you're the knight errant. The world needs people like you. I'm just a workaday drone. I have a hard enough time just keeping my own nose clean."

She lifted her cafeteria tray and got up. "CAT scanning's getting to be a real high-risk business," she said. "Hear about that case in New Jersey?"

52

"No," said Ryan, glumly.

"Jury awarded some psychic a couple of million," said Ann. "It seems the CAT scan stripped her of her psychic powers."

"They didn't call me to testify about that one," said Ryan.

"Oh, they'll be calling from now on, I'm sure," Ann said, and she carried her tray over to the tray rack and scooted out of the cafeteria with both of us looking after her.

CHAPTER
10

There was one lesson that it took me a long time to absorb and that was that Mrs. Bromley is never wrong. She had told me to give up that bus drivers' clinic, and I had dragged my feet. That Wednesday they had four drivers who needed notes to go back to work, and I listened to their stories thinking, "Is this why I went to medical school?" Stories so transparent even the drivers didn't look as if they believed them. They all added up to the same thing—use your sick pay or lose it. So I nodded through them and signed the forms, and everyone was happy. Then the drug company man stuck his head in my door. He told me Lydell Brown was back—and I had to tell him his drug screens were positive for heroin.

They had Lydell in an examining room with his shirt off. He was staring at the floor when I stepped in, but he looked up quickly, his eyes crawling up and down my face and following every move I made.

"You got trouble, Lydell," I told him.

"Don't I know it, Doc. I never felt like this before."

"I'm sorry about this."

"I'm scared, Doc. I never felt this way before. Now there's blood in my pee."

"Blood?"

"I just pees blood."

He'd noticed it two days before. He'd been getting short of breath walking a block, and his bedding was soaked with sweat every morning.

I looked at his fingernails. There were five straight brown lines that could have been splinter hemorrhages. I turned the lights off in the room and looked in his eyes with the ophthalmoscope. He had hemorrhages scattered in both.

I listened to his heart. He had a murmur a first-year medical student couldn't miss. But I had missed it when I saw him two days earlier because I hadn't listened to his heart. I had been the company doctor, interested only in collecting his blood and urine to hang him with. I'd missed the infection that was currently chewing up his heart valves and that would surely kill him if it wasn't treated promptly. It might kill him even if he were treated.

"Lydell," I said, "you're going to have to go into the hospital. Today."

"It's serious, Doc?"

"It's the most serious thing that ever happened to you. I'm not kidding. Today."

"Where you gonna take me, Doc?"

I didn't know what to say. It had never occurred to me that I might be asked to take care of him. But Lydell Brown didn't have a doctor. He was twenty-two and until that day the idea that he might ever need a doctor had never occurred to him.

"I work for the company, Lydell. I think you need your own doctor."

"I could pay you, Doc," he said. He was holding my hand in both of his hands. "I got insurance, at least until they fires me. I'm good for it."

"It's not that at all, Lydell. It's just . . ."

It was just the conflict of interest, which didn't matter a damn to

55

Lydell and, once I thought about it, didn't matter a damn to me. If I didn't admit him to St. George's, he'd wind up going to the emergency room at Elsewhere General, where they'd be as likely to miss the diagnosis as make it. I told him I'd admit him as my patient.

"Thanks, Doc. I'll never forget you."

I called the admitting resident from the phone in the examining room. He was very happy to have a case of subacute bacterial endocarditis. They'd admitted three ninety-year-old women with urinary tract infections that day and two eighty-year-old men with pneumonia. Lydell was the best case of the day.

Later that day, Ann paged me about the eighty-four-year-old lady with the constipation and the belly pain. The belly pain was caused by an inflamed appendix, just as Ann had predicted. Not just an inflamed appendix. A perforated appendix.

"That's what the mass was," Ann said. "A big, juicy abscess." The mass Ann had felt was a pus ball. The mass I had missed. A big, juicy abscess.

"Don't feel so bad," Ann said. "My surgical resident missed the mass, too."

"I feel much better," I said. "I'm a professor and I'm missing appendixes and abscesses."

"She'll do just fine," said Ann, laughing. "I'll have Ryan see her for the antibiotics. Ryan'll take care of her. A little blast-a-bug, what's left of that pus ball will just melt away. The important thing is that she's okay."

"That's one important thing."

"Buck up, professor. Things like this keep you humble."

I agreed and hung up. I was due to play professor in fifteen minutes.

For the month of September, the endocrine service at St. George's Hospital consisted of one second-year resident who looked like a young Gregory Peck; two adoring female medical students, one blond as a ghost, the other a dark Greek, neither of whom looked

56

old enough to be admitted to an R-rated movie; and me. They were a more eager and more compulsive group than usually rotated through Endocrine, which was thought to be a relatively undemanding service—you got to go home at night and there weren't many emergencies.

I would have liked them to make Rounds on Lydell Brown, to help me keep an eye on him, but Lydell steadfastly refused to develop a single endocrine problem, so I never was able to include him in our Rounds. I always had to go by afterward to see him by myself.

Endocrine consults were called into the department office, the resident handed them to the medical students, and the medical students presented the patients to me. Sometimes the consults were interesting, but mostly they were diabetics, "dumps" from the surgeons. The surgeons liked doing surgery but were bored by the drudgery of adjusting insulin levels and keeping post-op diabetics from blowing up in ketoacidosis. They put in consults for "diabetic management" on all their diabetics and handed them off to the intrepid endocrine service.

So we were doing sugar Rounds on the surgical wards.

It always surprises medical students when they first come face to face with the fact that diabetes mellitus did not roll over and die with the advent of bottled insulin. Diabetes being a disease of elevated blood sugars, and insulin being a hormone that can lower same, it seems to the average medical student that there should be no problem, and yet here we were making Rounds on diabetics with below-the-knee amputations (BKAs), diabetics with above-the-knee amputations (AKAs), blind diabetics, diabetics with premature coronary artery disease and heart attacks at age thirty, diabetics on dialysis, and diabetics with infections—all the fallout of small blood vessel disease wrought by blood sugar levels that just can't be kept quite normal by injecting insulin.

Before injectable insulin, diabetes wasted its victims quickly. Now it was the slow wet rot.

The blond student presented a forty-year-old man who had presented himself to the emergency room complaining of foot odor.

57

The ER doc discovered the head of a nail sticking out of the sole of his foot. Gangrene had already eaten through to the ankle, and he was now a BKA. He had never felt the nail—he had diabetic neuropathy. The student had read about neuropathy, but this was her first personal acquaintance.

"I just can't believe he couldn't feel that nail," she said. "Look at that thing."

The surgeons had taped it to his chart. It was an old galvanized nail, about two inches long.

"It was just that putrid stench," the BKA told us. "Of course, I can't see my foot"—he was blind—"but I could sure as hell smell something was wrong."

We wandered down the ward, past two more BKAs whose blood sugars were well controlled on stable doses of insulin, and then past an AKA who had refused to let them cut off his foot. He had lapsed into sepsis, then coma, and after he was unconscious for a day, the hospital ethics committee met and decided it was okay to cut off his foot to save his life, even though it was against his expressed wishes. Ann Payson had done the deed.

"If he wakes up and decides he doesn't like being alive, he can call his lawyer," Ann had said. "But right now he's not arguing with me, so I'll cut." He woke up and discovered that he was alive and missing one foot. He had been depressed and weepy ever since.

"Nice save, Ann," I told her. "You saved his life and he wishes you hadn't."

"He's got time to think," said Ann. "If he decides I did the wrong thing, he's still got options. If I'd let him go, he'd have no options today."

"That's what I like about surgeons," I told her. "No doubts."

"You guys already did the agonizing for me. That's what guys on the ethics committee are for."

"Oh, I see."

"I happened to agree with cutting or I wouldn't have done it," said Ann. "Give me a break."

So now he was an AKA, silent and saved.

We walked over to the obstetrics ward.

Obstetrics, of course, is the happiest place in the hospital, and it cheered me up just being there. We walked by the viewing room with the gooing fathers, and we stopped outside Cheryl Walker's room.

The brunette presented Cheryl, who was my own patient, but she did it formally for the benefit of the resident and the other student. Cheryl was a very nice twenty-four-year-old accountant for the Congressional Budget office who had lost her first baby the year before she became my patient. It was a ten-pounder who got hung up and died in the birth canal. Cheryl had been a diabetic since age twelve, and her GP had told her it was just fine to run her usual blood sugars of two hundred during pregnancy.

She had grown a ten-pound baby and she learned that you have to get the right advice when you're a diabetic or you can get burned. So she came to me and we kept her sugars under a hundred, and Cheryl got clammy and hypoglycemic several times a week, but she grew a nice little baby who sonograms showed was not going to get big enough to get stuck in the canal. But then Cheryl's eyes started to self-destruct, as diabetic eyes sometimes do during pregnancy, despite tight control.

I had to tell her we might have to abort.

Cheryl said, "Over my dead body."

I had a long and serious talk with her, explaining that she ran a very real risk of going blind by the time she delivered. I did my best to scare the hell out of her and to paint the blackest, scariest picture I could so she wouldn't be surprised no matter what happened. Cheryl said, "Okay, you can consider me warned. I've felt this baby move. There's no way I'd kill him."

Her husband wasn't quite as stalwart. The idea of living with a blind wife shook him, but Cheryl had enough steel for both of them. She delivered a lovely seven-pound, one-ounce baby boy, and her eyes made it through labor and delivery more or less intact. As the medical student put it, "It was all a very happy ending, more or less, mostly more."

They named the kid Jason Abraham Walker. The Abraham was for me.

"It's an undeserved honor," I said.

"You got me my baby," said Cheryl.

The medical student had followed her postpartum. Cheryl's sugars were perfectly controlled on half the dose she'd taken during her pregnancy.

"Her eyes look fine now. She's doing wonderfully," said the student. "Everything's going to be great."

"For a while at least," I said.

"What's that supposed to mean?" asked the student.

"Her long-term outlook is pretty bleak." I told them about the Joselin study. "The median maternal survival after delivery was eight years. That meant one out of five kids lost his mother by the time he was ten years old."

"How dismal," said the student.

"We've helped bring a little kid into the world who'll be a semi-orphan," I said.

"Better than no kid at all," said the blond student.

"That's not a question for science to answer," I said.

Amazing how often you wind up saying that in medicine.

CHAPTER
11

Lydell Brown had a rocky day Thursday, going into congestive heart failure and developing a fever. He was twice as sick from the minute he entered the hospital as he ever had been outside of it. I chose to think that simply meant I had hospitalized him not a moment too soon. I wasn't sure what Lydell Brown or his wife concluded. They might have thought the hospital had made him sick.

Ryan did the Infectious Diseases consult on him and was overseeing his antibiotics, but the bacteria living on his hypodermic needles had found a new home on his aortic valve and were currently chewing it up. Heroic doses of antibiotics, digoxin, and diuretics seemed to improve things by late Thursday.

Friday morning, Lydell could even walk to the bathroom, leaning hard on his rolling IV pole.

After listening to Lydell's heart and reassuring him he wasn't going to die today, for whatever such reassurances are worth, I dragged myself over to the ward with the lady whose appendix I had missed.

She greeted me with surprising vigor, in a voice much stronger than she looked. "You're a sorry excuse for a doctor," she said.

The daughter said something like we-are-very-grateful-for-all-you-did. I took that as my chance to escape.

I drove back to the office thinking about changing careers. Windsurfing instructor at Club Med maybe. They probably have bad days, too. I saw six patients that afternoon, but none of them had ruptured appendixes. Not that I detected anyway.

Friday evening I took Ann out to dinner. We both carried our beepers. Ann had a woman whose right lung kept collapsing and I had Lydell Brown, who could go sour quickly.

We met Ryan at a Vietnamese restaurant in Georgetown owned by an old friend of mine, Mai Nguyen, with whom Ryan had been deeply in love off and on for about three weeks. Mai seated us at her owner's table, as she always did when Ryan and Ann and I showed up, and food began appearing without benefit of menu.

Mai had lived in the States about seven years and spoke excellent English, but of course the hardest thing to acquire in a new language is the humor, especially that which plays on words.

Ryan told one of his favorite jokes, "What's the difference between a lawyer and a rooster?"

Ann said she didn't know and didn't want to know. I had heard Ryan do this routine too often, so busied myself with Mai's wonderful light spring rolls.

"The rooster clucks defiance!" roared Ryan, laughing, choking on his food. His face turned red, his eyes streamed with tears, and he couldn't breathe at all. Ann and I sat there trying to decide whether we should save him or let him die for his horrible jokes. Mai chopped him on his back and he recovered. He was still laughing.

"I don't get it," said Mai.

Ryan started to explain, but Ann cut him off with a hand on his arm. "Don't bother," she told Ryan. She was trying to look stern and unamused but not succeeding. Ryan enjoyed himself so thoroughly it was hard not laughing along with him.

Ann's beeper bleated. She disappeared behind the bar into Mai's office. We had eaten at Mai's place many times and felt at home.

"She's a lovely person," said Mai, about Ann. "If I ever need a surgeon, I want her."

"Me, too," I said.

Ann returned. With that easy grace that made routine courtesies sound important and charming, she told Mai how wonderful the food was. She said she had to go.

We had taken my car, so I stood up to take her to St. George's.

"What?" said Ryan. "Breaking up the party? And Mai's only up to the sixth course. You're coming back, Abe?"

As if in answer, my beeper went off. I, too, took the call in Mai's office. It was the intern on Lydell Brown. Lydell had slid into pulmonary edema, and the intern thought he could hear a new heart murmur. I asked him to call Nancy Colleo, chief of cardiac diagnostics, for an echocardiogram.

Then I slipped back into the restaurant, drew aside the maître d', and paid for our meal. Ann and Ryan were distracting Mai—she always protested our paying for our meals and we always went through the maître d'.

Ann and I said good-bye and walked out onto M Street, which was crowded with the Friday evening throngs. We walked down the hill under the Whitehurst Freeway, to my car. I took a back-route-cobblestone-street way to the hospital to avoid the Friday night congestion along Canal Road. I always hesitate going near Georgetown when I have a sick patient in the hospital and there's a chance I might have to get somewhere quickly. Friday nights in Georgetown the traffic may not move until Saturday morning. I wondered what Lydell would look like when I arrived. Ann looked out her window and was quiet.

We pulled into the parking lot and I put my plastic card in the box, hardly waiting for the wooden gate to rise before we shot past it.

"I might need your services tonight," I said.

Ann looked at me in the dark car. "Now that's the kind of opening that gets me listening."

"I mean your surgical services."

63

"This guy with the SBE?"

"Lydell Brown. May need a new aortic valve, if the intern's right. Nancy's supposed to be doing the ECHO."

"Depends how fast he needs it," said Ann. We were out of the car now and halfway to the hospital entrance. "This lady's going to take a while. The one I'm going to do right now."

"Who's backing you up tonight?"

"Your friend, the chief of surgery."

"No kidding?"

We were through the revolving glass doors now and moving down the main corridor. Ann was somewhere between a trot and a gallop, headed for the OR. I tried to keep within earshot.

"Would I kid you?" she shouted over her shoulder, disappearing into an elevator. "If he needs a valve tonight, and if I'm not finished with this case, your patient can have the big cheese do it."

CHAPTER
12

Lydell Brown was not in his room. Since internship I've always hated walking into a patient's room and finding him gone. It's disconcerting, not to mention disorienting. You have to go looking for a nurse, hoping her face won't change suddenly when you mention the patient's name. That facial transformation, followed by "Oh, didn't you hear?" Then quick directions to the morgue.

No, I don't like finding an empty bed at all.

But Lydell was not in the morgue. He was in the cardiac cath lab with Nancy Colleo. She was methodically setting out her instruments while Lydell's labored breathing got faster and faster and his eyes got bigger and bigger.

He was sitting bolt upright on the hard slab cath table because every time they made him lie flat he felt as if he were drowning. He looked happy to see me. His intern, a nice frightened-looking blond kid, stood in the corner of the lab wearing a lead apron. Lydell wasn't sure who Nancy was or what she was up to, but he wasn't keen to find out.

"Sure am glad to see your face, Doc," he said.

"How you doing, Lydell? Pretty fancy lab, isn't it?"

"What's happening to me, Doc?"

"Those bugs may be eating the valve," I told him, taking his wrist. His pulse was strong enough, but racing. "Dr. Colleo here is going to get a picture of it."

"I'll remember this day as long as I lives, Doc."

I thought that particularly poor phrasing.

Nancy looked up and caught my eye. She had found some irony in Lydell's choice of words, too. She finished laying out her instruments. Nancy was a willowy brunette, with good dark eyes and quick fingers that seemed connected to her cerebral cortex by a single synapse—every thought sent those fingers into reflexive action.

She nodded at the echocardiograms she had done before I arrived. I sifted through them. They showed progressive deterioration of Lydell's aortic valve as it shredded under the onslaught of *Staphylococcus aureus.*

Staph can be a very nasty bug, especially when it's on your aortic valve, where it has no business being. It almost never gets there unless you push dirty needles into your veins several times a day. Lydell had done that, and as the bus company drug man had observed, he was paying the price.

I had seen all this before, as an intern and a resident, but it was different seeing it now. In those days, the life of the intern puts you in a different frame of mind. Sleep deprivation engenders a baseline irritability that effortlessly escalates into an emotionally insulating hostility. It was easy to work up a nice functional hate for patients like Lydell Brown, who played with heroin and wound up with disintegrating heart valves, usually at four in the morning.

In those days I spent a lot of nights pushing Lasix and morphine and rotating tourniquets while some candy-ass attending hemmed and hawed about getting the patient through with medical therapy, meaning antibiotics, when it was patently obvious the patient was headed for a rendezvous with the surgeons. It was just a question of how long it would take the medical attending to swallow hard and push the button.

66

Now I was the attending, and I didn't live in the hospital. Sending a patient to be hooked up to a heart-lung machine and arranging for someone to cut out a large chunk of his heart and sew in a new valve did not seem like just another day at the office.

On the other hand, it was becoming increasingly clear there was no way to avoid it for Lydell Brown.

Nancy wanted to do a quick catheterization to look at the valve and to see the function of the main pumping chamber, so the surgeon would know how strong a heart he was working with.

She said, "You got the blades ready?"

"I came in with Ann Payson."

"Good."

"But she's doing another case. How long can we wait here?"

Nancy lowered her voice. "Not long, brother."

"Couple of hours?"

Nancy shook her head, sneaking a glance at Lydell to see if he was following all this. His eyes were closed.

"I'll get her backup," I said.

"Good idea."

I started for the wall phone and Nancy asked who Ann's backup was.

"Tom McIlheny."

Nancy had pulled a surgical mask up over her face, so all I could see was her eyes. I didn't like what I saw there.

Lydell's chest started to heave and I could hear him gurgle from my spot at the wall, a good eight feet away. The intern took a syringe marked "Lasix" and shoved it into Lydell's IV line and pushed in a hundred milligram bolus.

"We might use some rotating tourniquets and a touch of morphine before I give him the contrast," Nancy told the intern.

I dialed page. Lydell wasn't going to wait. Just watching him I could feel my pulse pound and my blood pressure double. Without an aortic valve he would be very quickly dead. As he lost more and more valve function, fluid backed up into his lungs and he started to drown all over again. But for the grace of Lasix, digoxin, morphine, and the tourniquets, he would have slid away from us.

67

I dialed a page from the wall phone. The operator told me she didn't know if Dr. McIlheny was in the hospital. "It's Friday night, you know. They do take time off," said the operator. Nothing was going to be easy this night.

"Doctors have no right to take time off," I said. "They're doctors, aren't they?" I hung up before she could respond.

A patient had said that once, when I told her I was covering for her doctor, who was out of town for the weekend. A memorable line. I knew it would come in handy. But it didn't help me with Lydell Brown.

A beeper sounded outside the lab door. Thomas McIlheny stepped in and fastened his gaze on each one of us in turn, Nancy, Lydell, the intern, and me. That was the quickest response to a page I'd ever seen. I thought he probably had changed in a phone booth and flown over before his beeper stopped beeping.

"Hello, Abrams," he said, as if he hadn't recognized me before. "You seem to spend all your nights here."

"I've noticed that too," I said. "And they told me my social life would pick up after internship."

The intern laughed, a little hysterically. I liked my little joke, but it wasn't that funny. Nancy smiled. Lydell Brown concentrated on breathing. McIlheny smiled a smile his lips had forgotten by the time it reached his eyes.

He stood there and watched the monitor above Lydell's table as Nancy injected contrast dye above the aortic valve. The dye cascaded down into the left ventricle like a bucket of water crashing through a wet paper bag.

"I think I see the problem," said McIlheny.

"Look at the ECHO," I said, handing him a strip of ultrasound paper.

"Let's see the complete study," he said.

I followed him into the adjoining room, where Nancy had spread out the echocardiograms on the workbenches. McIlheny stood looking at the long sheaves of paper jumbled in a heap, reached into his lab coat pocket, popped four Clorets into his mouth, and then took a look at the ECHOs, chewing gum.

There was something incongruous about his gum chewing—the patrician white-haired surgeon, in his starched white coat, not a hair out of place, chewing like a left fielder coming to bat.

I started to point out the valve fluttering when McIlheny stepped up to the workbench and said, "I don't know how anyone can think straight amid all this junk." He arranged all the folders and rulers and pencils into neat little rows and stacks until the top of the desk looked like a Boy Scout's tent before inspection. Then he went through the echocardiogram, page by page.

Finally he said, "No doubt about what he needs."

We walked back into the cath lab where Nancy was sewing up Lydell's artery.

McIlheny said: "Mr. Brown, you will have to have surgery tonight. I will replace your infected valve with a nice new one. It will take about four hours, from the time we have you in the operating room."

"You mean, like, surgery?" said Lydell. He had heard it, but he had not wanted to hear it. And his heart was not supplying all the oxygen his brain would have liked to deal with this announcement.

"Surgery, tonight," said McIlheny.

"I sure hope you done a few before," said Lydell.

"More than I can remember," said McIlheny with what he probably thought was a laugh. It came out more like a bark.

McIlheny looked at me and said, "It'll take me some time to get the pump team and everyone together and in the OR. You might want to diurese him and even phlebotomize him in the meantime. We've got the good phlebotomy bottles in the OR suite."

The intern left with McIlheny to get the bottles. I helped Nancy transfer Lydell onto a stretcher and started wheeling him toward the SICU, which would be the safest place to hold him until the OR called.

"He a good surgeon?" asked Lydell.

"He's the chief of surgery," I said.

"Oh." Lydell smiled, his head dropping back. "Good."

"You better clean up that ultrasound room," I told Nancy. "The

69

chief of surgery spent five minutes dusting and straightening the top of your desk."

Nancy suppressed a smile and shook her head. "Hey, you ought to see my cot in the on-call room since he's come. Pillowcase pressed. Blanket tight. You could bounce a quarter off it. I'm afraid to lie down on it, for fear of messing it up. Heaven forbid Dr. McIlheny should find a crease."

"Well, I'm glad he's finally got you slackards in shape."

Nancy looked at me a beat too long.

"Oh," she said, "there have been quite a few changes around here since Dr. McIlheny arrived."

I looked over to see how much of this Lydell Brown had heard, but he was still working hard on his breathing.

I wheeled him off down the long corridor to the SICU, pushing the stretcher from behind Lydell's head. He turned around, in a panic, to find me.

"Doc, you there, Doc?"

"Right here, Lydell."

"Don' leave me, Doc."

"I'll be right with you."

"You going be doing the surgery?"

"I'd just get in the way. Dr. McIlheny's a specialist."

"A specialist. Oh. That's wonderful, Doc."

"We're going to the intensive care unit until they're ready for you in the operating room," I told him.

"When they take me," Lydell rasped, "go talk to my wife."

"Where is she?"

"In the waiting room on the floor where my room is, Doc."

The intern was waiting for us at the SICU with the phlebotomy bottles. I took one end of the plastic tubes that came with them, unsheathed the metal tip, and drove it into Lydell's femoral artery. Blood came pulsing up the line. The intern connected the other end to the vacuum bottle—it was a liter bottle and it filled in less than twenty seconds.

Lydell smiled and said, "That's better. I can breathe."

70

McIlheny had told the intern it would be forty-five minutes until the team could be in place. They called for Lydell in thirty.

"The man wastes no time," said the intern. "He's ahead of schedule."

"Good luck, Lydell," I said.

"Tell my wife," he said, and waved as the nurses from the OR rolled him off.

CHAPTER

13

I found Lydell's wife in the waiting room on Seven South. She wasn't what I'd expected. I'm not sure what I expected—maybe something lumpish and slow and ungrammatical—but she was not that. She was Jamaican and spoke with that lovely island lilt.

They had met at college, where he was busy playing basketball and flunking out, and she was studying applied math. She was a senior and he a sophomore. They were married after her graduation and moved to Washington. She worked for Treasury.

That all came out fairly quickly and smoothly, and we were having a nice time until she decided to get down to business. She had about a dozen relevant questions, starting with what they were doing to her husband in the operating room and finishing with how well I knew the surgeon.

I think I satisfied her on everything but how well I knew McIlheny.

"Then he's new here?"

"He's chief of surgery."

"You said since January."

"That's right."

"And where was he before that?"

"A hospital in Chicago."

That hospital in Chicago hung in the air for a moment.

"And what is the risk of surgery?"

I never know how to answer that question. In this era of informed consent, full disclosure, litigation, Phil Donahue, *Sixty Minutes*, and maximal truth telling, I could just hear a pregnant voice intoning, "Now, what did the doctor tell you, Mrs. Brown?" And I could hear her answer, "The doctor said everything would be all right. And look at my husband now."

I drew in a breath and said, "The major risk of surgery is death on the operating table."

I don't think a solid right hook could have rocked her more. The enamel on her controlled exterior cracked, and I suddenly felt less besieged than sorry. I guess I had suffered through a few too many talk shows and magazine articles lambasting doctors for playing God, and too many hospital risk-management seminars run by lawyers. Mrs. Lydell Brown got it between the eyes for all of that.

Having said that, I was left to deal with the terror in her face. I felt as if I'd punched a woman whose hands were tied.

"I realize that," she said. "I meant, what can I expect?"

"You can expect your husband to be in intensive care after the surgery. Hopefully, replacing the valve will also take care of the infection."

I felt like a tape recording made by the hospital malpractice committee. I was being careful, dancing around her questions, staying on my toes, deflecting every parry. Only she didn't realize it was a sparring round. She was scared to death and looking for reassurance, and I was giving her the business. The risk-management people would be proud.

"Look," I said, "I think the surgery has risks, but not doing the surgery really wasn't an option. This procedure, replacing the aortic valve, is done all the time. It's more difficult when there's infection."

73

"But he was given antibiotics. How could there be an infection?"

"The antibiotics don't always kill enough bacteria, especially if the heart tissue itself is infiltrated with bacteria."

"Then he may die tonight," said Lydell Brown's wife. She was beginning to sway a little. I stepped up next to her, in case she lost control and headed for the floor.

"He's got the chief of surgery working on him. The guy wrote the book. He's going to be fine."

She grabbed my hand with an icy grip. "He could die."

"Nobody can write you a guarantee, Mrs. Brown, but he's not going to die. He's going to make it. He's going to be looking up at you from that stretcher in the intensive care unit in just a few hours. We don't let people die around here. The time he was really in danger was before he came to the hospital."

To hell with risk management.

She smiled weakly and dabbed away her tears.

"I know what you're saying," she said. "I'm sorry. I'm better now." She sat down on one of the vinyl chairs they fill waiting rooms with. "A coward dies a thousand deaths," she said.

"So does the brave man," I said. "If he's intelligent. He just doesn't talk about them."

"Well, now we've talked. Thank you."

"Can I do anything for you?"

"Are you going back to the surgery?"

"I'm not a surgeon."

"Oh," she said.

She didn't like that answer at all. "You mean," she said, "you're going home?"

The intelligent, straightforward, and honest answer at that point would have been: You bet I'm going home—it's almost midnight.

I said, "I'll stick around, if you'd like." That's how intelligent and straightforward I am.

"No," she said. "That's not fair. You've done all you can."

That is what in the trade is known as the perfect out. The smart thing to do was to say, "I'll keep in touch, and don't hesitate to

74

call," and to get out the door quickly. That being the obviously smart thing to do, I said, "I'll stick around. I'll stay in an on-call room. You can stay here or in your husband's room."

She wanted to stay in Lydell's room, but she refused to lie on his bed. "In case they want to bring him back tonight," she said.

"He'll be in the operating room until well past midnight, then in the intensive care unit at least until morning. Probably for a full day."

"I'm fine here," she said, taking up position in his bedside armchair.

I drew the folded white thermal blanket from his bed and handed it to her, and she wrapped herself in it.

"Go to your on-call room," she said. "I'll be fine. Really."

I reached the door and heard her speaking to my back.

"Thanks for staying."

I found an empty on-call room. It was your basic no-frills on-call room: telephone by the metal frame bed—a bed that wouldn't give an inch if it were struck squarely by a meteorite—wool blanket, and pillow. The pillow had seen service as a sandbag the last time the Potomac overflowed its banks, and had been retired to easy service. No window, no chair. Over the light bulb in the ceiling, a cracked glass fixture. I'll say this for St. George's on-call rooms —no bare light bulbs hanging from the ceiling. And no mice scampering behind the wainscoting. I'd spent nights in worse on-call rooms. I stretched out on the bed and looked at the ceiling in the dark.

Forty years old and I'm spending the night in an on-call room, alone. Nice to grow up and be a success. If I ever have a kid he'll go to law school.

I tried to comfort myself with the thought that life had changed for the better. Ten years earlier I had been an intern lying in an on-call room, staring at the ceiling, wondering how long it would be before the phone rang. But then I had forty sick-as-stink patients, sometimes twice that, whom they could call about. And they always did. Usually just when I had dropped off. Now I had

75

only one patient. The chances were excellent for at least two hours' sleep, since the surgery was scheduled to go four.

I was grown-up now. A real doctor. I lay there in the dark, adding up the pluses and minuses. In the plus column, I wasn't an intern anymore. That had to be progress. I made my own schedule now. But in a sense my schedule made itself, and my practice ran me. I was older and wiser, hair thinner and ten pounds heavier than my internship weight, most of it settling in places it'd never been before.

But I had definitely arrived. Medical students and residents stood up when I entered the room. My name on the coatrack in the doctors' coatroom. A clinical professor of medicine. Somewhere in some medical school catalog was my name with that title next to it. That and a quarter would buy me coffee. Of course, I had college friends who are now presidents of banks who drink three-martini lunches, who know about tax shelters and vacation in Europe. I ate from vending machines when I had time for lunch.

I had definitely arrived. Every third weekend on call, and every weekday night. Two weeks' unpaid vacation every year. There should be a corporate ladder for doctors to climb. So you'd know when you had really, definitely arrived.

Whom was I trying to kid? Life was soft now. Easy street. No problems—except a patient with his rib cage pulled open, heart flayed, a surgeon I hardly knew but had chosen, squeezing and pulling. The wife waiting. And I had put him there.

As an intern I'd always laughed long and loud when I heard older docs talk about the burden of responsibility, the weight of decision making, the things that turn your hair gray. Give me the weight and the burden, but let me sleep through the night, I said. Trade places anytime. Interns don't make the big decisions, they just stay up all night executing them. Make me a general. The decisions are obvious most of the times—you don't lose sleep. All that was coming back to me now—with a vengeance. The decision with Lydell Brown was obvious. I told his wife as much. The surgeon told me it was obvious. So did Nancy Colleo. Everyone

76

knew what had to be done. But it might have been Ann Payson in there sewing Lydell's heart if I'd played my cards right. Instead, it was the new unknown, Thomas McIlheny. A man who did an occasional radical neck dissection. A man one might doubt. I had put Lydell Brown in his hands. And why? Because he'd shown up. I could have stepped back and said I wanted to think about it. But I'd handed Lydell over on a platter.

Console yourself, Abrams. You gave the case to the chief of surgery. Ann told you to. They don't make guys chief for nothing.

Since January, Lydell Brown's wife had said. An accusation.

It was like that for half an hour or so. Usually I'd had no trouble falling asleep in on-call rooms. But, as I said, I had arrived.

I awoke not knowing what time it was. Groping around in the unfamiliar room, so dark I couldn't see my watch, I finally felt a light switch. The light blinded me momentarily, until I made out the watch face: four o'clock. In the a.m. They'd been in surgery four hours. I splashed some water in my face at the sink and considered taking a shower. But I was wide awake. I walked through shadowy wards to Lydell's room, hoping McIlheny had finished and hoping he had talked to Mrs. Brown and told her everything had gone well.

Mrs. Brown was dozing in her chair.

"Are they through?" she asked.

"Don't know."

"They said four hours."

"I know."

"Could you check?"

I was afraid she'd say that.

CHAPTER

14

The doors to the operating room suite swing open only for those who know. They have no handles and cannot be pushed open with a shoulder. The secret is a metal plate on the wall six feet down the hall. I hit the plate and the doors swung open, and I murmured, "Open Sesame," for luck, as I had done since medical school.

I walked past the yawning doors and faced a nurse in blue OR scrubs sitting behind the tall desk. Behind her was the OR posting board, and I scanned it for the room where McIlheny worked on Lydell Brown. There were no cases posted. That was easy to understand, it being after 4:00 A.M.—there were probably not too many cases being done.

"They're in Room G," said the nurse, looking up from her day-old newspaper just long enough to see me staring at her board.

"Where are the gowns?"

"Dr. McIlheny does not allow anyone in the OR in gowns," she said slowly, and I thought a little ironically. "You'll have to change into scrubs. And get your hat on straight, tie band at the back.

Nothing in your pockets. Bootie straps in. Dr. McIlheny may just decompensate if your scrub suit's not just right. A sloppy scrub suit, a sloppy surgeon, you know."

She was a middle-aged nurse, which is to say older than me, younger than my mother, gray-haired, a little overweight but in an athletic way. She looked as if she'd been through more than one new chief of surgery in her time. She smiled at me.

"I'm not a surgeon," I said. "That's my patient he's doing in there."

"I know who you are. You're Dr. Abrams. You did grand Rounds on that pheo lady we had up here last year."

Local hero. Someone remembered my only home run. I took that as a good omen. She pointed out the locker room, and I changed into scrubs and presented myself for inspection to the desk nurse, who adjusted my hat and mask and gave me directions to Room G.

I found my way into the OR as the nurse had directed, through the scrub room, with the sinks with foot pedals, where the surgeons scrub before gowning and gloving in the operating room. I put a shoulder to the door and slid in, folding my arms. If you're not totally at home in an operating room, fold your arms—it's the only way to be sure you don't touch something sterile and send the nurses into great snits. Operating rooms are like ice-skating rinks for expert skaters. You're allowed to glide around as long as you're graceful, but fall down or get sloppy and you get shoved toward the door. I positioned myself so I wouldn't be hit by the door if any-one swung it open and I tried to figure out who was who.

Everyone was gowned, and there were more than half a dozen people in the room, so it took me a few moments.

McIlheny had his back to me. Next to him, on a platform, with all the instruments spread out before her on a tray, the scrub nurse was leaning in his direction, trying to hear the names of the instru-ments he was calling for. On the other side of him was a tall male figure, probably a surgical resident. Across the table were two more residents. At the head of the table was the anesthesiologist. I could see only the top of his scrub hat, but I could hear him pressing methodically on the bag with which he was breathing Lydell Brown. The anesthesiologist is the one guy you don't want falling asleep during your surgery. If the surgeon nods off, somebody'll wake him before any damage is done, but if the anesthesiologist falls asleep you're not breathing. Very nasty, as Mrs. Bromley would say. By the opposite wall were two pump team people, sitting whispering to each other. A circulating nurse in blue scrubs sailed between the heart-lung machine, the trays of instruments, and other paraphernalia, plucking wrapped parcels out of glass and metal storage bins around the OR and emptying them on the tray in front of the scrub nurse.

It was very quiet. The heart-lung machine made a low droning noise, and occasionally came the hiss of the Bovie cautery blade, and I could hear McIlheny's voice low and muffled by his mask, and the nasal replies of the scrub nurse, who seemed to be having trouble getting his requests for instruments straight.

McIlheny worked hunched over and with a lot of twisting and shoulder motion, like a very frenzied orchestra conductor not very happy with what he was hearing and not sure where the problem was. He never looked up at the scrub nurse, simply held up his hand, into which she'd slap an instrument.

She slapped a clamp into his hand, he looked at it for a moment, and then suddenly flipped it with a quick snap of his wrist over his back. The silvery clamp spun across the room and bounced off the tiled wall not more than a foot from my head. It left a white scratch on the green tile.

"I said a Kelly, not a mosquito. Give me what I ask for," said McIlheny. The voice was controlled, but there was a fury in it that sounded ugly.

"I'm sorry," said the scrub nurse. Her accent made her Filipino, but she spoke very clearly. "I am having trouble understanding you."

McIlheny looked up, away from the surgical field, craning his neck to see into the corners of the room. He found the circulating nurse and barked at her, "Get me a scrub nurse who speaks English, for crissake. And I mean now, madam."

80

No one moved. Not the scrub nurse. Not the residents. Not the anesthesiologists, not the pump team people. The silence was as thick as embalming fluid and twice as suffocating.

Then the circulating nurse pulled another nurse from near the heart-lung machine and sent her to the scrub room, from which she emerged ten minutes later with dripping hands and arms ready to be gowned. McIlheny watched as the circulating nurse helped her gown and glove.

Then his eye caught something and he grabbed the resident next to him by the wrist, "Not so much traction. Jesus H. Christ. Those are arteries you're crushing."

He looked up again. "Where's that scrub?"

The new scrub nurse stepped up onto the raised platform, still pulling the waist belt of her scrub gown to tie it fast. The first scrub nurse stepped down in defeat and walked fast, past me toward the door.

Eyes are about the only thing you can see in those scrub caps and gowns, and her eyes were brimming with tears.

"Jesus H. Christ," McIlheny said. "Now the suction's crapping out."

Thomas McIlheny did not run a relaxed OR. I decided not to ask how it was going. He'd probably throw a scalpel at me.

I backed out of the swinging door, unseen by McIlheny, and walked back to the locker room, showered, and dressed.

Back at the front desk the banished nurse had her cap and mask off. She was pretty, Filipino, mid-twenties, and her face was blotchy red. She was talking to the desk nurse, who was looking sympathetic.

"I speak English," said the scrub nurse. "I speak better than he does. At least I don't mumble. He mumbles into his chest and then he blows up when you hand him the wrong thing."

"You're not the first, honey," said the desk nurse. "You won't be the last. If he throws you out, count your blessings. At least you don't have to stay in there with him."

"But Sheila didn't even stand up for me," said the scrub nurse, clearly not mollified. She wasn't doing this kind of work, up at

81

this hour, for the overtime. She was a scrub nurse. There was pride working there. She had probably scrubbed on dozens of aortic valve replacements and she knew what instrument the surgeon would ask for two steps ahead of his request. She was part of the team and she'd been yanked from the lineup, humiliated.

"They just baby him," said the desk nurse. "He's a prima donna. If things go bad, they don't want him to be able to blame it on nursing."

CHAPTER
15

Not wanting to go back to Mrs. Brown, I wandered over to the
SICU. What could I tell Mrs. Brown? Your husband's still alive
but the surgeon is throwing tantrums so the outcome is still in
doubt.

Besides, I learned in medical school about premature announce-
ments of all's well. Once, as a third-year student, a patient's wife
had asked me to run up to the OR to see how things were going. It
was my opportunity to be useful and important, as third-year students rarely are, so I ran up six flights of stairs to the OR and
popped my head in. The surgeons were closing the chest and said
it had gone well. I ran down six flights of stairs and breathlessly
blabbed the good news. For that I got a hug, grateful tears, and a
warm feeling inside. I retired to the coffee room, where I rewarded
myself with a bagel, and shot the breeze with two nurses who
showed a lot of leg and were reputed to know how to use it.
Halfway through the bagel a loud wail stopped me mid-bite. It was
the wife, of course, who was in the waiting room with the surgeon. In the twenty minutes it had taken me to reach the floor,

tell the wife, butter my bagel, and schmooze with the nurses, the patient had been sent to the recovery room, where a ligature had slipped off the pulmonary artery, and he had exsanguinated. Dead, the surgeon told the wife, minutes after my glad tidings.

So I didn't want to talk to Mrs. Brown, and I couldn't see going back to the on-call room or going back to sleep while Mrs. Brown thought I was in the OR with her husband. They'd take Lydell to the SICU when they were done, assuming they didn't take him to the morgue.

In the SICU Ann Payson was writing a note on her lady with the collapsing lung.

"Don't we have fun," she said, looking up when I sat down beside her. "Friday night and the gang's all here."

"Saturday morning."

"Time flies," she said, "when you're having a good time. How's your man with the SBE?"

"I'm waiting to find out. McIlheny's still in there with him."

"He told me he was doing him. I saw him just before I went in to do my lady."

"I just popped in to see how things were going," I said. "Wish I hadn't."

Ann didn't say anything. She was supposed to ask why, but she just sat there waiting for me to go on.

"Why is that, you ask?" I said. "Because Dr. McIlheny was throwing everything from instruments to nurses around the OR."

The controlled expression didn't change on Ann's face. "He's a bit of a tyrant in the OR, I hear."

"It's not exactly the *Brandenburg* Concerto," I said. I'd been in Ann's OR a few times. She often had that playing. She also liked Rickie Lee Jones and James Taylor. She ran a very relaxed OR. People hummed, and the surgery seemed to bounce along on the rhythm. Nobody threw anything in Ann's OR.

"Everyone has his own style," Ann shrugged. "It's the outcome that counts."

"Seems like I've heard that line before. Bottom line. I don't buy it."

84

"Some real good surgeons have short fuses," said Ann.

"Is McIlheny a real good surgeon?"

"He's the chief of surgery," said Ann. Her eyes grew opaque, and she drew up a smile that had no business on her face.

"That's not what I asked," I said, trying to keep the anger out of my voice and failing. "I asked you, and you pointed me at him. You recommended him."

A look of pure surprise crossed Ann's face. She said: "They don't make people chief for looking pretty in scrubs."

"He's still in there."

"Would you like me to stick my head in?"

"Give him a few minutes."

"It'll turn out just fine. In an hour Brown'll be out here, eyes open, and you'll wonder why you ever doubted."

"I know that line," I said. "I used something like it on his wife."

I don't know who was writing the script that night, but as if on cue the double doors swung open, and Lydell Brown came rolling in. He didn't exactly look like the picture of health—tubes and IV bags and a hemovac dangling, but he was breathing on his own. They rolled his gurney over to a stall and transferred him to the bed. I watched the nurses go over him and listened while the OR nurses gave report to the SICU nurse. Then a resident came in with Lydell's chart, sat down at the work station, and scribbled an op note.

"How'd it go?" I asked.

He looked up from his scrawl. His eyes were bloodshot and the scrub mask had made a deep crease across his face. His hair was matted with sweat.

"He's got his valve. He's alive."

Ann was sitting next to him and asked, "Good tissue to work with?"

"Oh, sure," said the resident. I didn't like the look in his eyes. "If you don't mind sewing wet Kleenex."

Ann tossed me a look I couldn't read. I looked around for McIlheny, but he hadn't come to the SICU. He must have headed directly for bed. It was almost 5:00 A.M.

85

I walked over and listened to Lydell's heart. The new valve made a clicking sound as the silastic ball struck the metal struts of its cage with each ventricular contraction. McIlheny had put in a Starr Edwards valve, the new improved version of the same type Sam Sawyer was carrying around. The anesthesia still had Lydell in its grip, so he wasn't answering any questions.

There didn't seem to be much more to do.

I turned around and found Ann standing there.

"Can I walk you home?" I asked.

She laughed. "I drive," she said. She looked at the nurse working on Lydell and nodded me toward the door. We walked out into the corridor, and the electric doors closed the SICU off behind us.

"There's enough speculation about my love life without feeding the SICU nurses material," she said, taking my arm, pecking me on the cheek. "He'll do fine."

"Think McIlheny will talk to the wife?"

"I'm sure that's where he is, even as we speak."

I stopped at a hallway phone and called Lydell's room phone number. I got a recording telling me they turned the patients' phones off after 9:00 P.M.

"I better drop in and talk to her."

"What are you going to tell her?"

"She asked me to check on how things were going."

"McIlheny will give it to her from the horse's mouth."

"You're right. She doesn't need me now," I said.

"How nice," said Ann. "You're available."

I drew her to me and spun her into a convenient utility room. She put her face up to be kissed. She was nice to kiss. She had a nice body and you missed none of it in that sheer cotton scrub suit.

"Not here," she said.

"Where's your on-call room?"

"Déclassé." She smiled. "No, you go home and get some sleep and call me around four this afternoon, if you still want to. You can take me out to dinner and get me in a receptive mood, which you've never had trouble doing."

"You're sleeping to four?"

"No, I have to get up and take my insulin, and eat. Then I'm going back to sleep until four."

"You're staying here?"

"Until breakfast. Why?"

"I was trying to figure out how I'm going to get home. I'll take a cab."

"Your car is in the hospital lot." She laughed. "You picked me up, and we went to Mai's place together."

She was right about that.

"That's right, Doctor," I said. "We went to dinner last night. Seems like ages."

CHAPTER

16

The next morning I was in the SICU at eleven. I had been home, gotten four hours' sleep. Lightly breakfasted, showered, and shaved, I walked onto the SICU.

It was Saturday, my office was closed, and I had no place special to be until dinner, which meant I had time to look Lydell over carefully. There wasn't much in his chart—just a brief operative note by the resident—no complications, to the SICU in stable condition, and so on.

I looked over the flow charts they keep on big boards on the wall of each patient's stall. Lydell's urine output had been good initially, but was now dropping off, and his respiratory rate was climbing. I listened to his lungs and to his heart.

The redheaded nurse who had handled that blowout I had watched with Ryan came into the stall while I went over Lydell. Having seen her in action the night her patient blew a suture, I was glad she was Lydell's nurse.

"His urine output's down," she said, "and his wedge is up."

"He didn't have that murmur when he came out of surgery last night," I told her.

"I think he's in failure," she said. "Why is anybody's guess. I called the resident twice already. He keeps telling me to push the Lasix."

"Lasix isn't going to help much if his valve is working loose."

"What can I do?" she said with the same vehemence I'd heard that time before, when her patient's chest had filled with blood. "I call and I call. All I get is, 'Push the Lasix.'"

"I guess they're pretty wiped out after all night in the OR," I said.

"That doesn't help him a whole lot," she said, nodding at Lydell. "And if they're wiped, they ought to have someone covering who isn't."

I couldn't argue with that.

"I haven't taken care of post-op patients a whole lot since medical school," I said. "But seems to me if he has a new murmur, he could be unseating his valve."

"I called the resident twice already," said the nurse. "He's not getting out of bed. We're all very spit and polish around here now," she said. Her eyes narrowed, and she was holding it all back, but finally it all came out in a rush. "Name tags on straight, creases pressed. But getting that valve sewn in so it doesn't leak, we're not so swift on that."

"Who's the doctor for the SICU?"

"José Cruz. The anesthesiologists cover."

I asked José Cruz to look at Lydell.

José was a fat Mexican who always looked as if someone were standing on his foot but he was too polite to say anything about it. He went over things carefully enough. Then he said, "This is Dr. McIlheny's patient?"

"Yes," said the redheaded nurse.

"Maureen," said José Cruz with his Mexican intonation. "This is Dr. McIlheny's patient. I think he maybe might be unseating the valve. But Dr. McIlheny does not like to hear bad news, you know. I will call first the resident. I am just an anesthesiologist. We should let the surgeons have a look."

89

"Let's not waste time with the resident," I said. "He could blow any time."

"Of course," said José Cruz. "But you do not know Dr. McIlheny as we do. He is very sensitive. We should go through channels. The chain of command, he calls it."

"I'm pretty sensitive about my patients blowing valves," I said. "I'll call McIlheny."

McIlheny answered the phone in a sleep-thickened growl. I apologized for waking him and presented the information—the rising lung pressures and signs of fluid backing up there, the increasing heart murmur, the falling urine—all of which added up to a failing heart and a loosening valve. There was a long pause during which I thought he had fallen back to sleep.

McIlheny said, "I'm on my way. Tell the resident to call the pump team in and to get the thoracic team together."

I hung up. The nurse, Maureen, was listening on another phone nearby. She was smiling, beam to beam.

"You must swing some weight," she said.

I picked the phone up again and asked page for Nancy Colleo's home phone number. Nancy answered breathlessly. She had been working in the garden and had to run in, she said.

"Well, wash your hands off. I want you to restudy Lydell Brown. I think his new valve may be unseating. Tom McIlheny's on his way to replace it."

"Oh, lovely," said Nancy. "I'm on my way. Oh, and Abe?"

"Yes?"

"I've got to talk to you about your man, Sawyer."

"You did him?"

"I'll show you his studies. Hard to believe he's got it so long after he had the valve put in."

"One thing at a time, Nancy. Right now let's do Lydell Brown. Then you can hit me over the head with Sam Sawyer."

When it rains it pours. Lydell Brown literally tearing apart and now Sam Sawyer. Times like that I'm glad I don't smoke—I'd go through a pack just waiting for people to show up.

"Why didn't you call Nancy before you called Dr. McIlheny?" asked José Cruz.

"If she sees what I think she's going to see, I want him taken right to surgery."

"Boy, you got guts," said José.

I looked at Lydell, tubes coming out of places even his expert junkie hands would never have dared jab, flat on his back, flaccid, sliding away from us.

"It's all in your perspective," I told José. "You got to deal with Dr. McIlheny. I got to deal with this guy's wife."

CHAPTER

17

Ann Payson lived in a town house about half a mile from the hospital on Reservoir Road, overlooking the canal, thirty steps straight up from the street. You could get chest pains with clean coronary arteries climbing up those stairs. Before I knew Ann I would drive by those town houses on the way to the hospital and wonder who lived there. No one much past forty could lug groceries up those stairs. Ann could, though. She was in great shape. Jogged every morning along the canal all the way to Key Bridge and back. Probably took those stairs two at a time with a bag of groceries in each arm. She was ready to go when I arrived.

"You must have come straight from the hospital," she said. "You look like you could use a drink."

"I could use a shower," I said. "But I'll settle for the use of your sink."

She followed me into the bathroom and watched me wash my hands, face, and finally my hair until I felt clean and revived.

We walked back into her living room, across her green Oriental rugs. Ann liked green. Green, the color of spring, new life, the greening of things. All her rugs were green. I slumped onto her dark green sofa, and she rubbed my neck while I watched her strange fish whip around in her fish tank. The tank was no bigger than a beer truck and had one of those oxygen pumps that make very sedating noises. I'd kid Ann about the fish once in a while, but she liked them. They were companionable and they were quiet, and they never paged her or bothered her on the phone. I don't know what kinds she had, but looking at them was very restful, almost hypnotic.

"How's Brown?" she asked.

"Alive."

"They redid the valve?"

"Had to. He's back in the SICU now."

The first valve Thomas McIlheny had sewn into Lydell Brown had pulled loose, the sutures tearing away from their moorings in the soggy, inflamed tissue the *Staphylococcus aureus* had left. McIlheny took him back to surgery and put in another valve. I was left to explain it all to Mrs. Brown. It had been a lovely day.

"Want to go out, or just stay home?" Ann asked.

"Out," I said.

"Where?"

"What place feels far away but isn't?"

The answer was Adams-Morgan, which is the only place in Washington that never feels like Washington. We took the scenic route, along Calvert Street past the Russian compound with all its rooftop antennae bugging out, bugging Washington, past the vice-president's house with the big white anchors and the guards at the gate, through Woodley Park with all its Victorian homes. We popped out across Connecticut Avenue, and suddenly there was the city again.

It was a cool night, and crisp for late September in Washington, and the sidewalks were full along Columbia Road. Men and women in their twenties, black women with white men, white women with black men, Asians, Hispanics, old people, homosexuals holding hands—people as you see them in New York and

93

never think about it. Somehow in Washington it all seemed exotic. Washington can be such a stiff, pious, policed town. Too much of that old plantation-life influence. Adams-Morgan was a place where you could imagine people cared about different things than the rest of Washington cared about. There was energy, eccentricity, people breaking rules, people living lives that had nothing to do with government, politics, celebrity, or image. In short, it felt alive and very far away.

We looked at the menus outside an Ethiopian place, kept walking past Indian, Afghan, Chinese, Mexican, Greek, Italian, and finally went into a Spanish restaurant, La Plaza. Four people waited on a line in front of us. A thin man with wiry hair pushed by us and called over the maître d'. He announced he was Doctor Somebody, as if he expected the maître d' and perhaps the entire staff of waiters and cooks to come out and genuflect before him. He apparently had a reservation, his wife and friends were on their way in, and he had told everybody he would take care of the table.

"But our reservation was for eight," he was saying.

"But the table is not ready, señor," the maître d' said in his nasal Spanish tones. "People do not always finish their meals on time."

"That's no excuse."

"Doctor, I wait sometimes an hour in my doctor's office. Do you always see your patients on time?"

"I make a point of always being on time," he said.

The four people on line in front of us laughed.

"Can we take this guy out and shoot him?" Ann whispered in my ear.

We had no reservation, but we were seated no more than two minutes after the doctor, who we decided wasn't a real doctor but a psychiatrist. We had no way of knowing that, but we wanted to believe it. We didn't want him to be one of us.

They put us next to a couple with a baby. The baby was asleep in a portable baby carrier, but I asked Ann if she wanted to wait for another table. I wanted to talk to her and I didn't want to have to shout over screams.

94

"Don't be ridiculous," said Ann. "This is just the place to be." She sat down next to the baby and smiled in the direction of the soft pink face. It was a nice enough baby, but they usually are when they're sleeping. The parents noticed Ann smiling, and she asked how old, and they said five months, and Ann told them they had a beautiful child.

The wine waiter appeared, and I waved him off. Alcohol did no favors for her diabetes, and Ann rarely drank. The real waiter came. Ann had eaten at La Plaza before and ordered for us, some kind of fish thing, with rice. I hardly noticed. I was thinking about Lydell Brown.

"Sounds like he had nothing to work with—staph's a nasty bug in the heart," Ann said.

"I didn't say it was McIlheny's fault," I said. "The moral of the story is, you don't go with a surgeon you don't know. Especially for something like this."

"The moral of the story is," said Ann, "you don't inject your veins with dirty needles."

The baby woke up and sneezed a couple of times, and Ann cooed and waved at him. He waved his arms and legs. Then she turned back to me and said, "No surgeon in the world's going to have any luck sewing in infected tissue." She looked at the baby, then looked back to me. "And it sounds like he didn't fool around deciding to take Brown back to the OR."

"I know all that," I said. "But if you'd done the surgery and all this had happened, I'd have no second thoughts now. You go with the ace and if you get shelled out, well, them's the breaks."

"I'm the ace?"

"You're the ace."

"I like that," said Ann. "Sounds so superior."

"It is. The ace of the staff is the best pitcher you have."

"Don't let that get back to the chief of surgery."

The food arrived, and the smell of it started to revive me. Ann had chosen well.

"He's got to earn his way, like everyone else," I said.

95

"He will," she said. "But I'm on good terms with him now, and I don't want to get rumored into some kind of competition. It's bad enough as it is."

"How is it?"

"Whenever you get the new regime, there's going to be problems," Ann said, scooping rice and fish on her fork, holding it poised before she continued. "McIlheny has his fans—John Toland and one or two others who were on the selection committee —and he brought some guys with him. But there are a lot of guys from the old guard who were here when he came who are just waiting for him to screw up."

"How's he done so far?"

"What do I know? He's in his OR, I'm in mine," said Ann, her eyes everywhere but on mine.

"But surely you've formed some impression."

"Well, there is one thing."

"Which is?"

"He shouldn't have done the radical neck on that lady you were so lathered up about," said Ann. "The surgery was clean enough," she continued, now looking me straight in the eye. "It's just the judgment behind it. I mean, radical necks went out with leeches. But I guess that's arguable."

"Not when you leave the lady bereft of parathyroid glands, and she needs calcium and vitamin D for the rest of her life."

Ann shrugged and continued eating.

"Are you really that forgiving?" I asked. "Or are you just trying to be diplomatic?"

"It's not a matter of being forgiving or diplomatic," Ann snapped. "I'm just not rushing to judgment. And before you get all self-righteous, tell me how many internists gone to seed you've cast stones at lately?"

Her face was tight, and her voice sharpened to an edge, and none of it was lost on the baby, who had been studying every feature of Ann's face and sensed Ann was angry. Kids pick up on that. The baby started bawling at good volume.

"Oh, I scared you," said Ann, reaching down for the red-faced,

96

squirmy thing who was waving his arms. "May I?" she asked the mother.

Ann put the screamer on her shoulder and patted him into submission. A pretty substantial burp erupted, and he fell asleep instantly. Ann laid him down perfectly, and the mother rocked the portable baby contraption with her foot.

"You ought to get one of those for yourself," I said.

Ann smiled at the sleeping child and shook her head. She said, "I'd never get to work. I'd just nuzzle it all day."

"Some days you would," I said. "Some days you'd tear yourself away and save lives."

"It would be nice," she said.

"Good, it's settled then. Let's run off and buy a Volvo and have a baby and get married—not necessarily in that order."

"I think we've played this scene before," she said. Her eyes grew opaque. Sometimes you could look into Ann's eyes and see a long way in. Sometimes you might as well have looked at a couple of bottle tops. "I'd love to have your baby. I'd love to live happily ever after. But that's not the hand I've been dealt."

She was right, of course. A thirty-seven-year-old diabetic who'd been on insulin since internship would have a thrilling time with pregnancy. At best, it would be a mess, with the tight control and the hypoglycemia we'd have to impose. She might not be able to operate for a lot of that nine months. She might not make it through pregnancy. The kid might not make it.

"This is not one of my favorite topics," she said in a low voice, not looking up from her plate.

"Sometimes you've got to just say what-the-hell and do it," I said.

"Why don't you find yourself a nice healthy girl with a good pelvis and have some kids," said Ann. She had hauled up a look over her face she thought was a smile. It wasn't a smile. She just thought it was a smile. "Some nice Catholic nurse like that cute little redhead I've seen you ogling in the SICU. Maureen, with the nice legs. Doesn't believe in birth control, I bet. You should do that."

97

"I don't want a redhead with nice legs," I said, "even if Ryan says she's great in bed."

"Ryan told you that? I thought Maureen had more sense than to fool with Ryan."

"He wears down their resistance. Like I'm trying to do with you."

"You wore me down long ago," said Ann. "And nobody else could."

"Look, we don't have to get married. We'll move in together. I'll even feed your fish. But throw away the diaphragm and take some chances."

"You just like the idea of being a young widower with kids and no wife to bother him."

"You'll outlive your doctors," I said.

This was an old wound for Ann, and she seemed to enjoy rubbing salt in it occasionally. Why was I wasting my time with her? She was not going to live a normal life span or a normal life. She might well go blind or wind up in renal failure someday. She was living on borrowed time. She was diabetic. She had no hopes for kids, or for marriage, or for anything more than her town house with her expensive Oriental carpets and her exotic fish. And she had her career.

"Ben," she said. "We have a good time. I get all gooey inside just standing next to you in an elevator. You want forever, you're looking at the wrong lady. I'm going to be a double amputee on a dialysis machine someday. You want to bring the kids by to see that?"

"I won't let that happen."

Ann laughed. It was a lovely, tinkling laugh, without anger, a beautiful sound.

"You really are precious," she said. "So earnest. You really think you can protect me."

"I can."

"My hero."

"I can."

"Against all odds. Against all the slings and arrows."

98

"I will."

"Let's change the subject," she said. "We're safer with medicine. We never get too emotional with that."

"Heaven forbid we should get emotional."

The baby left with its companions. I asked for the check, and Ann tried to grab it.

"You got the last one," she said.

"I invited you," I said.

"No, you've been working all day," she said. "And I can deduct it. Legit. I'm taking out a doc who refers me patients."

"I'm a business expense," I said. "Terrific."

So she paid, and we walked out into the cold night air. Ann was wearing a sweater under a thick Harris tweed jacket, but she shivered and drew me into a doorway and pressed up against me.

"You're no expense," she said, and she kissed me. "No expense at all."

I didn't want her to stop and held her, but she pushed away.

We walked back to my car, Ann holding onto my arm. We walked down Columbia Road with the other late-night couples. It had turned quite cold, and we talked as we walked, our breaths mingling in the air. I watched the evanescent puffs flowing together, blending into one and dying before my eyes.

CHAPTER

18

Monday morning there were thunderstorms. I sat in my car and watched the water sweeping like curtains of swung glass beads across the lot next to my office. Thunderclaps followed. The concussions shook the car, and it got dark as night. It was much more fun than going to work, but I was already ten minutes late, so I made a run for it.

Mrs. Bromley helped me off with my raincoat.

"Nasty, nasty," she said, spearing the dripping thing with a hanger and suspending it in the front closet like something her husband had pulled from the Potomac. "How was your weekend? Spend it lolling by the health club pool?"

Being English, Mrs. Bromley had an active fantasy life about how Americans spend their weekends. She usually spent hers gardening.

"Not exactly. I spent quite a lot of it with Lydell Brown."

"The bus driver who likes to shove dirty needles in his veins? Where did you stash him?"

"Surgical intensive care at St. George's."

"Oh, you're doing surgery now?"

"I just stand around and wring my hands a lot. Chant incantations. That kind of thing."

"And what happened to Mr. Brown?"

"Where did you leave the story last week?"

"He had bacteria behaving like a pack of starving termites chewing up his valve."

"Yes, that was Thursday or Friday."

"Friday."

"So Friday night I'm out to dinner and he went into rip-roaring congestive heart failure and tried very hard to die."

"But you wouldn't let him?"

"The surgeons wouldn't let him. They sewed in a new valve, but the tissue they had to sew it to was soggy, like Jell-O, and the sutures wouldn't hold, and the valve started to come out."

"Oh, splendid."

"Oh, it gets better. So they took him back to the OR Saturday and sewed in a second valve, and Sunday he strokes, and now he can't move his left arm or leg, and his face droops on the right."

"So he's a nice mess. You saved him and he wishes you hadn't."

"Actually, that's the worst part. He's very grateful for everything. I saw him yesterday. He can't even raise his left hand off the bed and he looks up at me and says, 'Thanks, Doc. I knew you'd get me through.'"

"Nothing like a grateful patient."

"I may change careers."

"You may have to. Does Mr. Brown have a wife with a lawyer?"

"He has a wife. I'm sure the lawyers will find her."

"Well, you did all you could. It's not your fault."

"That's just the kind of cases lawyers like best. They win more of those than any other."

"Curious system."

"Oh, you should see it in action. They'll haul this poor guy in front of six taxi drivers and a bowling alley owner and five housewives, and they'll lift his arm and let it fall with a sickening thud, and they'll turn to me in the witness box and ask, 'Now Dr. Abrams, do you regret sending this patient to surgery?'"

"I presume there was no other alternative."

"There are always other alternatives. I was pretty sure that the others all added up to letting him die. Try telling the jury that. They're sitting there looking at him drool."

"Maybe they'll take it out on the surgeon."

"Oh, they'll sue everyone in the chart."

"The most disconcerting part of this weekend, aside from what happened to Brown, was that it happened with a surgeon I'd never used before. Your friend, the chief of surgery."

"My friend?"

"You told Sawyer all about him referring me patients."

"Well, sounds like you got your money's worth from him."

"He did earn his fee," I admitted. "But one of the nurses in the SICU said something. When it became evident that Brown was going to have to go back for a second time, I said something like, 'Oh, well, at least we've got the chief of surgery.' And the nurse says, 'The chief ought to be good at going back in a second time, he does it often enough.'"

"My word," said Mrs. Bromley, raising her eyebrows. "Not exactly a vote of confidence from the nursing staff."

"Not exactly."

"Do you think it was the surgeon's fault?"

"I don't know what to think. Ann Payson says it would've happened to anyone. Don't blame the surgeon for the disease."

"Oh, we saw Dr. Payson this weekend, did we? You were a busy man," said Mrs. Bromley. An annoyingly knowing smile crossed her lips, despite her best efforts to control it. "Well, that sounds like a surgeon talking. How is she, the good Dr. Payson?"

"She sends her regards."

"And why didn't she do the surgery?"

"She was doing another case, or believe me she'd have had it."

"Well, you went with experience and stature."

I found that small comfort somehow. I couldn't get the image of

102

Lydell Brown lying there with a flaccid arm and leg out of my mind.

Mrs. Bromley and I walked back to the examining room, which had the refrigerator and the coffee machine. She made some coffee. We heard the front door to the office opening.

"That must be your first patient."

"I've got patients this morning?" I asked, trying to keep the disappointment out of my voice.

"Now, now, that is what we are here for. We do run a medical office. Heal the sick. Minister to the suffering."

"Keep the lawyers fat."

"It's your barber with the big breasts. I'll ask if he has a lawyer."

He didn't admit to knowing any lawyers. His breasts were bigger, his adrenal glands harbored no tumors, and his testicles were clean. I couldn't figure out where his extra estrogen was coming from. I was pretty sure he wasn't making extra estrogen—but he had no known exposure. His wife didn't use estrogen vaginal creams and he took no medicines.

As he was leaving he looked at my hair and said, "Hey, Doc. Your hair's getting a little thin in front. I got this cream I rub in make it nice and thick."

"Sure, Mario," I said. "And I got some snake oil makes you young again."

"No, Doc. You should see this guy I rub it in. His hair's so thick now."

As I said, I get preoccupied and miss things. He mentioned that the first time, and it went right by me, but somehow now it hit me in the face, and I couldn't walk away from it.

"You have the cream with you, Mario?"

"No, Doc. I keep it in the shop."

"What's the name?"

"I don't know. I can call the shop and find out."

He called the shop, and they fetched the tube and read the name out over the phone, and I looked it up. It was loaded with estrogen. It had so much estrogen a guy could start menstruating just sniffing it.

103

"This is what's growing you breasts, Mario. You're rubbing it in this guy's scalp. You're rubbing it in your hands."

Mario couldn't have looked more surprised if the tube had materialized and bitten him. "But you should see his hair, Doc," he squawked.

"Have you checked his breasts?" I said.

Mario looked at me in horror. It wasn't like I was asking him about his sexual preference. What did he know?

"Let him rub his own scalp cream in, Mario."

He went away shaking his head, looking at his hands as if he had blood on them, and checking his breasts.

We had five other patients that morning: three feeling dizzy's, one chest pain of three months' duration, and one cough. None of them very sick. They all had clean heart valves and they could all move both arms and legs.

CHAPTER

19

I could hear my phone ringing through the door when I got home. I almost took the hinges off getting to it by the fifth ring.

"Oh, I'm so glad I got you." It was Mrs. Bromley. "I thought you might have gone out for one of your walks by the river."

"I just got home," I said.

"You raced by me and I quite forgot to tell you Dr. Payson called while you were with your last patient."

"Did she want me to call her back?"

"She wanted you to call her at home tonight."

No answer at Ann's home phone. I called the hospital. She was in the OR. Seven o'clock in the evening, where else would she be? She spoke to me over the special speaker phone in the OR.

"That Mr. Seagram," she said. "The guy I did with the BKA, the one who wanted to die and then didn't say a word after I took his foot off, remember?"

"How could I forget?"

"I'm worried about his other foot now. He spiked to thirty-nine today, his sugar's four-twenty, and he's got a spot on his big toe that's draining."

"And the resident on Endocrine has gone home for the night?"

"That's about the size of it, Doc," said Ann. "We can have dinner after you finish seeing him."

It didn't take long to bring Mr. Seagram's sugar down to where it belonged. Afterward, Ann and I and two residents raised our blood cholesterols eating pizza. Ann wanted to treat the residents who had helped her with her late case, so she ordered out.

"Now, isn't this a nice reward?" said Ann. "Don't we all feel virtuous? Saving lives, supporting a struggling pizza industry?"

"I can feel my coronary arteries clogging up even as I eat," said one of the residents, biting into his slice happily. "I want you to do my bypass."

"What?" I said. "For a St. George's house officer, only the chief of surgery will do."

The look that passed between the two residents could not have been missed in a sandstorm on a moonless night. Ann kept her eyes on her plate, but her ears turned crimson.

The resident said, "Thank you, no. I'll have Dr. Payson do mine."

I waited for him to say more, but all the surgeons at the table suddenly found the Formica tabletop intensely interesting.

I looked from one to another and finally said, "Well, silence does speak eloquently."

A long column of seconds marched by at half step until finally the other resident said, "You wouldn't see me hanging around on my night off to do a case with anyone but Dr. Payson."

Ann said, "What he means is that he knows I'm a soft touch for a free meal after the case is done."

"Only next time," said the resident, "order Chinese. This cholesterol pie is taking years off my life."

"Look at these guys," said Ann. "Spoil them and they take advantage of you."

When the residents left, Ann and I walked to her on-call room.

106

"Really amazing how eager everyone is to talk about the new chief," I said, as Ann closed the door and pulled her blue scrub shirt off over her head.

"They're not eager to share anything with you right now," said Ann. "Not until they've made up their minds." She slid off her scrub pants. I could see the spot on her belly where she had injected her insulin that morning. She had hit a small blood vessel, and it left a bruise. Ann had lovely skin, all a single tone, and the bruise stood out.

"Looked to me like they've made them up already."

Ann shrugged but didn't answer. She reached into her closet and pulled out a knit dress. I looked at the fine muscles move in her shoulders as she slid on the dress. Her surgical life kept her in fine shape. They were all a sort of athlete, those thoracic surgeons. Anyone who could stand up that long in one spot had to be.

In my overheated youth, I looked at women as if they were statues—any flaw detracted from the aesthetic experience of them. With Ann, flaws were not important. I was always excited just being with her.

My beeper intruded with its annoying, insistent blurt.

"Oh, this is going to be a wonderful night," I said.

It was the postpartum nurse on Cheryl Walker.

"She's all goofy and confused, and her blood sugar's fifty-six," said the nurse.

"Feed her," I said. "I'll be right over."

Ann and I walked down to her ward together.

Cheryl was drinking orange juice when we arrived. She looked and sounded fine.

"I'm so embarrassed they called you," said Cheryl. "I knew it was just my sugar dropping."

"Better to call too often than not often enough," I told her. I looked at Ann to see if she was laughing at me. She had to endure my post-phone call tirades all the times patients called for no good reason. But I liked Cheryl and I really didn't mind

107

her calling. She didn't abuse it. Besides, it was the nurse who called this time. Ann said nothing—she just smiled at me and at Cheryl.

Ann and I walked out to the parking lot and took my car to Thirty-fourth Street, parked, and walked down the steep hill to M Street. She held my arm as we descended.

"Oh, I don't mind if you call," said Ann. "Call me anytime. Better too often than not often enough."

"Well, she never calls."

"She's awfully cute," said Ann. "And she adores you."

"Oh, phooey."

"She does. And she's got you wrapped around her little finger. Those big baby blues—bats those lashes."

"She damn well should adore me," I said. "She lost her first baby because her LMD thought she shouldn't worry about her diabetes during pregnancy. Now she has a nice little seven-pounder, thanks to my hounding her for nine months."

We reached M Street and walked out onto Key Bridge, toward the blaze of lights in the Roslyn buildings across the river.

"She must have had quite a time," said Ann, leaning over the stone wall of the bridge and looking down into the dark water rushing by below.

"Not too bad," I said. "All's well that ends well. Mother and baby doing well. Happy endings all around."

"That's a nice story," said Ann. "I like happy endings."

We walked a little farther. An airplane roared overhead.

"But the story isn't over," said Ann. "She's got the baby. Now she has to live to see it grow up."

"Who are we talking about now?" I asked.

"Cheryl," said Ann. "And me and you."

"If your diabetes disappeared tomorrow, you still wouldn't go off with me and have babies."

"Oh, I'd have lots of babies."

"No, you'd have to give up too much. The operating room, the pizza with adoring residents. The life. Admit it."

108

"I could have kids and surgery. Look at Jane Dickson. She has three and operates every day."

"But you couldn't."

She looked up. "I can do anything I want to do."

I looked at her. There were cars going by on the bridge, and their headlights caught her face in waves. It made no difference whether she was in light or dark—her eyes were flat as nickels.

CHAPTER
20

Lydell Brown could move his left hand. He could move his left foot, too, if you badgered him. He could hold a hollow rubber ball in his left hand, wrap his fingers around it, and squeeze enough to dent it maybe a quarter of an inch. My two-year-old nephew could have collapsed that ball in one hand. Lydell was making progress, though.

His heart sounded good, and his lungs were clear. He could smile nicely now, no lopsided face. He was alive.

You needed perspective at times like that.

His wife walked in as I was finishing. She wasn't smiling, but she was polite, as always. She asked me how he was, and I told her he was better without trying to make it sound as if I thought she ought to be happy or grateful. I let her know I realized he was still a disaster as far as she was concerned.

She stroked his forehead and kissed his cheek, and he smiled at her.

"I's doing better," he told her, showing her what he could do to the rubber ball.

"Oh, that's so good," she said, and she looked up to me with a look that made me uncomfortable. Look at what we're calling success now.

My beeper went off. For once I was glad to hear its chirpy, insistent voice. It saved me from the usual tête-à-tête in the hallway with Mrs. Brown, who asked me every day all the questions I'd be asking if I were in her position—how much better will he get, how long will it take, why did this happen—questions for which there were either no answers, no good answers, or answers she didn't want to hear.

The man who paged me was the chief of medicine, and I nearly knocked him down flying out of the room. He caught me with both arms like a lineman smothering a quarterback.

Chiefs of medicine come in two varieties: elder statesmen and young Turks. Dennis Rallston was a young Turk, gray-haired at just shy of forty, stocky, aggressive, and abrupt.

"Just the man I wanted to see," he said.

"Call my secretary," I said. "It's by appointment only with Dr. Abrams."

"I run this joint." He grinned. "You'll come with me to the command post or suffer the consequences."

"I suffer, either way."

We walked down the long corridor to his office. He hadn't changed it much since assuming command of the department of medicine. Not that you'd want to. His predecessor, Dr. von Dernhoffer, had done a very nice job on the office. There were enough Persian carpets in inventory to start a small store, and they lay on top of a wall-to-wall carpet deep enough to sink into and never be heard from again. And that was just the waiting room. Dennis's own office had the requisite sweeping oak desk made from the hull of a presidential yacht, and two full-size couches facing each other across a maroon Oriental for which the hospital must have traded in an old CAT scanner.

Dennis sank into one of the couches and I into the other, and we grinned at each other like a pair of Chicago aldermen who had just stolen the election.

111

"You rent this place out for weddings on weekends?" I asked.

"On weekends I move my family in," he said. "Better than going to a hotel."

"You could buy your own hotel."

"Power at the university hospital does not translate readily into money," said Dennis. "Not for the chief of medicine."

"I can tell," I said, "by the BMW you got in the doctors' lot. That is the space that says 'chief of medicine' with the BMW?"

"Damn guy keeps stealing my spot." Dennis grinned. "Mine's the sixty-four Honda next to it."

"Next to it is an even bigger Mercedes, which belongs to the even newer chief of surgery, if I'm not mistaken. At least that's what it says on the wall."

"That's his car, all right. I hear you're buddies now."

"Good news travels fast," I said. "You hear about the patient?"

"I hear he's still alive," said Dennis. "And he doesn't have much right to be."

"You chiefs always stick up for each other."

"You got a beef about McIlheny saving that guy for you?"

"No," I said. "The patient can move half his body. Why should I beef?"

"As I said, he's alive. The wife going to sue?"

"Not you. Me, if she does."

"Good, I got enough in the way of lawyers right now."

"Already?"

"One I inherited. One I just heard about."

"Welcome to the real world. You've been hiding in the ivory tower too long."

"You know what Kissinger said about university politics?"

"No. But I'm sure I'm about to learn."

"The reason they're so vicious," said Dennis, "is that there's so little at stake."

He laughed. I laughed.

"What happened before you got here?"

"Oh, a beaut. Local lawyer's visiting his eighty-year-old mother on Seven North. Mother arrests right in front of him. He calls a

112

nurse, who calls a code. Everyone rushes in. The resident running the code asks him to step out. Resident looks at his three-by-five card sign-out file he carries in his pocket."

"This is before you changed the coverage system?"

"Of course. This is when the interns had patients on six different floors and the coverage chart looked like a map of the solar system."

"So?"

"So listen, the resident consults his sign-out cards. He does not look in the patient's chart, mind you. He sees that Mrs. Browning is a no-code, do not resuscitate, and he cancels the arrest." Rallston fixed me with his dark brown eyes. "Trouble is, he had the wrong Mrs. Browning."

"Offhand, I'd think you better settle."

"I got two-hundred-dollar-an-hour lawyers telling me that in sixteen-page memos. I need your advice."

"I'll send you a bill."

"You collect much?"

"Some of my patients pay their bills. If they can't or don't want to, they call their lawyers. Then I hear about how I nearly did them in and we call it even."

"Why not get out of the rat race?"

"But it's such fun. Healing the sick, giving depositions."

"You thought about my offer? You can get out of the rat race."

"But I'm having such a good time in private practice. How could I come here and let the hospital buy me Persian rugs for my office, pay for my secretary, my life insurance, my malpractice? Where's the thrill in that?"

"Abe, I got to fill the Endocrine spot," Dennis said, standing, offering his hand. "Think about it."

I had thought about it. It was a very attractive offer, as they say in the business world. No more worries about meeting the end-of-the-month bills—the hospital would give me an office, phones, even let me keep Mrs. Bromley, and provide malpractice coverage —which was becoming a big budget item—plus life insurance, health insurance, retirement, that steady monthly check.

My big worries in solo practice coalesced around the dollar. Insurance companies shuffled and hemmed and hawed and paid six months after I saw patients, and my landlord was standing there the first of every month with his hand out. Patients paid or didn't pay, often late, frequently only partially, and it was a constant struggle, mailing checks on a timed schedule so nothing bounced and so no penalties accrued, managing cash flow, things like that, things I never learned about in medical school and wished I never had to learn.

So a steady check and no overhead looked very good. There were so many reasons to do it, I knew there had to be some very good reason not to.

Nothing is that black-and-white.

The problem was time. I owned my own day now. I made my own schedule. Actually, Mrs. Bromley made my schedule, but, in theory, she worked for me. And despite the need to keep to some semblance of a schedule in the office, I could take an hour with a patient without looking over my shoulder. I had no partners to get resentful that I was seeing only half as many patients as they were. There was no administrator looking at my appointment book to be sure I was "productive." I love that word. I had friends who worked in a health maintenance organization until "productive" drove them out. Administrators thought that seeing patients was like manufacturing widgets—you could do time and motion studies in clinics and count the number of patients a doc saw and figure out what he was worth to the organization.

There's no such thing as free money. Let someone put you on salary and you let him own you in ways you don't like to think about.

Dennis wanted his Endocrine department put in shape, but he also wanted his man in place. There was more to it than just taking care of patients and keeping the interns out of trouble. There was loyalty. Organization men knew all about loyalty and being a team player, making yourself forgive things in your boss you wouldn't forgive in anyone else, and being nice because your

114

mortgage payments depended on it, rather than because you had any real sympathy.

That's called being a grown-up, Ann would say. You can't be snide and obnoxious to whomever you please if you want to drive expensive cars and live in elegant neighborhoods. You have to be civilized. Adult.

She was right, of course. Ann could have it.

CHAPTER

21

Coming out of Dennis Rallston's office, I was paged twice in rapid succession. The first page was from Mrs. Bromley, reminding me we had a patient scheduled and I was to be on time.

The second page was from a surgical resident in the SICU. Dr. McIlheny had asked him to call me about a ward case he had done with the residents. The patient was now post-op with a temperature of a hundred and four, and they wanted me down there right away.

I ran down the four flights to the SICU. I should know better than to do that. I arrived breathless and unable to hear a word the resident was saying for the first three minutes. When oxygen returned to my brain, I tuned in on a sixty-year-old woman who was previously healthy except for some colicky abdominal pain until the blades took her gall bladder out. By the time they got her to the SICU her temp was skyrocketing, her pulse was a hundred and sixty and irregular, and her cardiogram showed that her heart was hurtling toward a precipice, sixty-year-old hearts not being overly fond of beating a hundred and sixty times a minute.

"She was afebrile pre-op?" I asked the resident, who was looking pretty shaky himself.

"She was fine. We took her in and had that gall bag out in under seventy minutes. Then the gas man tells us she's flipped into AF, so we get out as quick as we can and bail out. Figured she'd flipped an embolus. But her gases were fine, and she's hot as a pistol."

He looked at me for some answers. I didn't have any.

"What could make her spike a temp like that? I mean, in thirty minutes or so."

"Sepsis."

"She wouldn't have gotten septic that fast. And her pressure's fine. No way she's septic."

"Let me take a look at her," I said, stalling for time. That's always a safe thing to say when you don't know what to do. Go into the room, stick a stethoscope in both ears, and block out all the nurses and interns and think.

"We thought maybe postanesthesia hyperthermia," the resident said.

I walked over to the patient. She was awake, but her eyes were closed, and she was beet-red, glistening with sweat, and breathing at about twice the normal rate. Her monitor showed the racing heart rate.

The nurse was my favorite redhead—her nameplate said Maureen Flaherty. "Another McIlheny gift," said Maureen.

I plugged my stethoscope in, put the bell on her chest, and tried to think. Usually when I listen to a heart I lay a finger on the carotid artery in the neck, and that paid off this time. Her neck was where the answer lay.

I called to the surgical resident, who hopped into the stall.

"You notice something here?" I said, pointing to the patient's neck. At the base, just above the collarbone was a bulging mass. It looked like she'd swallowed a grapefruit whole, and it lodged there, unable to descend into the chest.

"Christ," he said, reaching out and lightly running his finger over her neck. "Where'd that come from?"

117

"It didn't just pop up overnight," I said. "Thyroids take time to grow. Someone missed that goiter. Who examined her pre-op?"

"The intern," he growled. I pitied that poor intern. The resident was supposed to check his work, and now they both looked bad, not to mention how bad the patient looked. Of course, McIlheny was supposed to check the resident.

They'd taken a lady to surgery who was probably hyperthyroid at the time they admitted her. They'd put her under general anesthesia, operated, and now she was in thyroid storm. People died in thyroid storm if you didn't do just the right things for them, and sometimes they died even if you did.

I told the resident what to do and watched him copy the orders into the order book.

"Draw up a milligram of propanolol for me, Maureen," I asked.

I handed the syringe to the resident. "Be my guest," I said.

He injected it slowly into her IV tubing, and we watched the monitor above her bed. It took about thirty seconds, and suddenly she flipped back into normal sinus rhythm at ninety a minute.

"Neat," said Maureen.

The resident said, "Thanks." He felt better for having been the one to push the drug in. The resident walked back to the center observation area to call his intern.

Maureen looked at me meaningfully. "How's your man?" she said.

"Better today."

"Still stroked out?"

"Getting some movement back."

"You hear the latest about McIlheny?"

"You're a regular one-woman fan club."

"He's closing up a belly yesterday. Scrub nurse tells him the sponge count is off by one. He has her recount, and she does, and it's still off by one. He says something smart-ass—she's wrong, he's right, that kind of thing. They close the patient up."

"I'm waiting for the punch line," I said. "Surprise me."

"No surprise. We bring a portable X-ray up here and, of course, there's the sponge, still in the belly."

118

"McIlheny's not the first surgeon that's ever happened to."

"He denies the nurse ever told him about the sponge count."

"Says who?"

"Says McIlheny."

"You heard him deny the nurse told him?"

"Kathy told me about it."

"Sounds pretty thirdhand to me."

"You just don't want to hear about him, do you?" said Maureen. "Ryan doesn't, either. None of the docs do."

CHAPTER

22

Driving home along the parkway that hugged the C & O canal into Maryland, the fetid breath of the canal dogged me. Some kind of algae grew in the water every September and it stank like something colonic, something deep and rank. But another rancid odor had been lurking in the recesses of my olfactory lobe before I reached the canal. It had been there in the hospital, there on the SICU.

I followed the parkway, driving automatically, thinking about what Maureen had said. McIlheny had no fan in her. A new chief needs all the friends he can get, but I didn't suppose his fate would ever hang on what the nurses thought of him.

Closing up with a sponge inside happens to everyone. But when the nurse tells you the sponge count is off, it should give you pause. So the guy has a big ego. Don't they all? You don't get through thoracic surgery training without believing in yourself. Even Ann. They're all like that in greater or lesser measure. They're so sure of how well they do things, they can't bear to see anyone else do it, and they won't trust anyone else's work before

120

their own. Try telling Ann to take Canal Road into Georgetown instead of winding through the back way on Thirty-fourth Street. Ann knows how to do things. She's more diplomatic about it, but she's just as cocksure as any surgeon. She's thought about how to do it, whatever the task, and she's sure she knows the best way. Ann can barely restrain herself whenever I try to open a bottle of champagne. She knows she can have it open in two seconds flat while I'm fumbling with the wire on the cork. She bites the inside of her cheek to keep from telling me how to do it. So McIlheny doesn't trust the nurse to know more than he does about the sponge in the abdomen. Nothing unusual in that.

If only it were just that one thing. More and more, little things kept accumulating in McIlheny's vicinity, swirling around him like flies around raw meat: hyperthyroid ladies who get cut on uncovered, unprotected by antithyroid medication, bus drivers whose valves pull loose. It wasn't just one thing, one sponge left behind. It was a feeling building.

Ann's Jaguar was parked in front of my house when I arrived. That fancy green car stood out like spats at a country fair in front of my bungalow, across the street from the house with the car up on blocks in what might once have been a lawn. In my neighborhood, big-time home and yard care was a plastic Santa on the front lawn at Christmas. My house is walking distance from the river. It has a front porch and a backyard and I like it, but upscale it is not.

Ann was sitting in the better rocker—the one without the broken rattan back—on my porch. She waved. She was drinking wine from my only true wineglass.

"Did I have wine?" I asked.

"You never have wine. I brought this from my own cellar. The glass is yours."

I walked in through the door she had left open. She had opened the windows, too. Give a woman the key, and she acts as if she owns the place.

"What is this with the windows?" I asked. "Open house?"

"Mrs. Bromley is right about you," she said. "You're going to be a fussy old bachelor someday."

121

"Mrs. Bromley said that?"

Ann smiled, wrapped her arms around my neck, and kissed me. She knew how to do that very nicely, too. She was good at the important things in life. Like opening champagne bottles.

"The place was stale as a coffin," she said. "And it's such a gorgeous evening."

She was right. It was the last day of September, and fresh winds were blowing into town, the advance guard of autumn. In Washington, summer doesn't just pack up and split town overnight. Summer lingers down here. It's a sleepy giant, and Lilliputian winds have to push it and prod it, and finally it gets the idea that it's time to move on, and it rolls out of bed. Lately, there had been those nights when you could see your breath in the air, and in the past few nights an autumnal chill had displaced the sultry summer air, and you slept under blankets with the windows open.

Ann followed me in and continued on into the bathroom while I phoned my answering service. I could hear the bathwater running.

I was put on hold, as I always am when I call my service, and I felt her arms wrap around my shoulders from behind. She kissed my neck.

"You're late," she said.

"I was cleaning up after surgeons," I said. "On the SICU."

"You're becoming a regular item over there."

"Oh, yes. The nurses all know my name."

The answering service operator came on and told me I was clear. I hung up and turned in Ann's arms.

"They always knew your name," she said. "They all have hot pants for you."

"They tell me things now," I said.

"What things?" she said. Her face changed suddenly. She let her arms fall. She walked back into the bathroom, and I followed her and watched her pull her L. L. Bean shirtdress over her head and off.

"Things about your fearless leader," I said.

122

"Nurses always have an ax to grind. You're either a hero or a goat with them."

"No doubt to which category McIlheny belongs."

"They're not even giving him a chance."

She slipped out of her bra and panties and glided into the tub, skin pinking up in the steamy water.

"It's not just the nurses," I said. "Today I saw a patient of his who had a goiter big as a grapefruit, had to be hot as a pistol pre-op—obviously nobody ever examined her before they tried to take out her gall bag—in storm."

"Hand me the wine," she said.

I handed her her half-empty wineglass and looked at her. Her eyes were closed. She brought the glass unerringly to her lips and sipped.

"This is heaven," she said.

"You don't want to hear horror stories right now: Is that what you're saying?"

Her eyes stayed closed.

"I am bone-tired and hypoglycemic. There is a steak defrosting on your kitchen table and a Giant salad-bar salad in your refrigerator. I came bearing gifts and all I get is recrimination."

"We are relaxing after a hard day's work?" I said. "Is that what we're doing now?"

"That's the picture," she said, eyes open now.

She wore my bathrobe for dinner. After the steak, we finished the wine on the porch and watched the car lights go by up on MacArthur Boulevard.

"What time do you start tomorrow?" I asked.

"Eight."

"Can you stay?"

"Only if you promise not to mention the hospital, surgical cases, or any person whose name ends in 'M.D.'"

That did not leave us with much to talk about, but strangely enough the lack of conversation didn't seem to hurt our evening at all.

123

CHAPTER
23

Morbidity and Mortality Rounds were held in a small auditorium on the fourth floor halfway between the offices of the departments of Surgery and Medicine. There was a podium in the front with a blackboard and projector screen, a sloping gallery with soft blue plush theater seats, and a slide projector setup in the rear.

It was Wednesday, and I was late getting there. There wasn't a seat left, except for the one Ryan had saved for me in the front row. I was late because I hadn't known they were going to present Lydell Brown until Ryan called me that morning, and we had to rearrange appointments at the office so I could escape.

The packed house wasn't unusual for M & M Rounds. It was one of the livelier conferences at St. George's. It was where everyone took the gloves off. The choice of location was no accident— no-man's-land—not on the surgeon's turf, not on the medical people's turf. Any case the pathologists thought "instructive" could be presented. Of course, the most instructive cases were often the worst foul-ups, often where someone had done something overtly stupid, more often where someone had simply not thought of a diagnostic possibility. When the cases were from Surgery, they were often cases of surgeons who got carried away and tried to be heroes, tried to do too much. Or they were the cases the medical house staff liked the most—cases where the surgeons had overlooked a medical diagnosis and tried to cure the patient with a Bard-Parker scalpel, when any medical doctor worth his salt would have recognized that to operate was folly—cases like pancreatitis masquerading and misdiagnosed as intestinal obstruction. The medical house staff could then shake their heads and suppress smug smiles. The surgeons didn't like those cases. They liked the cases where the medical house staff had missed a bursting diverticulum, thinking the patient had pancreatitis.

We sat on the left. In the right front row was McIlheny, flanked by a couple of his chief residents. He was starched and crisp as always, blue oxford-cloth shirt and a maroon Harvard tie, skin looking ruddier than usual.

A short, grizzled gray-haired man in a white lab coat stood behind the podium and cleared his throat, calling for quiet. He was the chief of pathology. He summoned a surgical resident to the podium.

I recognized the resident as one of those who had worked on Lydell Brown. He wore a white tunic buttoned to the top button and looked as fresh and pressed as all the other surgeons. One thing you could say for McIlheny, he had spruced up his department: The surgical residents all looked presentable. Spit and polish, the SICU nurse Maureen had said. The resident presented the case from memory, the way they did at Harvard, and he had obviously rehearsed it well. He covered all the main points crisply, in the prescribed format, and without inflection or any indication of whether or not he thought the case was interesting. He might have been describing the workings of an airplane engine. He described the condition of the infected valve, the original replacement procedure, the second surgery, the stroke, and the current status of Lydell Brown.

The Pathology chief stood up and said, "Any questions about the presentation?"

McIlheny was on his feet. "Not a question, Milt, just a comment, just to clarify a few points that might not have been emphasized. By the way, that was a very nice presentation of a very complicated case."

I had to agree with him there, but I couldn't understand what he was interrupting for—they hadn't even got warmed up yet.

"I did want to point out that Mr. Brown was in extremis, to say the least, when he reached the OR. He had been treated unsuccessfully medically and failed an intensive antibiotic trial. He was in pulmonary edema, with wide-open aortic regurgitation. As is often the case in such circumstances, we had a great deal of difficulty finding tissue that would even hold sutures. It didn't surprise me that we had to take him back to the OR. There was precious little to work with in the first place."

I hadn't heard anything in the presentation to suggest anything else. I suspected the pathologists were going to show us a bunch of slides of the chewed-up valve they'd taken out of Lydell Brown, emphasizing the point McIlheny was trying to make, but he wasn't giving anyone a chance.

McIlheny turned to me and said, "Did you want to add anything from the medical side, Dr. Abrams?"

I said I had nothing to add. I wanted to see the pathology slides.

A crusty old gentleman in a white coat, with his name embroidered above "Department of Surgery," spoke up from the middle of the grandstands. "I think the man's lucky to be alive. Dr. McIlheny didn't give him his heroin habit or his dirty needles. He just gave him a new aortic valve. The patient could have stroked whether or not the surgery was ever done. Perhaps more likely without surgery."

The Pathology chief said, "Nobody is suggesting anything different. These case discussions are intended as educational exercises."

"Inquisitions, more like it," said the old gent. "Problem cases. This guy's no problem. He's a save. He's lucky to be alive— stroke or no stroke. I congratulate Dr. McIlheny for getting him off the table alive."

126

They showed the slides then. The valve McIlheny removed looked like a piece of old shoe after a pack of Doberman pinschers had got through gnawing on it. Nobody had a chance to say much about the first prosthetic valve unseating.

Ryan and I took an elevator down to the vending-machine room after the conference. There was a nurse in the elevator for two floors. When she got off I said, "Who was that old customer who rose to McIlheny's defense?"

"John Toland. He was on the search committee that brought McIlheny here from Chicago. He knew McIlheny from Chicago. Toland was on staff there during the ice ages, before he semiretired down here. Semiretired means six instead of ten cases a day. Nobody from his old place can do wrong. He's lucky when he can get two functioning neurons to rub together."

"He added a little life to the proceedings."

"The blades were a little defensive, didn't you think? Did you see how McIlheny jumped right up?"

"What do you think of him?"

We got out of the elevator and made straight for the Dr Pepper machine. Ryan plugged coins in, and we watched the cup fill as he considered my question. He put in a coin for me, and we watched my cup fill, too, before he answered.

"He's a disaster," Ryan said in a low rumble. He looked at me for a long minute, and all the boyishness drained out of his face. He was as sober as a hangman and twice as deliberate.

"How do you know?"

"How do you ever know? You hear things. A little here. A little there. First the SICU nurses. Then the floor nurses. His patients don't always do so well post-op."

"Nobody's patients always do well post-op."

"There are some cases you don't wonder about a guy if they don't go well," said Ryan. "Like this guy they presented just now. Your guy."

A patient in a bathrobe pulling a rolling IV pole walked into the vending room area with her family trailing behind, and Ryan nod-

127

ded to the door, and we walked out. We stood in a quiet part of the hallway, away from stairwells and corners where passersby might wander into our conversation.

I said, "So he takes on the tough cases. What do nurses know?"

"Nobody's bad all the time," said Ryan. "I'm sure McIlheny's got a dozen patients who'll swear on a stack of Bibles that if it weren't for him they'd be pushing up daisies today." Ryan checked the hallway and dropped his voice. "But it's not just the nurses. Nancy's in a position to know. She wouldn't send him her worst enemy."

"Nancy Colleo? She was right there the night I gave him Lydell Brown. She didn't say boo."

"I know. I know. But you'd paged McIlheny, and he showed up in thirty seconds. She thought you were calling someone else. McIlheny's there in the flesh. What's she going to say? You'd already given the case away."

"Nice to hear about it like this. Why doesn't she do something about it?"

"Like what? Send out a letter?"

"If he's a dirtball, get the word out."

"We're all trying. You just got caught in a bad spot."

"He's only been here since January. How can you be so sure he's that bad?"

"Who do they call when they get post-op infections? They've been keeping me busy since McIlheny's arrived. Not busy enough so you could build a case on numbers alone. It's the *kind* of case I get called to see. You got a minute?"

I had a minute. I followed him up to the SICU. There in a dimly lighted stall was a kid about three years old all hooked up to monitors, IVs, endotracheal tube coming out of his mouth hooked up to a respirator, hair plastered wet on his forehead.

"One of the chief's less famous therapeutic triumphs," said Ryan. "Patent ductus. No sweat, right? Not this kid. Mediastinitis, temps spiking to a hundred and five every night on blast-a-bug. You name it, we've tried it. Right now he's on vancomycin. Look at that kid and tell me if you've still got doubts."

128

I looked at him, a little blond kid who couldn't have weighed more than forty pounds, floppy and dazed the way kids are when they're really sick. I felt myself being persuaded, but not by intellect. I resisted that kind of persuasion.

"A patent ductus?" I said.

"Nothing is simple for Dr. McIlheny," said Ryan in a hoarse whisper. "He makes the routine stuff exciting."

"So why hasn't anybody done anything about it?"

Ryan looked around as if he expected to be arrested at any moment.

"Let's get out of here."

We walked to his office. I don't think we said a word the whole way. He was letting the image of that kid on the respirator sink in. Ryan spun into the swivel chair behind his desk and put his feet up, hands clasped behind his head, leaning back.

"Nice mess, huh?" he said.

"So far all you've given me is anecdotes. For every nurse who says his patients don't do well, he'll have two patients willing to do testimonials for him. You got any numbers?"

"Where am I going to get numbers? Especially without McIlheny knowing?"

"I should think Surgery would keep numbers."

"You want to ask McIlheny for the numbers on his cases? Tell him you're investigating his morbidity and mortality so you can prove he's unsafe at any speed? Who's going to hang him, big boy?" croaked Ryan. He reached into his desk, set up two tumblers, and filled each with anisette from a small bottle. "Suppose I get you numbers. Suppose the mortality rate for every procedure he does is ten times what everyone else's is. Numbers don't mean shit. He'll say he does all the tough cases. There's always ways of playing with numbers."

"We just have to collect them right," I said. "If they're good, solid numbers, they'll convince people." I tried to make that sound convincing, but I don't think I could have sold it to a drunken sailor.

"Who you going to show the numbers?"

129

"Isn't there some kind of review committee for chiefs?"

"I looked into that. They give 'em three years before they review 'em. And then it's more of an academic thing. How many guys he's attracted, what kind of research they're doing, how high the residency program rated in the match, that kind of shit."

"I can't believe he's above review for his surgery."

"I told you, I looked into it. He reviews his department. Nobody reviews the chief. He reviews them. He is a citizen above suspicion."

"There's always the dean of the medical school."

Ryan laughed. His face turned red, and he sounded a little hysterical. "The dean? That's priceless. Now there's a likely player. The dean's the guy who named the committee who chose McIlheny in the first place. Guys like John Toland. The dean's set foot in the hospital maybe twice in the last six months."

"Somebody must know the program's in trouble."

"The program is not in trouble. Patients are in trouble. You've got Ann Payson and two or three others who are always going to attract good residents here, who are always going to make the place look good. McIlheny's a burr under the saddle, but as long as you don't sit on it, you'll never know."

"I cannot believe nobody will notice."

"Somebody will notice. Somebody already has. But she's just a nurse, and nobody's listening. McIlheny's untouchable—ask your friend Ann Payson."

"Maybe I will," I said. "But first, let's get some nice, unemotional numbers. See if we've got anything real."

"Oh, we've got something all right. There's just not a damn thing we can do about it."

130

CHAPTER
24

Saturday, the leaves were moving in the trees, the ducks were swooping down all along the canal and river, and staying indoors would have constituted a form of acute mental illness. Summer was finally washed away.

It was the kind of crisp, energizing weather that brings out the hikers and the bird-watchers, the cheerleaders and the footballs, the kind of day people used to call glorious, the kind of day you might get a smile from the park policeman's horse.

Ann telephoned early and asked if I wanted to walk down the canal into Georgetown with her and her five-year-old niece, who was spending the weekend with her.

We started out at nine that morning and made it to Fletcher's Boat House before it became apparent that no five-year-old was going to make it to Georgetown and back in anything under two days. So we rented bicycles, one with a kid seat, at Fletcher's. I hoisted the niece up into the bicycle seat and tied her in. She was a pretty, freckled little kid, looked a little like Ann about the eyes. Her name was also Ann, the daughter of Ann's younger sister. We bumped along the dirt and pebble towpath, avoiding joggers and bird-watchers.

Ann rode ahead, and I watched her hair flying in the wind. She had taken off her sweater and tied it around her neck. It was an orange Fair Isle sweater and it waved below her rich-looking hair, and she looked very lovely. I felt like the father of a little family pedaling along.

Coming toward us along the towpath on a bicycle was Thomas McIlheny. He was wearing an Irish fisherman's knit sweater, and next to him was a teenager who looked enough like him to be his clone.

McIlheny recognized Ann and pulled his bike to a halt, and we all clotted the path.

"Well, hello," said McIlheny. His face looked ruddy in the wind, and he looked healthier, less tired, and more relaxed than I'd ever seen him. "And who is this?" he said, looking at the younger Ann.

Aunt Ann made the introductions as McIlheny looked me over and looked Ann and Ann's niece over, drawing conclusions. Aunt Ann looked uncomfortable, not embarrassed, but uncomfortable, as if she did not want to share this part of herself with the chief of surgery.

McIlheny's son was introduced, a sullen adolescent who looked about as happy to be among us as a shanghaied sailor. But that's what adolescents are supposed to look like in the presence of parents. He couldn't see much of his father. Surgeons' sons never do. This must be the father-and-son big-afternoon-together fathers feel obligated toward and sons resign themselves to.

We said good-bye, and I looked back over my shoulder at McIlheny and son fading away from us down the towpath. It seemed incongruous, yet strangely calming, seeing him out in the real world, in natural light, out from under the glare of the ICU lights, away from the intensity of the hospital. Made me think maybe we were imagining problems, Ryan and I. Maybe he was all right after all.

We ate at the Foundry. The younger Ann gobbled down two

132

Cokes, an immense cheeseburger, and a large heap of french fries.

"This is good," said little Ann.

"We feed you well in Washington," said Ann. Her niece was from Boston. "It's a nice town."

"It's very pretty," said Ann the younger.

"Well, this is Georgetown," said Aunt Ann. "If you didn't like it here, we'd have to take you over to the hospital and have the shrinks examine your brain."

"Oh, no. Not the shrinks!" The five-year-old laughed. It was some kind of game between them. "Anything but the shrinks."

We rode back to Ann's place. The younger Ann announced that she was done in and went for a nap, which I thought was pretty grown-up for a five-year-old. Maybe she was just trying to give me some time alone with her aunt, which would have been even more grown-up. Whatever, Ann and I sat out on her porch and watched the leaves move in the beech trees and drank iced tea.

"I didn't know McIlheny had a kid," I said.

"Three," said Ann, sipping her tea. "Just like a real person. Father, surgeon, respected member of the community. Kind of guy takes his kid out for a bike ride."

"He must have a feeling for kids," I said. "Having his own."

Ann looked at me for meaning, an eyebrow arched, knowing I was setting something up.

"Made me feel better seeing him like that, in a sweater, on a bike," I said. "Made me think maybe he isn't some maniac with a scalpel and a black heart."

"You listen to Ryan and the nurses too much."

"I'd like to believe that," I said. "I'd sleep easier."

"Nobody goes to med school and through surgical residency so he can butcher people."

"Nobody starts out that way maybe," I said. "But along the way some must find out they just don't have it. Only they can't admit it to themselves. They start making excuses."

"It's true," said Ann. "There're some big egos on some bad surgeons."

"Maybe it's like that with McIlheny."

"Maybe, maybe not," said Ann, glancing over, as if she were only passingly interested. "But you're not going to find out about him by talking to nurses."

"I know. I have to go to Morbidity and Mortality Rounds to see him in action."

"How'd that go? They rake him over the coals, or what?"

"He didn't give them a chance. He jumped right up and told 'em how sick Lydell Brown was and how it was amazing he survived at all, and everyone said Hosanna."

"But you weren't convinced?"

"I didn't know what to think. Then Ryan took me up to see this little kid McIlheny had done, and done badly."

Ann looked at me, and her eyes grew dull, and she said nothing. But she was listening.

"On a respirator," I said. "Mediastinitis. All floppy and glazed eyes. Three years old."

"So what do you do now?"

"I don't refer any more patients to him, obviously. But the question is, what do you do?"

"You mean am I going to shoot it out with him at high noon, or what?"

"You going to let him go around messing up little kids?"

"What am I, the American Board of Surgery?" said Ann, a little too quickly, I thought. She had thought about this and she had her speech worked out. "Harvard College, Harvard Medical School, the Massachusetts General Hospital, St. George's Medical School all say this guy's a certified genius and a qualified surgeon. Who is Ann Payson or Benjamin Abrams to disagree?"

"Tell that to the kid on the respirator."

"Crissake," said Ann, finally looking at me. "I've seen a few of his disasters. Don't we all have some? Nobody's shown me any of his good cases."

"Maybe he doesn't have any."

"Ever read his textbook?" she said hoarsely. "He has some."

I tried to hold her eye, but she swung around and stared at a cardinal in the beech tree.

134

"You wouldn't just let him get away with it," I said, "if you really thought he was dangerous, just because nobody's put an indictment in your hands?"

"So who am I? Jack Anderson?"

"You'd let him cut on little kids and mess them up?"

"I don't even know there's a problem."

"But if you did," I said. "Just for the sake of discussion. I'm curious."

"He's the chief of surgery," she said. "There's nobody to go to about him."

"Nobody's supposed to be above the law."

"He's not breaking any laws. He's just maybe not raising the practice of surgery to new heights."

"He's supposed to be teaching residents. He could do a lot of harm if he's bad."

"Any of us could."

"Three-year-old with a hole in his heart," I said. "Should have been easy. Now his chest is all infected. Sick as stink. You know how little kids look when they've given up?"

Ann's eyes grew hard as she exhaled harshly. "It's not my fault if they hired a turkey. And I still don't know he's a turkey."

"Silence implies consent."

She turned on me and nearly shouted, "Now what do you expect me to do?"

"Keep your eyes open. You're around the OR. You're on the floors. You can hear things."

"I wish to Christ I didn't hear half the things I get told. Hearing things is the worst investment someone in my position can make."

"And what is your position?"

"Untenured," said Ann, exhausted. "A holdover from the old regime. The new king's in power, and there's nothing either of us can do about it. I'm just trying to do my cases, take care of my patients, and stay out of politics."

"That's not enough," I said.

"And what are you going to do about it?"

"Collect data."

"Collect data?"

"Yes."

"Oh, is that all?" Ann laughed. "And all this time I thought you were pushing me really to do something."

"You've got to start someplace."

"Well, if it makes you feel better." Ann smiled. "Eases your conscience. Can't get you into trouble."

She was right, of course. But I didn't like to hear it.

CHAPTER

25

Coming out of the hospital cafeteria line Monday, I spotted Dr. John Toland eating by himself over in a corner table. He was making a desultory attempt at pretending to read a surgery journal, looking as sour and dyspeptic as he had at Morbidity and Mortality Rounds. I asked him if I could join him and sat down before he had a chance to throw his tray at me.

Toland must have been sixty, but he was built like a fullback just past his prime. He was the kind who would arrive at the operating room every morning at seven-thirty no matter what the weather, would round on his patients twice a day, would demolish some young surgical resident at squash for lunch, and his kids probably only saw him at graduations and funerals.

He looked up at me, trying to decide whether to bite my nose off or just ignore me.

I said: "I was interested in what you said at Morbidity Rounds."

"Witch hunt," he grunted, not looking up from his journal, biting off a piece of ham-and-cheese sandwich.

"Academic inquiry," I said. "Pure and simple."

That got his attention. He looked up and looked me over. He was used to intimidating people my age. He was used to backing people down by the force of his personality. I'd learned that game from my father. You stand your ground with people like that. Especially if you're in the department of medicine and he's in Surgery.

The surprise registered on his florid face. He opened his wrinkled eyelids a little and tried to stare me down.

I didn't give him the pleasure. "That was my patient they were presenting. I had as much right to feel defensive as anyone. But I decided not to."

"You didn't do the surgery," barked Toland. "How long have you been on staff here?" His tone was evening out.

"Four years."

"How many times have you had a patient presented at M & M Rounds?"

"Once."

"Tom McIlheny's been here nine months. This is the second time they've hauled him up before that kangaroo court," Toland snorted. He glanced around the cafeteria then back to me as if he were letting me in on something. "At that rate he'll have ten cases to every one of yours."

"Who chooses the cases for those Rounds?"

"It doesn't matter. Tom's making enemies getting Surgery into shape. He's pushing hard, rubbing noses. So now they're trying to take him down."

"So you see conspiracy hiding in smiles and affability?"

Toland smiled a smile you could have broken granite with. He said: "I'll show you Caesar's wounds, and bid them speak for me."

"You like him, don't you?"

That seemed to defuse him a little. He said, "He's invented more procedures than half the guys on staff here can even do. He was the best chief resident they've ever seen at Mass General."

"In the days of the giants," I said. I tried not to sound ironic, and I have a hard time not sounding ironic, but I guess I succeeded this time because he smiled at that.

138

"We lived in the hospital then," he said. "We were on every other night for four years and every weekend for the first year, every other after that. But you learned surgery. Not like these candy-ass kids now."

Toland looked off into that lost and distant world.

"And McIlheny got to be a good one?"

He came back from the days of the giants and looked at me, a little annoyed. "Those morons who bring his cases up for M & M Rounds should live to be half the surgeon Tom McIlheny is."

He said that with enough force to stop a charging bull. Nothing loud or threatening, just bedrock conviction.

"You know what this whole thing reminds me of?" Toland said, leaning forward. I half expected him to grab me by the collar. "Friend of mine worked in Saudi Arabia once. All the Americans stayed in a compound behind the hospital. One morning he looks out his window and sees a crowd of people gathered around his car parked out back. He goes out to investigate. Seems that during the night a bedouin has crawled up in front of his car and died. The police arrive and ask who owns the car. He says 'I do,' like a damn fool. They arrest him."

"Arrest him?" I said involuntarily.

"Sure, the bedouin had died in front of his car, hadn't he? They held him until he was missed, and someone from the King Faisal Hospital came and bailed him out. Had to pay the family 'blood money.'

"Well, that's what happened to Tom McIlheny with this case. Intravenous drug abuser lands on his doorstep and he gets the blame."

I sat back and looked at Toland. The analogy was not a close one, but I got his point.

"Let me ask you something," I said. "Not about Tom McIlheny now, but in general. How would anyone ever know if a surgeon lost his edge?"

Toland looked at me with something that might have been close to interest. He said, "That you only know by working with a man day in and day out."

139

CHAPTER
26

Tuesday was a better day. Some days everything seems to go well, some days just the opposite. Lydell Brown actually took three steps with a walker and two nurses, and his wife was there to see it. His heart sounded fine, and he hadn't had a fever for a week. His urine was flowing; his lungs clear; bowels moving. He was almost a new man.

I arrived at the office feeling better. Lydell Brown was walking. Mrs. Bromley followed me back to my office. She had arranged a stack of mail on my desk. I opened the top letter while she talked to the top of my head. And there was a check from the great blue insurance company in the sky for a lady whom we had written off as a nonpayer. I waved the check at her and said the patient's name.

"It's about time," said Mrs. Bromley. "What did they think you were paying your rent with these last four months?"

"Doctors don't have to worry about money," I told her.

"Crikey, their secretaries do."

"You have to learn to be above all that."

"Do you know how much money is owed us at this very instant, not counting the people you saw today in hospital?"

"I don't, but I'm sure I'm about to hear."

"Took me all yesterday afternoon to tally it up."

"Keep it your own little secret for today."

Mrs. Bromley wanted to talk about sending some miscreants to collection, but I kept quiet on that. They may not pay their bills, but unless I sent them to collection they wouldn't sue me, either. And if they had to pay, they'd find a lawyer who would convince them they'd been mistreated. I managed to divert her by telling her about the progress Lydell Brown was making.

"Mr. Lydell Brown, you'll be pleased to hear, is walking."

"I'm very happy for him," said Mrs. Bromley. "But what are you going to do about that surgeon?"

"Do about him?" I asked, all innocence. "Just yesterday I had lunch with a surgeon who thinks McIlheny's the best thing since general anesthesia."

"Isn't there an automatic review, some sort of quality control on all the surgeons?"

"Well, there's accreditation, board certification, but everyone who takes those exams knows what they're worth—they're about as discriminating as a fast game of Russian roulette. The guys who pass them heave a sigh of relief and tell you how much fun it was, and the guys who don't aren't around to talk about it."

"Besides, I imagine one can pass an exam when he's young and dwindle pretty badly as he gets on," said Mrs. Bromley.

"Do we have patients this morning?" I asked. One of her favorite topics.

It didn't work. She could not be diverted from McIlheny.

"I just cannot fathom why they don't keep records on surgeons. Don't they investigate these things, like airplane crashes?"

"You're not talking about baseball players. Nobody keeps statistics on wins and losses, strikeouts and hits. It's not that clear-cut with surgeons."

"Well, surely if a patient dies, that's not a win."

"It may be a no-decision. Sick patient who would have died without surgery, like Lydell. Was he a loss or a save?"

"I wouldn't call him a win."

"I wouldn't call him a loss. He's alive. Now whether or not he would have had a stroke if any other surgeon had done him is unanswerable."

"But surely there is some system for review."

"How would you do it?"

"Keep records. If a surgeon has more than a certain number, call him in. Review him. Put him on notice, and if he doesn't improve, give him the sack."

"Ah, Mrs. Bromley, you've lived in Washington too long."

"I beg your pardon?" She laughed. She always liked hearing how American she was becoming. It amused her husband.

"You want to set up a regulatory agency. As soon as you do that, all the regulated will start organizing their lives around the rules—like what happened with income taxes."

"No reason not to try."

"Suppose you decide to monitor all the patients in the SICU. Logical place to look for complications following surgery, right? The surgeons start rushing their patients out of there. People who should benefit from the SICU are rocketed right out of there."

"So you throw up your hands in despair and allow a man to continue to ravage the unsuspecting population?"

"As a matter of fact, Dr. Ryan is supposed to come by this morning so we can plot our review of a certain famous surgeon."

"You mean you're out to get him now?"

"We are objectively reviewing the data," I said. "Objectively and secretly, and that information is to go no further than this room."

"By all means," said Mrs. Bromley, rising. There was a noise of someone coming through the front door. She went out to see who it was.

She rang through on the intercom, "Dr. Ryan of the data review committee is here to see you."

Ryan arrived carrying a beat-up leather attaché case.

"This was supposed to be a big secret. What was that crack about the data review committee?"

"Mrs. Bromley is safe. Besides, I couldn't hide anything from her if I tried."

"Well, let's be careful. This wasn't so easy to get. I don't want to compromise my sources, as the newspaper hacks say."

He worked the combination lock on his attaché and pulled out a computer spread sheet, spread it before me on my desk, and stood behind me while I went over it. It was a list of the names and medical record numbers of all the patients McIlheny had done since arriving.

"How'd you get this?"

"A friend in Medical Records," Ryan said with his bad-boy smile. "She's good with the computer."

I looked up at him. "Is there any department in that place where they employ young women you don't know?"

"I sure as hell hope not," Ryan said earnestly. The idea shocked and disturbed him. "I haven't done a formal survey, of course."

"Maybe you could get your friend in Personnel to run it on her computer for you."

"Not a bad idea," he said, eyes drifting off to survey the possibilities of young lovelies in Accounting or the Laundry he might not know. Then he came back to earth and said, "This stuff should never have been run off—she did it as a personal favor to me. Cost me a dinner at Clyde's."

"My lips are sealed."

"And be sure Mrs. Bromley's lips are sealed. Judging from that crack out front, she's not too careful."

"Ryan, you think they've got my intercom bugged? There's nobody in the office."

"This stuff could get to be highly explosive, is all," he said. "I don't think you appreciate how easily we could get burned. We've already probably committed some crime or other just breaking into the Medical Records computer file."

"There are over one hundred cases here. The guy's only been here nine months," I said. "How could this be right?"

143

"I don't know how many of those are cases he's scrubbed in on that the residents did, but his name goes on as the physician of record."

"We're going to have to pull and review one hundred charts," I said. "You got that kind of time?"

"No. Do you?"

"No way."

"Guess that does it, then. Nobody's paying us to play policeman." Ryan started to scoop up his spread sheet.

I clamped a paw on his paper, pinning it on the desk. "We need help. Not just anyone, as you said. Mrs. Bromley could help, but she wouldn't know what to look for. We need people who can read the charts and know what they're looking at."

Ryan looked at me with the pity of a priest walking a man to the gallows. "You're not thinking of asking those nurses?"

"No," I said.

Ryan's shoulders relaxed.

"You're going to be the one to ask those nurses," I said.

"What?"

"They know you. I hardly know their names. What is it? Maureen Somebody and her buddy, Kathy."

"You really want to go through with this?"

"What'd you take me up to see that kid in the SICU for? You think that got you off the hook? Like fifty Hail Marys or something? You raised the fucking issue—you can help resolve it."

"What am I going to tell these ladies? We're investigating McIlheny 'cause we think maybe he should be deposed and we need your help but don't tell a soul? It'd be all over the hospital in five seconds."

"Tell them you want to talk to them about something they've expressed concern about. Tell them you want to do it away from the hospital, at Mai's restaurant. Tell them it's secret and it could all go up in smoke if they talk. They won't say anything. They want McIlheny worse than anyone."

"Oh, fine. Just what we need for an unbiased chart review."

144

"It'll be numbers," I said. "Numbers don't lie."

"Except when you want them to," said Ryan.

He gathered up his computer papers and stuffed them back into his attaché case.

"You tell Ann about this?"

"Last Saturday."

"Can we count on her?"

"She's in a bad position."

"Aren't we all?" said Ryan. "Aren't we all?"

He disappeared out my door.

I swung my feet up onto the desk and thought about McIlheny and about Lydell Brown and about John Toland and about the lady who had stormed out post-op because nobody had recognized she was hyperthyroid before they took her to surgery. And then I thought about that little kid on the respirator.

Maybe it was just a bad streak.

Sometimes the pitches are there, and you can hit them, and sometimes all you see is junk and bad luck, and you just can't seem to do anything right. Who knows whether the same thing would have happened to any surgeon? I could make up a good story, if I were a lawyer, using all the techniques fiction lawyers use. I could make McIlheny look like Jack the Ripper. Throw in that scene in the OR, with him heaving instruments and nurses around, and you could paint a very damning picture indeed.

But that's what's so nice about the austere simplicity of fiction— you can edit out whatever doesn't fit. Like McIlheny getting right up and coming back to redo Lydell Brown's valve without a whisper of complaint. The man who wrote the book. The man who Toland thought was one of the great surgeons of the Western world.

The tangled woof of fact doesn't make such a clean story, but it was all I had to work with until we could look at all the medical records, one by one.

Mrs. Bromley interrupted my ruminations with a buzz over the intercom. My next patient, Samuel Sawyer, had just walked in.

Sam stood in my doorway looking unsure about whether to come in or not. He had a cap in his hands, which he twisted one way, then the other.

"Come on in, Sam," I said. "You look like the guy waiting for his bill at the garage."

"More like the guy come to identify the body at the morgue," said Sam. "I want to know, but I don't want to see."

He sat down on the patient's side of the desk, and I swung into my swivel chair.

"I talked to Nancy Colleo about your studies," I said. "You need a new heart valve, Sam."

"I guessed that from the look on her puss when she was doing the ECHO," he said. "She wouldn't say anything about that or the phonocardiogram. She just said she'd send you a report. Don't know why they feel they can only talk to another doctor, like I don't speak English."

"That's so I won't have to hear the news from you. It's supposed to be the other way 'round."

"When's this valve have to be replaced?"

"It doesn't have to be done today, but let's not let a week or two go by."

"That fast?" he said. His eyebrows were saluting, and his face flushed tomato-red. He was still smiling but he wasn't happy. He was in control, but his eyes were glazing over, and I could see I was going to have to repeat myself a lot—he wasn't really listening now.

"You're going to need to see a surgeon," I said.

"Why not the best?" said Sam, snapping out of his fog.

That surprised me. I thought I was going to have to repeat myself a hundred times, go through his refusal to believe he needed surgery, but he must have worked all that out before he came.

"Who's that?"

"The chief of surgery."

I tried to laugh, but it came out sounding more like a sob. I said: "You always were impressed by titles."

146

"Don't you think he'd take my case if you asked him?"

"Oh, he'd take you all right," I said.

"I don't want to put you in a tough position," said Sam, almost apologetically. "I imagine he's got more people coming to him than he can possibly handle."

"It's not that at all. I'm just not sure he's the right man for this particular job."

"You see his write-up in the *Washington* magazine?" asked Sam. He drew a folded magazine out of his jacket pocket and handed it to me.

On the magazine cover was a fetching young thing in hot-red tights bending over and looking at me through her legs. A Redskin cheerleader, I think.

Inside was an article entitled "The Best Doctors in Washington." It was pretty much a list of the chiefs of departments at the local medical schools.

There was Thomas McIlheny's name, big and bold. The choice of *Washington* magazine. Last month it had been the fifty best restaurants. This month it was doctors. The editors might even have eaten at a few of the restaurants. I wondered if anyone on the staff had ever had his chest opened by Thomas McIlheny.

"These magazines," I said. "What the hell." I can be bold and decisive in the clutch.

"Nice little write-up. Harvard College. Harvard Med. Cum laude. Sounds like quite a guy."

"Look, he's only been in town a few months. I really haven't had a lot of experience with the guy."

"Hell, he wrote the textbook of surgery," said Sam. Sam the teacher. Sam, for whom authority came in printed letters, wrapped in book jackets. "How bad could he be?" he said.

"Fame isn't much of a qualification when it comes to surgeons. Says more about his press agent than about his skill."

"Well, if you don't think he'd take me." He sounded a little hurt.

"Look, why don't you see the surgeon I've used a lot, Ann Payson." I could see that made about as much impression as the ball

147

makes on the bat. "See McIlheny, if you like, but see my surgeon, too. You'll need a second opinion for your insurance company anyway, won't you?"

"Sure," said Sam, shrugging. "I'll see 'em both."

"Then, after you've had a chance to talk with each, you can pick the one you want."

"Good plan," said Sam.

He walked out the door a happy man, or at least a man with a plan. For all I knew, he'd like McIlheny better and want him. But what could I do? The man wants to book passage on the best ship ever made—so the name's *Titanic*? What does he know? He just reads the papers, and the *Washington* magazine.

CHAPTER
27

There was a reception at the medical school that afternoon I had promised Dennis Rallston I'd attend. He had a smile jacked up and he was shaking everyone's hand too vigorously when I arrived.

"Damn," he said, grinning, "I hate these things."

"Who's here?"

"Everybody who's anybody, big boy."

I spotted Thomas McIlheny talking to a big-busted lady in a sequined dress.

"Who's Mae West?" I asked Dennis.

Dennis said some name. I don't remember. "Most important honcho on the board of governors," said Dennis. "Let's go press her flesh."

McIlheny looked relieved to see us walk up. Reinforcements to help him deal with the board of governors of St. George's Hospital.

The sequined dress barely contained her big white bosom, and she was either very nearsighted or she enjoyed pressing it up against Thomas McIlheny, who kept trying to back away and interpose his gin-and-tonic glass between him and the advancing breasts.

We were introduced, and she turned her bosom loose on me.

"And how do the private practitioners feel about DRGs?" she asked, as if she were asking for the opinion from some underclass nobody ever thinks to ask.

"The Gallup poll isn't done yet," I said.

She didn't like that answer much. She was in the far end of her fifth decade, a platinum blonde—the color may have been real or may have been an expensive job—and she had that nearly albino skin some blondes have that doesn't really look healthy. Her eyes looked unfocused, as if she weren't wearing her glasses but needed to. I wasn't sure whether she planned to drag me into the nearest closet and pull my pants down or spit in my eye.

"I was asking for your opinion about the DRGs," she said. "But you can just be cute, if you want to."

The DRGs were a new system for paying doctors and hospitals based on the diagnosis the patient was admitted with. You got so much for a pneumonia, so much for a heart attack, and so forth. If you got the patient out of the hospital fast, you got to keep the difference. If the patient refused to get better, it came out of your hide. It had all the private docs pushing their patients out of the hospital as soon as the patients could breathe deeply, which is just what the government wanted, but it didn't do much for the patient.

"I've been thinking about bringing my ten sickest patients in and admitting 'em all," I told her. "One of them has twelve bona fide diagnoses. I figure he's worth half a million. He gets along okay at home. But in the hospital his diabetes, lupus, chronic gall bladder disease, and anemia would be worth plenty."

She laughed and her bosom shook. McIlheny and Dennis tried laughing, too. It wasn't that funny.

"Oh, that's just priceless," she said. "You boys are just priceless." She spied someone across the room and waved and called out and slid away from us.

"Whew," said McIlheny, smiling and looking relieved.

"She's a handful," said Dennis.

"Every board of trustees of every hospital I've ever known has

150

one of those," said McIlheny, smiling. "You've got to strain just to be polite."

"That's part of the territory," I said, "if the hospital pays your rent."

"Don't rub it in." McIlheny laughed. "It's bad enough visiting the palaces of my friends in private practice without having to think about that."

"Well, they're paying their own malpractice," I said.

"The corporation pays their malpractice," McIlheny said, smiling, friendly. He was standing there holding his drink, with the other hand in his pocket, looking atypically relaxed, and I felt like staying and listening for once, rather than running away.

"I've had three men resign from the faculty since I've arrived. I've offered positions to six good surgeons and got no takers. They all told me that in private practice they could get twice what I could pay them."

"Is that right?" I said.

"They probably can," he said. "But what the hell they'd go to medical school for? You want to be a millionaire, live in a palace, you go to Harvard Business School. Go into stocks and bonds. That's not what medicine's about."

"Well, they're still surgeons," I said. "What's the difference except the size of the check? Why do the same work for less?"

"It's not the same when you're thinking about what to do with your seventeen-week vacation every year."

Dennis said, "Hell, I can't even get Abrams to come on faculty, and he'd make more money with me than he does in that every-patient-gets-two-hours practice of his."

McIlheny looked me over approvingly, as if he were just now seeing me for the first time. "You just keep practicing good medicine," he said. "You look back over thirty years and you'll be a happier man. Don't worry about the money. You won't starve."

I could see why Sam Sawyer would like him. He said all the right things. His heart was in the right place, and he'd been to the right schools.

151

Thomas McIlheny had *me* liking him. The guy inspired confidence.

I watched him hold his drink, surveying the action at the reception, looking amused, slightly reproachful. He looked like the kind of guy I wouldn't mind going fishing with. The problem was, I wasn't sure I'd want him cutting through my chest.

CHAPTER
28

I left the reception early, with McIlheny propped up against a wall listening to Dennis Rallston's observations on the frustrations of chairmanship. I was supposed to collect Ann and Ryan, and we were all going out to Mai's restaurant for dinner and some serious discussion. Ann didn't know about the discussion part yet. We were due for dinner. I called Ann's office, and her secretary told me she was in the ER. I paged Ryan and told him to meet me there.

Ryan was standing outside the ER when I arrived. He had a sly little grin on that altar-boy face and he looked as if he'd just seen the headmaster kissing one of the nuns.

"There's action down here" was all he said.

The ER at St. George's was very well run. This was dinnertime, and things should have been slow, but the nurses were flying around, and there were men in dark suits with little gold stars in their lapels standing around.

"Car wreck," the charge nurse told us. "Got the secretary of state or defense or whatever in three. That's where Dr. Payson is."

Ryan and I headed for stall number three and were stopped by two of the men in dark suits. Ryan was wearing his white coat with his picture ID clipped to the pocket, and I wasn't wearing anything particularly identifying beyond a stethoscope.

"Name, please," said the guy in the dark suit. He was one of those clean-cut guys you have to dislike immediately. Looked like Pat Boone.

"I'm Dr. Ryan, and this is Dr. Abrams, and Dr. Payson in there needs our assistance."

"Let 'em in." Ann's voice carried out to us through the curtain.

They let us in.

Ann was wearing rubber gloves and blue scrubs and she was standing at the head of the bed with a surgical resident and an ER nurse. The secretary of something important was lying on his back on the stretcher not breathing particularly well. He looked like his pictures. Except now he was shirtless, breathing hard, and his face was a little gray. I couldn't remember whether he was defense or state or possibly the CIA, but he had an acute need for a chest tube, which Ann was in the process of providing him.

"You guys arrived just in time," Ann said.

The secretary opened his eyes briefly to look us over, but wasn't impressed, so he closed them and went back to concentrating on his breathing.

There was another dark-suited guy with a hand-held radio in the corner, trying to be unobtrusive, but keeping a fish-eye on everyone.

"I'm sure we did," said Ryan.

Ann plunged the tip of the thoracotomy tube, which looked like a small spear, into the secretary's chest, which must have looked to the guy in the dark suit as if she were trying to murder him. A nurse hooked the tube up to the hemovac, and Ann checked the connections; the nurse turned on the vacuum, and as blood emptied out of the secretary's chest into the hemovac, he pinked up very nicely. Even the guy in the dark suit could see that.

Ann listened to the secretary's chest and spoke to him. "You feel it's easier to breathe now?"

154

"Much," said the secretary. "You do nice work."

"Good." She laughed. "You remember that next time my passport expires and I need a favor."

"Any favors you need, Doctor, you check with me first."

Ann laughed and patted his shoulder and led Ryan and me out to the work station where she wrote a note. The dark-suited guy followed her and asked where the secretary would be taken next. They had to clear the path, to sweep the way for mines or whatever.

He left, and Ann looked up at Ryan and me. She said, "Do you believe this? I'm going to be late for dinner."

"How come the chief of surgery was not asked to do the honors?" asked Ryan.

"The chief is tied up in surgery," said Ann. "He asked me to see this guy." She wasn't smiling.

Ryan could see he had kidded her on a sore topic. He said, "You stood in nicely. We're your witnesses."

"Thanks," she said. "And I'm going to keep everyone from eating at a reasonable hour, so let me take care of things here, and you guys go on ahead."

"Ryan can go," I said. "I'll hang around."

CHAPTER
29

Ann and I headed for the SICU. She wanted to be sure the secretary was plugged in and everyone knew what to look for before she left.

On the way, I mentioned I'd been at the reception and seen her boss.

"He wasn't tied up in surgery," I said. "He was smiling ingratiatingly at various provosts and members of the board of trustees."

"Which is what he's supposed to be doing as chief," said Ann. "I can handle chest tubes on car wrecks."

I was about to agree that the secretary was better off in her hands when we rounded a corner and nearly collided with Thomas McIlheny himself.

His eyes weren't quite focused, and he looked as if he'd probably had one or two more gin-and-tonics listening to Dennis Rallston or whomever he had to listen to before making his escape from the reception.

He said, "Good heavens."

We looked at him. He wasn't exactly weaving down the hall, but he clearly wouldn't have made it past a sobriety roadblock.

"You're right." He smiled, looking at us look at him. "I am not totally sober. In fact, I am headed right for the on-call room to sleep it off. Won't even drive home."

"You're sure you can find it?" Ann laughed.

"Not without considerable error," he said, draping one arm around Ann and one around me. His breath could have pickled a school of herring. "I understand you have been saving the republic, Dr. Payson. Be careful, you lose this secretary and they'll call you a communist. Sympathizer at least. Pink down to your underpanties."

"He's out of the woods," said Ann. "He's got his chest tube. We're just going up to see him in the SICU."

"Give him my regards. Make my excuses. The chief cannot hold his liquor."

"You were tied up in surgery," said Ann. "I already told him."

"You are a gentleman and a scholar," said McIlheny. "And your friend here is the last of the real physicians."

"No kidding?" said Ann.

"Don't believe him," I said. "He's drunk."

"No, no. I'm serious. Spends two hours with a patient every now and then. I have it on the highest authority. Chief of medicine told me. Chief was trying to turn Abrams's head with a lot of money."

Ann shot me a quizzical look.

"Aha! I can see you didn't know this." McIlheny laughed. "Dr. Abrams turned down power and riches to continue as a humble country doc, healing the sick for modest fees. You say I'm drunk. Well, I am. I'd take care of him. You know what's ruining medicine?"

"Lawyers," said Ann.

"Worse than that. Money," McIlheny rasped. "Too many kids getting out nowadays expecting to drive Cadillacs, live in mansions, and retire by the time they're fifty. What ever happened to

157

the old country doc who made house calls and charged a dollar for an office visit? Now all the offices have twenty women working computers and doing the billing. You couldn't buy coffee for the office staff for what the old country doc charged to bring a new life into this world."

"Jesus, you are drunk, Tom," said Ann. She was laughing at him. She might have been his daughter, delighted at his disorder, happy to be a little in control of him, scolding him. It was interesting seeing them together. I'd never appreciated the father-daughter aspect of their relationship. But seeing them, I knew that enlisting Ann into any action aimed at McIlheny was not going to be easy.

That would make the dinner plans Ryan and I had set for Mai's place a little sticky.

We had reached the on-call rooms, and Ann slipped from under one of McIlheny's arms and opened the door. We helped him into bed.

He waved regally. "Call my wife," he croaked. "Tell her the bastards got her husband drunk. She won't believe you. Haven't been drunk since the end of chief residency. We got drunk together that night."

"Okay," said Ann.

"No, have Abrams call," said McIlheny. "Can't have a woman calling my wife telling her I won't be home tonight."

"Okay," I said.

"Stay pure, Abrams," roared McIlheny.

We closed the door behind us, and headed for the SICU.

"I've never seen him even high," Ann laughed.

"He's stewed now," I said.

"What did Dennis Rallston offer you?" Ann asked as we slipped into the elevator. She pushed the button for the SICU floor. "What rich and powerful position have you turned down now?"

"Don't listen to drunks."

"He's no drunk. He's just drunk now. What rich and powerful job?"

158

"Chief of Endocrine."

"And you turned it down?"

"What do I want with rich and powerful? I've got what I need."

"You are a strange and wondrous human being."

"I keep telling you that. You don't believe it till you hear it from the chief of surgery."

The elevator door opened and we hurried down the hall to the SICU.

They had turned the SICU into a circus. The security men were buzzing around with everything but bomb-sniffing dogs, which I'm sure they would have used if the SICU head nurse had allowed dogs to cross her threshold.

José Cruz was the physician working the SICU that night. He was fiddling with the respirator on that little kid with the mediastinitis, who didn't look any better that night than he had five days earlier.

Ann stood near his stall watching José work and tried not to look at the kid, crossing and uncrossing her arms, her face growing tight and her jaw muscles knotting. She cleared her throat a couple of times to get José's attention, but he didn't notice her. I could have walked over and tapped him on the shoulder, but I wanted Ann to have to walk right by that kid, something she was apparently determined not to do.

Finally José noticed and smiled his nervous smile. He hurried over to talk to Ann.

"A real train wreck, that kid," I said to José.

José looked as if he had a full bladder and couldn't find the bathroom—his eyes darted back and forth between Ann and me. He wasn't sure what to say.

"Dr. McIlheny won't win the Halsted prize for surgery on that kid," I said.

A foxy glitter rose behind José's eyes. He smiled and looked around, then said in a sly undertone, "I don't think Dr. McIlheny gonna win no prize for surgery nohow. If you know what I mean."

I grinned, urging him on silently. Ann remained stone-faced.

159

"His patients don't do too well, José?" I said.

"He's a dangerous man," said José. "Somebody got to do something."

"There's a man coming up with a chest tube, José," said Ann, as if we had been talking about things of no more concern to her than the weather in Altoona, until that moment. "He's a big mucky-muck in the government."

"Oh?" said José, eyebrow arching. "Who is this guy?"

"Just don't let his men get in your way. He's got lungs and the same anatomy as any other man. Just be sure the tubes are draining and listen to his chest and all the usual things. You want to put in a Swan, do it. Just like a regular patient."

José looked around the SICU and noticed the dark-suited men taking up positions in various corners, and he started to look sweaty and nervous. He began wringing his hands.

"Who is this guy?" he said.

"Same as any man," said Ann. "Understand, José? He's the secretary of state."

"Oh, my," said José.

"You going to be okay?" asked Ann.

"The secretary of state," José said, as if he'd just had a close encounter of the third kind.

"Don't let it rattle you," said Ann. "They breathe and pee just like you and me."

We took my car to Mai's restaurant. Ann was laughing about José.

"Did you see his eyes?" she said. "His eyes were bugging out. I mean, he looked like Peter Lorre."

"I'm never sure how much he understands."

"He understands everything. He doesn't understand what he doesn't want to, José. His English is fine."

"Well, the nurses will keep those G-men off his back. They didn't look like they were going to take any guff from the feds."

"What a production." Ann laughed. She seemed to be in an artificially good mood. She still hadn't mentioned the little kid on the respirator. "They all enjoy it so much. The storm troopers.

160

Never smile. Notice that? They just love to play that ultraserious organization man role."

"It makes them feel important."

"They all love it. The guys they're protecting, the guys doing it. It's such theater."

"It's the only way those guys would ever get on stage, even as bit players," I said. "See that kid?"

"Yes," said Ann abruptly. "What of it?"

"He's still in the SICU. Ryan says he's getting better."

"Thank God."

"Tom McIlheny did that."

"Ben," said Ann. "Let up for a bit, okay?"

At the restaurant, Mai had our usual table, food stacked high, waiters coming from all directions.

"Dr. Payson," said Mai. "Tonight we are especially honored."

"Why's that?" asked Ann, taking her place between Ryan and me.

"I understand you have been saving important lives tonight."

"They're all important, Mai," said Ann with a smile that tried to be warm but looked pretty grim. "Rank gets left at the hospital door," said Ann.

Mai smiled one of her demure and deferential smiles, a smile I'd seen her use on Ryan when she was steering him in some direction he had no idea he was being taken. She said, "I'm glad to hear you say it."

Ann looked at her. "I meant it."

Mai smiled and reached for a spring roll, not looking at Ann now. "Yes, there is nothing more important than a single life."

Ryan had obviously told Mai about the problem in the department of surgery. But that was as direct as she would get, if I knew Mai.

Ann was chewing, chewing on what Mai had said and looking at Ryan, who made sure to stare intently at his plate. She finally swallowed and said, "You must have seen a lot of people given the VIP treatment in your country."

It was a graceful way of deflecting us. I felt a little embarrassed.

161

We had asked Ann out to dinner and then cornered her. She didn't want to talk about life and death and the problem of Thomas McIlheny. She was out to dinner. I could never have been as smooth. That kind of social polish is really a talent.

Mai said something about the different expectations in different countries. The rich and powerful were expected to be treated better in her Vietnam. It was the order of things. She had that same social grace Ann had.

I kept thinking about the two nurses Ryan had invited to join us for dessert, and plotting how I could get Ann out of here before they arrived. It had seemed like a good idea when we talked about it the day before, but I could see now how unfair it would be to invite Ann out to dinner and then surround her and put her on the spot to join our plot.

We were finishing what I guessed was the main course—you could never tell how many main courses Mai would serve—and I said, "I promised the president I'd get Ann back to take care of the secretary."

Everyone looked up in confusion, especially Ann, because she had no plans to go back to the hospital. Ryan and Mai looked puzzled. Ryan caught my look and seemed to understand. He shrugged an if-you-want-to-play-it-that-way shrug.

Ann, not knowing what was planned, said, "The secretary is all tucked in. What are you talking about?"

I looked at my watch, then said to Ryan, "What time are your friends arriving?"

"Our friends are due at eight-thirty," said Ryan.

"I guess I better explain," I said.

Ann put her fork down and looked at me, eyes wide-open, face cool and controlled, but alert.

"I was trying to give you an opening to back out," I told Ann. "We had an ulterior motive for dinner tonight. In addition to all the usual motives."

The corners of Ann's mouth turned down and she looked directly at me. She said, "What ulterior motive?"

"As you know, I've been concerned about McIlheny. And I'm not the only one. Ryan, a number of the nurses, and apparently José Cruz have some questions about whether he's safe at any speed. Is it just that he takes on tough cases, or is he just quality-insufficient?"

Ann started to speak, but Ryan cut her off. "Just let him finish, Ann."

"Ryan and I and two SICU nurses—volunteers—are going to review every chart on every patient Thomas McIlheny has done since he's arrived. We were going to invite you in on the party."

Ann looked around the table at Mai and Ryan and then at me. She was trying to decide how to react. The corners of her mouth gradually straightened, then curled up, and she laughed a short, sharp laugh, like the coed who winds up in the bedroom and appreciates her circumstances for the first time. "Oh, no, ladies and gentlemen. Not me."

"Ann, the guy's a train wreck," said Ryan. "He's the Cabin John Bridge in a snowstorm—he's an accident that can't wait to happen."

"He's also my boss," said Ann very nicely but very firmly and, as before, with enough grace under fire to make me feel like a heel for putting her on the spot.

"Okay," I said. "Fair enough. We didn't want to do this behind your back. But we can't involve you, given your position, if you've not made up your mind yet."

"I've made up my mind," she said with deadly politeness. "To mind my own store and keep my nose clean."

"Fair enough," I said again.

"When are these nurses arriving?" asked Ann.

Ryan said, "Any minute now."

"Then I'd better be running along," said Ann. Then to Mai, "It really was a lovely meal, as always."

Mai smiled and looked disappointed.

I started to get up.

163

"No, you stay for your meeting," said Ann. "I can get a cab."

She stood up and pulled her purse up under her arm and walked out the door.

Ryan looked up. "I guess she's not on the team."

"Apparently not," I said. "I shouldn't have done it this way."

"We, big boy," said Ryan. "From now on, it's we."

"I don't understand Ann," said Ryan. "I've never seen her run away from a fight before."

"And if patients are dying," said Mai.

"Nobody's died," I said. "Not that I know of, anyway. And I can see it from her point of view."

"How?" asked Mai.

"Right now all she's heard are rumors. Nothing she's seen with her own eyes. No case she's actually been in on."

"You show her that kid in the SICU?" asked Ryan.

"So what? So the kid's sick, and McIlheny did the surgery. What's that prove to Ann? She sees patients of his go through the unit all the time who do fine."

"Not from what I hear."

"What you hear does not constitute hard data. That is the stuff of hearsay."

"So we're gonna get some hard data."

A few minutes later the two nurses from the SICU arrived. One was the redhead, Maureen Flaherty, and her friend, a willowy brunette named Kathy Kennedy. I watched them come in the door and give their names to the maître d'. They wore similar tweed blazers and slacks and they didn't look a bit like the dressed-for-action athletes they looked like in scrub dresses. Looking at them standing there gazing about the restaurant, the hospital and the SICU seemed very far away. The maître d' brought them over and Ryan introduced everyone to everyone, ordered beer all around, then said to me, "What's the plan?"

I said, "I understand we've all noticed the same phenomenon, concerning a certain chief of surgery and his patients."

"We've noticed he's a disaster, if that's what you mean," said Maureen.

"Let me play a role, for a moment," I said. "Tell me, Miss Flaherty, have you been trained as a thoracic surgeon?"

Maureen looked confused and shot a look at her friend Kathy, who said, "I thought you agreed with us."

"I do, but I'm trying to show what we're going to run up against. Now, Miss Flaherty, why should we believe that you are capable of evaluating a thoracic surgeon—a certified genius and the chief of surgery?"

"I see what his patients look like post-op."

"And what is Dr. McIlheny's postoperative mortality rate for aortic valve replacements in patients with preoperative reduced left ventricular ejection fractions?"

Maureen reddened, and her eyes grew hard. "Whatever it is, it's a helluva lot worse than everyone else's. I can tell you that."

"You mean the other thoracic surgeons at St. George's do better? What is their mortality rate for this procedure in this group of patients?"

Maureen said nothing. She crossed her arms and shifted in her chair as far away from me as possible. She looked as if she'd just discovered I didn't change my underwear more than once a year.

"What is this?" asked Kathy Kennedy. "We all know—"

"We all suspect," I cut her off. "We don't *know* a thing yet. We've seen enough to form a hypothesis that we all have a gut

166

feeling is true. We think he's a disaster. Now we've got to prove it."

We talked about what had to be done, how to go over the patients' charts, how to organize the data, what to look for, how to divide up the work.

After all the details were worked out, Kathy said, "So, with this chart we show what we all know—that his patients are dropping like flies—wound dehiscence, valves unseating, bleeds, infections. What do we do with this great chart once we've got it?"

"That depends how damning it is," I said.

"Suppose it's as bad as we think it's going to be?"

"We'll take it to the dean of the medical school," I said. I tried to say that with a lot of conviction.

Maureen said, "And what's he going to do with it?"

I looked at Ryan. He looked at me with an amused smile, eyebrows raised as if to say, "Yes, Doctor, what is the dean going to do with all this information?"

"What he does with it is his problem. Once we present it, we've done all we can do."

Both nurses rolled their eyes and then looked at each other. They didn't say "What have we been wasting our time for?" but they looked it.

Maureen said, "So you just wash your hands?"

Kathy said, "And let him go on operating?"

"And what would you suggest?" I asked. I turned to Ryan. "You got a better idea?"

"Call the papers," said Maureen.

"You could do that now," I said.

Maureen chewed her lower lip on that.

"Maybe you could sell your story to a willing buyer, if it's a slow time in the newspaper business," I said.

"We could call up some families," said Kathy. "Like Mr. Manfredi's wife. He died. She ought to know."

"You wouldn't be the first nurse to do that," I said. "McIlheny will call his malpractice insurer, who'll call their lawyers, and he'll go right on practicing."

167

"But if he gets enough suits . . ." said Kathy Kennedy.

"He'll go right on. Thoracic surgery's a high-risk specialty. You really buy that lawyers' line about lawyers being able to make doctors shape up? Even the lawyers don't believe that. They just say it to defend themselves."

"And they'll call you as a witness, once they find out who put the buzz in the wife's ear," said Ryan.

"And when they do," I said, "you better have some facts. Know what a fact is? Lawyers love facts. It's something about which there is no controversy. And the lawyers will trot out some expert witness who'll make your impressions look pretty sick."

"So what's this dean going to do?" asked Maureen.

"He could appoint a committee to investigate our charges. He might just bury the whole thing. But he's the only guy over McIlheny."

"A committee," groaned Kathy. "Great. Patients dehiscing in the SICU, and we've got a committee looking into it."

No one said anything.

"I'm going to go through those charts," I said. "You want to help, I'll be happy."

"You know what they call him now?" said Maureen. "McIlheinous. That's our chief of surgery. Dr. McIlheinous."

The meeting broke up a few beers later when my beeper went off. I recognized the number the operator gave me immediately. It was the SICU. I tried to think of whom I had in the hospital, which patient could have wound up on the SICU that night. For one delirious moment I thought it might be Ann, forgiving me for setting her up, wanting to spend the night at my place.

It wasn't Ann. It was a nurse telling me that Mr. Crutchfield had made another curtain call.

It was a quick drive from Georgetown to St. George's. M Street to Foxhall on a weekday night clears out by eight. Government workers are in bed early. Washington is not a late-night town.

The lights were down on the SICU. I scanned the room looking for José, but didn't find him. My eyes stopped at the stall with the little kid McIlheny had done, the kid with the mediastinitis. Ann was standing by his bed, flipping through the pages of his chart as if she weren't really reading it, as if she were just leafing through a magazine not seeing much of interest.

But she was interested. She wasn't looking up. She read each note carefully, checked lab reports, moved on, read a nurse's note, went through the temperature charts. She didn't notice me standing by her for several minutes. Then she noticed me and she looked up.

"How's he doing?" I asked.

"White count's down. Afebrile for two days. Wound's growing out staph aureus. He's coming along."

"Exciting reading, that chart," I said. "He's doing better, but it was tough sledding and he's not out of the woods yet."

"No," said Ann, shaking her head, with a voice short of air, as if she'd been punched in the solar plexus. "He's definitely not out of the woods yet."

We looked at him. He actually looked more alert than the first night Ryan had dragged me up to see him, but he was a long way from looking totally viable. His skin was a skim-milk color, and his eyes were still glazed, but he moved them more now and he occasionally focused on things. They had removed the tube he'd had in his trachea and taken him off the respirator. He had IV lines in each of his puffy little arms, and his chest was taped over with an enormous bandage out of which ran two drainage tubes.

"He's had a rough time," Ann said.

Her eyes were filling, and she took a tissue from her pocket and wiped them.

I was getting a little teary myself watching her, watching him, and watching her look at him. I decided it was time to change the subject.

"I'm sorry about tonight. I had no right to—"

She cut me off. "Don't apologize. You did what you felt you had to do."

169

She met my eyes, and I couldn't read a thing in hers.

"Well, I'm sorry anyway."

Ann turned back to the kid. She lifted his hand and let it fall to the bed like a rag doll's arm. Her eyes were reddening again.

"You do what you have to do," she said. "You put the patient first."

CHAPTER
31

Lydell Brown's wife was watching him negotiate the parallel bars when I found them in the physical therapy room. She stood at the far end of the bars as he lurched toward her, and she smiled and nodded and made encouraging noises. He leaned heavily on his arms, listing to the right, then to the left, but finally reaching her. She took his head on her shoulder and ran her hand over the back of his head and congratulated him. He had walked eight feet.

Her eyes changed when they saw me, hardening at first, then more neutral. She managed a smile.

I hadn't seen Lydell for two days.

Lydell was being helped into his wheelchair by a physical therapist. He was sitting down before he noticed me.

"Hey, Doc," he said, offering an open palm for me to slap. "How's it going, man?" The real warmth in all that made his wife's reserve seem all the more cold.

I told him it was going fine with me and asked how it was going with him. "Real good. I just walked the whole way down that thing."

"It's good to see a doctor," said Mrs. Brown. "I was beginning to think the doctors didn't come to the hospital anymore."

"Isn't the physical therapy doctor seeing Lydell?"

"But I meant Lydell's doctors. Dr. McIlheny hasn't been in."

"Oh, he's a very busy man," said Lydell. "A specialist."

"I suppose the surgeons feel they don't have much more to offer," I said, trying to convince myself that was a good excuse for not making rounds on a patient after you'd cut his heart open and put in a new heart valve.

"Have you discussed Lydell's case with Dr. McIlheny recently?"

"Not since Lydell was transferred to rehab," I said. "I talked to Dr. Stevens yesterday." Dr. Stevens ran the physical therapy rehabilitation center.

"But Dr. McIlheny did this . . ." said Mrs. Brown, waving in the general direction of Lydell. "I would like him to tell us what to expect with this new heart valve. We ask the therapists, but they just say, 'Ask the surgeons.' I mean, is there anything he shouldn't do? Should he change his diet? Can he exercise?"

"The main thing is to increase the activity slowly, gradually, and systematically," I said. I had the feeling I was shouting in the wind. "I'll ask Dr. McIlheny to stop by."

I walked out of the room knowing I'd never ask McIlheny to see Lydell Brown. For one thing, I doubted it would do much good, and for another, I wasn't sure I wanted him to see Lydell. I was more and more sure I didn't want him seeing any of my patients.

I could see it from Mrs. Brown's point of view, though. The physical therapist might be nice enough, but he hadn't been the master wizard. He hadn't opened Lydell's heart and sewn it back together so it worked, and he hadn't given Lydell his stroke.

For McIlheny, of course, Lydell was just one more problem dealt with. Lydell had had a stormy course, a manageable complication, but he was past needing any more surgery and he was someone else's problem now.

Every time I softened on McIlheny, I had only to stop in and see Lydell. I felt guilty if I missed seeing him a single day. McIlheny had mentally signed off the case. Of course, there were rational-

172

izations—I was Lydell's primary physician. McIlheny was only a consult.

None of that washed with me. McIlheny just didn't have the guts to show up. McIlheny wasn't stopping by to see Lydell because he couldn't face Lydell. Things had gone wrong with Lydell. Lydell was an embarrassment. That's exactly when you have to stop in every day, when it might have been your fault. That's when you hang in there like a terrier.

There are always those patients. Patients you feel like leaving as soon as you walk in their rooms, as soon as you walk on the ward. You just don't want to face them. Those are the ones you have to force yourself to sit down with. Those are the very ones you have to be with. You've got nothing more to offer them than time and sympathy, and you've got to do it, as bad as it gets.

McIlheny could be charming. He could tell you that you don't follow the calling of medicine for money, that you had to remain pure. But the right words, having your heart in the right place, good looks, a wall full of diplomas aren't enough when you're a surgeon. You've got to be able to cut, and you've got to stay with your patient no matter what.

I couldn't be sure if that valve pulling loose was McIlheny's fault or not. But I knew one thing. He hadn't kept up with Lydell Brown.

CHAPTER
32

Sam Sawyer was in Ann Payson's office, sitting in front of her desk. Ann looked up when I came in and said, "Your friends make the most interesting patients."

Sam laughed. "Just what I never wanted to be, an interesting patient."

I took a chair next to Sam on the customer side of the desk, and we watched Ann examine the echocardiograms spread out on her desk.

"Nancy does such nice work," Ann said, not looking up. Nancy Colleo did do nice work. You could see the problem in Sam's valve with no doubts hanging.

Sam looked at the fuzzy impressions of the sonogram from his side of the desk.

"Come over and look," said Ann. She pointed out what she was looking at, fished out a folder from a pile on the top of her desk, and placed a normal echocardiogram next to it. It didn't take four years of medical school to see that difference between Sam's study and the normal.

"So it's got to come out," said Sam.

"No question," said Ann.

Sam looked her over with an expression I couldn't read. He liked her, that much was clear, but there was something in his face that was more of the schoolteacher than the patient.

"What kind of time frame are we talking about?" asked Sam.

"I wouldn't slap you in the hospital tonight, necessarily," said Ann. "But I wouldn't want to see you go longer than, say, next week. That's a frayed rope you're hanging by. No telling when it'll snap."

Sam's eyes reacted to that. He looked hard at her, then at me.

"I wouldn't screw around too long making up your mind, Sam," I said.

"That valve's given me no trouble for all these years."

"With this particular problem, you may not have much in the way of symptoms or premonitions," said Ann. "Just goes kaplooey one day."

"Okay," said Sam. "You've read me the riot act. Let me go home and reconcile myself to it."

We shook hands all around, and I offered Sam a ride home. He said he had driven. Ann and I watched him walk out of the office.

"Lean on him, Abe," said Ann. "You know what those valves can do."

"I was in medical school, second year, doing autopsies," I recollected. "We had a lady who'd died suddenly in her garden. Just keeled over. Opened the heart and the metal basket was there, but no ball. The resident asked me where I thought the ball had gone. I had no idea. Then he takes that long incision down to the belly and sticks his hand in the iliac artery and comes up with half the ball valve."

"Pathologists know everything," said Ann. "But too late."

175

CHAPTER
33

A week after the plot was hatched at Mai's place, Ryan, the two nurses, and I had reviewed sixty charts altogether. Early returns did not look encouraging for defenders of faith in Dr. McIlheny, but I wasn't ready to predict the outcome before the polls had closed.

It was Wednesday morning, and I had been in the record room, much to the chagrin of Mrs. Bromley, who pointed out that every unpaid minute I spent there was a minute I could have been seeing patients for cold cash in the office. Mrs. Bromley had a most irritating practical streak.

Feeling guilty about having spent the morning earning no money at all, I wandered up to the medical intensive care unit, where I had only to stick my head in the door and some medical intern was likely to ask me to consult on some patient or another, and I could then call Mrs. Bromley and have her bill the patient. Showing up regularly at the MICU was good for business, and it kept Mrs. Bromley happy, but it was depressing and no fun at all.

The MICU had become an AIDS depository.

At any given time, it was at least half filled with AIDS patients, stripped of their immune systems, loaded with tumor, stricken by all complications known to man. It had become a circus of medical curiosities, rare infections, and endocrine zebras. The interns who rotated through wound up thinking the most common pneumonia was not pneumococcus but *Pneumocystis*, an organism that, before AIDS, was seen only rarely in some leukemics. AIDS patients died in droves of previously bizarre and happily uncommon things like Kaposi's sarcoma, things I'd never even seen once when I was an intern, and cryptococcal meningitis, so rare in my day that any intern making the diagnosis was given a free meal in the cafeteria. Now cryptococcus was bread-and-butter stuff to the interns at St. George's. It was enough to make me feel obsolete, and I was only a dozen years beyond residency.

So I dreaded setting foot in the MICU. This particular Wednesday I had no sooner stuck my head in the door when I heard my name ring out, and Dennis Rallston grabbed me. He wanted me to see a patient with a low sodium and AIDS, who I knew had inappropriate ADH from his two-sentence description, even before laying eyes on him. Having laid eyes on him, I wished I hadn't. The patient was a forty-year-old homosexual window dresser for Giorgio's, in Chevy Chase, slumped over in bed, skin lumpy with purplish Kaposi's that riddled every organ, *Pneumocystis* caking his lungs, making every breath problematic.

His low sodium was the least of his problems.

Dennis Rallston pulled me aside and said, "You know who invented this disease?" He looked over his shoulder. "It wasn't the Africans. It wasn't the Jamaicans. It was the fucking hospital administrators."

I watched his sly eyes glitter. He said, "DRGs, shortened hospital stays, falling bed occupancy—ever hear those administrators talk about all that? They get all choked up. But then along comes AIDS and the ICUs fill up, and the beds are full, and you can't get the patients home 'cause they're sick as stink. Those guys did it."

An intern came up as I was listening to Dennis, and I was sure he was about to ask me to see another AIDS patient, and I began

177

looking around for somewhere to hide when my beeper went off, for once just when I needed it.

The phone had a very agitated surgical resident on the other end. McIlheny had asked him to call. The resident sounded as if someone had kneed him in the wrong place and he was still trying to catch his breath. They had operated on a kid with an acute abdomen—abdominal pain, vomiting, tender belly—looking for an appendix, but the appendix was normal.

"That happens," I said, trying to sound astute and trying to imagine why he was calling an endocrinologist to tell me about a kid with an appendix.

"The thing is," the resident said, squeaking out his words, "his blood. It looked like tomato soup with sour cream."

"Tomato soup?" I asked.

"I noticed it when I drew his bloods pre-op and I mentioned it to Dr. McIlheny. But he wanted to go ahead."

"It looked like it had a cream layer on top?"

"Yeah, in the tubes. You could see it floating, like."

I told him I'd be right over.

The kid was in the SICU, and my friend Maureen Flaherty of the red hair and sharp tongue had assigned herself to him. I had a pretty good idea what the problem was, so I drew some blood and asked her to spin it down in the centrifuge and to put it in the refrigerator.

Just looking at it coming out in the Vacutainer, I was sure what the kid had. There was a cream layer on top even before it was spun down.

He was about seven years old, a pale little boy with red hair—to look at him he could have been Maureen's kid brother—and he was still coming out of anesthesia. His hands kept traveling down to his belly—he still had pain. Not that that should have been surprising—someone had just cut open his belly, and that can smart a bit. Especially if it was the wrong belly to cut. His eyes were squeezed shut, and his mouth turned into an inverted horseshoe.

178

He had Type One hyperlipidemia, and surgery's never been known to chase away triglyceride levels of five thousand, which is what the kid had, along with some pancreatitis, which isn't charmed by a surgeon's gloved hands, either. In fact, the kid had troubles enough before McIlheny opened his belly, but now he was really in for it.

"Where is Dr. McIlheny now?" I asked Maureen.

"In the OR," she said, letting me know by the way she said it exactly what she thought of the idea of his being in the OR at that moment. "Doing an emergency bypass, if you can believe that."

"What do you think he's doing in the OR?" I asked.

"Hiding from this kid's parents," she said, mouth hard, chin up. She looked like a ten-year-old trying to look tough.

"Sometimes bypasses need to be done on an emergency basis," I said.

"Well, he's there anyway."

That provided the next cue. It was getting to be a very stagy morning. Just as she finished saying that, a female surgical resident rushed into the SICU and said, "Dr. Abrams?"

My problem was that I didn't know my lines. I just stared at her.

The resident was still wearing her booties and her OR hat, her mask pulled down, so I could see the panicked look on her face.

"Could you come with me, right now?" she said.

I was trying to figure out how she knew I was there in the SICU, which was not a place I had been frequenting much until lately. Then I realized if McIlheny had asked the other resident to call me in to see the kid, he knew I was there, and he might have sent this resident out to get me.

A nice guess, but as it turned out, very wrong. In fact, sending her out to fetch me was not at all McIlheny's idea, nor even one he liked.

"Where are we going?" I asked her.

She looked around. The nurses were staring at her from their stalls. "The OR," she said softly, so only I could hear. "You are needed in the OR, stat, very stat."

179

"What's the problem?" I asked. Surgeons didn't often ask for my help in the operating room.

"Just come," she said, "please."

I followed her into the operating room suite.

"Change in here," she said, walking into the men's locker room. I stood before the locker looking at her and wondering whether she was going to stand there and watch, or what.

The expression on her face was just as urgent as it had been in the SICU. "Go on," she said. "No time to be modest. Change. I'll tell you."

So I stripped down as she spoke.

"We're starting a bypass, when the anesthesiologist says the patient's pressure's up—two-twenty over one-twenty."

"I'm listening," I said, pulling off clothes and throwing them into the locker.

"I'm telling you." She tossed me some blue scrub pants.

I'd gotten down to my underpants by this time and pulled on scrub pants, still not understanding who wanted me in the OR, or why.

"Okay. So it's high. But McIlheny looks up and says, 'One-twenty diastolic—this man's got a pheochromocytoma!'"

"What?"

"A pheochromocytoma," she deadpanned, spacing each syllable, with increasing irony as she went along. She did everything but roll her eyes.

"Interesting thought," I said, trying to sound neutral and trying hard not to laugh.

"Well, okay, so McIlheny likes zebras," she continued. "But wait." Her voice dropped to a hush and she kept me dangling there a hung instant. "This is why I'm dragging you in there," she said. Her eyes grew wider, and there was a tremor in her voice as she fought for control. "He tells us to close the chest and tells the nurses to set up for abdominal surgery." Her voice was now a rumbling current, as ominous as a drum roll. "He's going in after the pheo."

180

The room spun a little when she said that. There was so much wrong with it, it overloaded my circuits momentarily. I could see why she was the color of bleached bread. I probably blanched a few shades myself.

The blood pressure was high, high enough even to be a pheo—a tumor of the adrenal glands that makes hormones that can send the blood pressure through the roof—but pheos are rare birds, and anesthetized patients get hypertensive for dozens of reasons, all of which were far more likely.

But all right, the question had been raised. The thing to do at that point is to close up the patient very quietly, give thanks that you got through the procedure you'd done, and get him to the recovery room posthaste.

Patients with pheos tend to explode rudely if you operate on them without protecting them with drugs beforehand. It's called "blockading" the patient, and you'd no sooner put your hand on a belly with a pheo in it without blockade than you'd stick your wet hand into an electrical outlet without turning off the fuse.

If McIlheny thought he'd stumbled onto a patient with a pheo, he had no business continuing surgery, much less going after it without making the diagnosis first and then protecting the patient with drugs before trying to handle a potential bomb.

"He's going to explore the adrenals," said the resident with a voice so pregnant it could have delivered on the spot.

By now I had my scrubs on, complete with hat, mask, and booties.

"He kept talking about how he found one just like this at Mass General, and how they had it out with just nitroprusside coverage," the resident was saying. "They just stumbled on it doing a nephrectomy. It's like he's trying to relive this great triumph of his days at the General."

I started for the OR, but she stopped me.

"Let me look at you. He'll throw you out if you've got your hat on crooked."

She looked me over, adjusted my hat, and led me to the OR.

181

The resident stopped me outside the door. "Let me go in first, and give me a minute. I don't want him knowing who called you in. He'd skin me alive."

I waited outside the door a minute, thinking about McIlheny in there cutting on that belly that could explode if he was correct about the pheo. When I couldn't stand it anymore, I entered through the scrub room, pushing the swinging door into the OR proper.

CHAPTER

34

I stood there looking around, trying to figure out who was who—they were all covered up in masks and caps and surgical gowns. I spotted McIlheny, tall and stooping over the belly.

McIlheny was making the skin incision. He looked up and shot me a look that could have stopped a fullback at the goal line.

I was wearing my mask and cap, and he didn't know who I was. "Benjamin Abrams, Dr. McIlheny," I said, trying to sound cheerful and upbeat.

"What can I do for you?" he said in a voice cold enough to chill a good martini.

"Oh, you know me. I heard you'd found a pheo and I couldn't resist coming in for a look."

"Heard I'd found a pheo? How'd you hear that?"

I thought for a moment how not to blow the cover of the resident who had taken a chance to protect a patient on the table. If I got McIlheny's hackles bristling, there would be no stopping him. "I was just in the SICU. Word gets around."

"Who was talking about a pheo?" said McIlheny, searching the OR with narrowed eyes. The resident who had summoned me was already regowned and she was making herself busy with some retractors. She was looking intently at her own hands, trying very hard to disappear. Several people had left the OR with her during the time they took to reprep the patient for an abdominal incision, and some were still drifting back in. McIlheny couldn't know who had squealed.

"How'd they hear about it in the SICU?" he demanded.

"Oh, I don't know. Maybe they heard it over the intercom, calling for the abdominal tray. You know how the nurses are. Like listening to police calls on the shortwave."

"Can't do surgery without someone spying on you," he muttered into the wound. "Turn off that intercom," he barked at the circulating nurse.

The circulating nurse walked over to the intercom switch and turned it off with a resigned shrug and a flip of her wrist.

"Picked up one of these when I was chief resident at the General."

"No kidding?" I said, trying not to look at the resident, who was staring intently at the belly. "Great pickup," I said.

There was a flicker of eyes around the OR when I said that. Oh, well, if McIlheny was going to believe I was on his side, the nurses and residents would have to believe it, too. I knew one resident, at least, who knew where I stood.

McIlheny looked up. His eyes looked friendlier now. Friendlier, but still a little wary.

"What's the story this time?" I asked as he prepared to make the incision.

"Hypertensive crisis," he intoned. He had a nice, rich baritone, very authoritative. Would have convinced any jury in the land that the patient had a hypertensive crisis. Any jury but me and the residents, who knew that a transient blood pressure of two-twenty over one-twenty did not a hypertensive crisis make.

"No kidding?" I said, all ears. "Got to hand it to you. Not

184

many surgeons would have thought of pheo. That's supposed to be the internists' tumor."

McIlheny issued a grunting laugh and he glanced up. "That's what the internists call it." He looked around at his residents. They laughed obediently.

He looked at me. I laughed.

"Come over here," he said. "Get a better look."

I walked over, and the nurses set out a stool so I could look over McIlheny's shoulders. I hopped up on it and looked down as he stroked a foot-long incision down the belly.

"Got him pretty well blocked, have you?" I asked. A shudder went through the residents around the table. McIlheny's head sunk into his shoulders a little, as if I'd slapped the top of his head. Nobody said anything for a moment.

"Well, of course, we didn't have time for Dibenzyline. We're using nitroprusside," he said, his words coming in a rush. "You know they do that at the Cleveland clinic. Urology, nineteen-eighty, I think."

"Oh, that series. That was Breckenridge. You know I talked to him about that at the Endocrine Society meeting in June. He says they've stopped doing that single-agent stuff. Too many foul-ups. They've got an update coming out in December. *JAMA*, I think he said."

The residents held their breath. The scrub nurse looked out of the corners of her eyes at McIlheny. The circulating nurse looked at the floor, but her ears flicked like an antelope's listening for the crackle of brush under the lion's paw.

McIlheny stopped blunt dissecting and looked at me.

"Breckenridge said that?" he barked, halfway between laugh and howl.

"From his own lips," I said cheerfully.

"That's what I get for keeping up with the literature. The fashions go out of style before you can read the retractions."

"I told him the same thing. I said, 'Think how many pheos are going to be done under nitroprusside without blockade before your

185

retraction appears, and they'll get into the same trouble it took you a year to find out you were buying.'"

"What'd he say?" said McIlheny, looking at the wound now, but not moving his hands.

"He said, 'Oh, well, surgeons don't read the literature anyway. Probably won't do much harm.'"

McIlheny laughed. "Speak for yourself, white man," he growled.

The residents looked at him between their masks and hats. The nurses looked at me out of the corner of their eyes. Funny feeling you get in the operating room, with everything blocked out behind a screen of blue masks and gowns, just eyes looking at eyes. Nobody moved. Nobody said anything. The seconds crept by on tiptoe.

"Well, for crissake," said McIlheny.

"That Breckenridge," I said, "irresponsible. I mean, think how many pheos could be done before December. I mean, most of the time you're going to get away with it. But . . ."

"How long do you think it would take you to get this guy blocked?"

"Oh," I said. "Day. Maybe two, max."

McIlheny looked into the big OR light for a hung instant and said, "Well, let's block him, then." He sounded like John Wayne saying "Move 'em out." Then he looked to the anesthesiologist who had started this whole fiasco by reporting the blood pressure in the first place and he said, "How's the BP, José?"

José said in a high-pitched, hysterical voice, "One-sixty over ninety. He's hokay, chief."

"We've got time, then," said McIlheny. He turned to a resident. "Close him up, Mark. Dr. Abrams here just talked himself into a patient."

He said that with a hard edge of irony, as if he were having his arm twisted by a hard sell, but he was a big man, big enough to give a spunky lieutenant a chance to prove himself. We could blow the bugles and ride to the rescue the next day.

186

I could see the shoulders of all the residents and nurses relax.

McIlheny stepped away from the table and pulled off his gloves and his gown. He motioned me to the hallway door. We both headed down toward the locker room.

"You'll let me know as soon as he's ready?" he said, smiling, friendly, almost affectionate.

"First thing, chief," I said. I don't know why I said chief. It just seemed right at the time. It fit the scene we were all playing. I caught myself making a thumbs-up sign, just like in the movies.

CHAPTER
35

Showered and dressed, I pressed the electric wall plate, watched the doors swing open, and stepped out of the madness of the operating suite into the more familiar fluorescent glow of the SICU. I was looking for Ann. I found José Cruz writing a note at the foot of the stall containing the patient McIlheny had nearly explored for a pheochromocytoma.

José looked up from his chart, shaking his head. "That was juz very scary," he said, his voice not at all hushed. He was shaken and he didn't care who knew it. Maureen, who always seemed to be on duty when McIlheny was at his best, was taking a blood pressure on the patient, but even with a stethoscope in her ears, she was listening to us.

"Well, hell, José," I grinned. "You tell the man his patient's in hypertensive crisis—what do you expect?"

José didn't see I was kidding. His eyebrows flew skyward, and his whole face and neck swelled, eyes bulging.

"I didna say a thing about hypertensive crisis!" he squawked. "I only tell him the BP. He flew off the handle. He called for the abdominal tray. I thought I wet my pants."

His voice was rising through the octaves, and his forehead was popping out in little beads of sweat.

"Calm down, José," I said. "I know what happened."

"But that man's dangerous," croaked José.

As he was speaking, Ann walked up. She was smiling until she caught what José was saying. Then her face fell. She stood there trying to make up her mind about leaving.

"You better watch who you call dangerous, José," I said, grinning. The grin got him. He thought I wasn't taking him seriously. His neck veins started bulging, and he got all lathered in a hurry.

"He cuts open a belly looking for a pheo!" José sputtered. "You know that's not right. He says, 'Hang the nitroprusside.' That's gonna do one hell of a lot if he's got a pheo. You got to do something, Abe."

"Hey, wait a minute." I laughed. "This isn't even my department. This is a job for a surgeon." Saying that, I looked right at Ann.

The corners of Ann's mouth were angling toward the floor, and she looked as happy to be hearing all this as a priest at a prochoice rally.

"You stirring up the natives again, Ben?" she said.

"He's not doing nothing," barked José. "Something's gotta be done. We can't go on like this."

José described what happened in his rapid, accented English, breathless and with much body language. Ann listened impassively, with a face as close as a face can get to having no expression at all and still be alive. Her eyes were alert, though. She was listening. She was disturbed. Finally, when José started to go over it all again, trying to get a reaction out of her, she held up her hand and said, "Enough."

José looked to me in desperation, then back to Ann.

"I'm not the executive committee. I just work here."

189

"But, Ann," said José.

By now Maureen and half a dozen nurses and residents were staring at José, Ann, and me. Ann lowered her voice so it was audible only to José and me.

"This is hardly the time or the place, José. Pull yourself together."

José looked as if he'd been slapped and looked to me.

I shrugged.

He grimaced, shook his head, and went back to writing his note.

"Free for dinner?" I asked Ann.

"Cafeteria, maybe," said Ann. "I've got a case going on in forty minutes."

"When did you start this morning?" I asked. I knew what she'd say. She had started at seven-thirty. I'd checked the OR schedule. She'd done six cases in eight hours and she was starting another in forty minutes. She'd probably finish in the OR by midnight, make Rounds on her patients, and start all over again the next morning. You can have the life of the surgeon.

We walked out of the SICU and down the hall to the elevator.

"That wasn't fair, Ben," Ann said after I'd pushed the button and we leaned against the wall to wait.

"I can't keep José quiet."

"McIlheny isn't José's boss. You guys put me in the middle."

"We're all in the middle," I said.

CHAPTER
36

I stopped off to see Lydell Brown before I left St. George's that day. His wife was with him in his room. He was scheduled to be discharged the next morning. He could walk now, with a walker, and he could move both arms and both legs, but he would never hit a jump shot from outside the foul line again. He'd be lucky to hit a lay-up.

On the other hand, he was alive.

I still wasn't sure whether he owed McIlheny his life or his stroke. I never could be sure. The same events happening after surgery by Ann Payson would have only convinced me how lucky he was to be alive. Thinking of them in the context of what I'd just seen in the operating room made me feel very shaky.

His wife smiled when I came in. She said, "Oh, you're coming to say good-bye." She offered her hand and a warm smile, and I couldn't find a shred of irony or hostility. I think she really did feel grateful for what little I had done for her husband.

"It's been a long haul," I said.

Lydell said, "I can never thank you enough, Doc."

191

I didn't know what to say to that.

"You stuck by us through some very hard times," said his wife.

"My wife told me about you staying the night I had surgery. I don't remember much of that. But I want to thank you for all you done."

"You're going to have to come back to see me," I said, "to check on your new valve."

"Oh, sure, Doc. We made the appointment with your secretary already."

They each shook my hand, and I got out as fast as I could without running.

Funny who thanks you.

Maybe they were right. Whom was I kidding? The only role I had in his care was deciding he needed surgery in the first place, which would have been obvious to any intern, and then choosing the best surgeon to do the job. You pay your internist for all those conferences, hallway conversations, all those times he gossips about surgeons with other docs, finding out who can do the job and who to avoid. And on that score—picking the guy least likely to hurt you—I had dropped the ball.

On the other hand, there was no way I could have known about McIlheny until Lydell Brown, until the hyperthyroid lady he put into storm with surgery, until the little kid with abdominal pain and milky blood, until the man with high blood pressure who almost got his adrenal glands explored. . . .

But now I knew.

And what do you do when you know?

192

CHAPTER

37

Thursday morning I was working my way through the ten phone calls left with the answering service from the night before: coughs for a week demanding a prescription, runny noses and muscle aches adding up to flu for which antibiotics were requested and had to be denied, and, of course, the insomniacs. All of these grew fearful as the daylight waned and the darkness deepened, all called my office and were fended off by the answering service with a "Do you really want to bother the doctor about this tonight? Shall I call him at home and wake him up?"

I'd got through my sixth call, refusing steadfastly to prescribe antibiotics for viral illness, refusing to prescribe cough syrups, none of which work at all, refusing and refusing, explaining and explaining, getting disgruntled, ironic thanks for doing the right thing for the wrong type of patient. Telephone patients. Abusers and misusers. Modern-day people who want horse-and-buggy doctors who make house calls, but get doctors who carry beepers and use technology the way Madison Avenue says it should be used. Modern patients who don't know that antibiotics don't cure viral illness.

In the middle of all this, Mrs. Bromley buzzed. She had Bill
Ryan on the phone.

"Isn't Sam Sawyer a patient of yours?" he said.

My mouth went dry. I said he was.

"Well, I'm making Rounds on Seven South and whose name do
I see on the board but Sam Sawyer?" He paused for effect. Ryan
could be very dramatic at times. "And guess whose service he's
on?"

"Go ahead," I croaked. "Make my day."

"Dr. Thomas McIlheny, M.D. Esquire."

My head spun a little, and I gripped the phone hard. "No," I
said.

"I thought you might like to know."

We had four patients that morning, and I don't think I heard a
word a single one of them said. I was too busy thinking about Sam
Sawyer. He hadn't told me. I thought McIlheny had rushed him
in as an emergency, but Mrs. Bromley checked, and he was on the
operating room schedule for Friday afternoon for an aortic valve
replacement.

I had an hour between the morning and the afternoon patients.
I managed to dodge speed traps and traffic snarls to reach Sam's
room on Seven South by twelve-thirty.

"You don't talk to your friends anymore?" I said. "You check
into the hospital for a little major surgery and not a word to Dr.
Abrams?"

"Hey, Ben," said Sam. He was sitting in bed wrapped in one of
those ridiculous flowered hospital gowns reading the New York
Times, with his glasses on the tip of his nose. He looked up,
smiled, and offered me his hand. "I thought Dr. McIlheny would
tell you."

"After he did the job, maybe," I said.

Sam smiled, not catching my tone. "Well, here I am. Ready
and willing."

"More willing than ready, I think. Your blood pressure was

194

pretty high. That'll have to be brought under control before Dr. McIlheny does his work. And your blood sugar's a little high, too."

"Tell me your blood pressure wouldn't be up, coming in to have your heart cut open." Sam laughed. He had that inappropriate cheerfulness, somewhat hysterical, like a man who laughs as the bombs are falling.

"I thought you were going to let Ann Payson do the honors," I said.

"She's very nice, Abe. But I just thought I'd go with the more experienced man. You know, you and Ann still look like kids to me."

He laughed again when he said that, and I couldn't even manage a halfhearted smile. The laugh just hung in the air.

It was still hanging there when Thomas McIlheny strode into the room, followed by a gaggle of surgical residents. He hoisted up a smile, seeing me, but it didn't look particularly engaging. He said, "I see you've found each other. I was just going to call you."

"We ought to talk about his blood pressure," I said, scrounging for any excuse to delay surgery until I had a chance to talk Sam out of having McIlheny do it.

"One-eighty over ninety," said McIlheny. "Didn't look too bad."

Not a hypertensive crisis. Didn't require cutting his belly open in search of a pheochromocytoma. I said, "We ought to look at it."

McIlheny's eyes grew hard, and he grunted, "You clear him. We'll be ready when you are." Then he turned on his heels and swept out of the room with his retinue.

"We should talk, Sam," I said.

"Sure, Abe," he said, looking puzzled.

This was not going to go smoothly. How do you tell a patient that a doctor of whom you once spoke highly, or at least gave tacit approval, has lost your confidence? What do you say when he asks why? That a bunch of nurses told you they don't like him? That there's a kid on a respirator you don't know personally, but Ryan

195

told you about? That you're reviewing the surgeon's charts right now to look for evidence that he has lost his touch?

I had to be back at the office. Two patients were probably back there right now looking at their watches, and Mrs. Bromley was reaching for the phone to page me.

"I think we ought to talk about the best surgeon for your particular surgery," I said, leaving him there to chew on it.

CHAPTER

38

I hit the hallway at a pretty good trot. My beeper went off before I reached the elevator.

"You *are* planning to cure the sick this afternoon?" It was Mrs. Bromley. There were not two but three patients looking at their watches in the waiting room.

"I'm on my way. Really I am."

"I'll believe that when I see you walk through my door. Until then I shall try to divert the restless."

Dashing into the elevator, I almost knocked Ann off her feet.

"What is this, rugby practice?"

"The world is full of hard knocks," I said. There were people in the elevator. "Let's get off."

We stepped off on the second floor, which had the offices of the department of medicine. We stood in the hall.

"Sam Sawyer talk to you about scheduling his surgery?" I asked.

"Haven't heard from him since we saw him that time in my office."

"He's on McIlheny's service right now, Seven South."

"Well, he's made his choice, then."

"He doesn't have the information to make his choice. And I've made my choice. And you're it."

"That's not the way it works, Abe."

"You'd let McIlheny cut on Sam?"

"There's nothing I can do to stop it."

Her eyes were filmy now.

"If I could convince him he really wants Dr. Ann Payson, would you be willing?"

"If he asks me to do it, I've already offered. But I can't go steal a patient from Tom McIlheny's service. That wouldn't help anybody."

"But most of all, it wouldn't be good for untenured Ann Payson, M.D.," I said. I don't know how that slipped out, but I was late and worried I might not have such an easy time convincing Sam, and Ann was playing it at arm's length.

"That's not fair, Abe," said Ann. "That's really not fair."

"Fair? What's fair about letting Sam waltz unsuspectingly into McIlheny's clutches just because he reads *Washington* magazine and thinks you look a mite young?"

"Whoa!" said Ann, trying to smile. Her lips were curling properly, but her eyes were flashing. "Tom McIlheny does cases every day. You're not talking about rescuing Sam from some maniac's clutches."

"He does cases every day and he's got a mortality rate six times yours for similar cases, and his morbidity's so bad we haven't been able to calculate it yet."

She looked as if she'd been slapped. Ann covers as well as anyone, but I could see that one landed.

"Where do you get numbers like that?"

"You know very well where and how."

"If things look that bad," she said, "then present your stuff to a referee and do it properly. Don't go stabbing a guy behind his back so he can't defend himself."

"I'll do the proper through-channels thing as soon as I can figure out what the channels are. So far, all the channels I can find go right through McIlheny. But none of that helps Sam Sawyer. You've got to help Sam."

"So I'm supposed to do what? Sneak him off and do his AVR in a closet, or what?"

"Just be ready," I said, "when you're asked."

"Christ, Abe. I like Sam, but you're asking me to take a lot on faith. Evidence I've never seen. It's all your analysis of a bunch of charts, patients you didn't have anything to do with personally. He could kick me off staff for something like this, and for what?"

"You know enough without my evidence," I said. "You've seen enough on your own."

A look of something close to dread swept across her face. She knew what I was going to say. She wanted in the worst way not to hear it, but she knew she was going to hear it. She had tried to think about it, but she knew it was going to be hitting her between the eyes.

"Been to the SICU lately?"

She didn't say a word.

"Notice that little kid with the patent ductus and the mediastinitis isn't around anymore?"

"This isn't fair," she said. She turned to walk away, but I caught her arm.

"It wasn't fair for him, either," I said. "It wasn't fair that a little kid who never hurt anyone is lying on a cold slab in the morgue now."

She wrenched her arm free, ran the six feet to the stairwell, and flew away from me.

CHAPTER

39

Thursday night I went back and sat down by Sam's bedside. His blood pressures in the hospital had been frustratingly normal, as had his sugars, urinalysis, and chest X ray, and I couldn't make a case on any grounds to hold up surgery.

"Dr. McIlheny stopped by this evening," Sam said. "He's quite a guy. You know he rowed stroke for the Harvard crew?"

"No," I said. I could see this wasn't going to be easy. "I didn't know that."

"Quite a guy."

"Sam, I know you like McIlheny, and he's had a pretty impressive career in many ways, but I'd like you to consider having another surgeon do your surgery."

Sam's eyes didn't get any bigger than a pair of grapefruits, and his jaw landed somewhere around his collar bone. "I don't understand," he stammered.

I had thought about how to say this. I had four or five different speeches worked out, but none of them seemed to fit the confusion in Sam's eyes. None of them would play to this audience.

"Sam, I don't know how to say this except directly. There have been several cases, some of which I've been directly involved with, that have raised serious doubts in my mind about Dr. McIlheny's surgical skills and judgment."

Sam took a minute to react, then said, "Well, you said it pretty clearly."

"I can't hand you an indictment, but I can tell you that when you're talking about a guy who is literally going to be holding your heart in his hand, you shouldn't harbor any doubts."

"Of course," said Sam. "But why the doubts?"

"I can't get into the details of the cases, and it wouldn't be fair or even help much. Just let me say that I'm advising you not to have Dr. McIlheny do your surgery."

"And what the hell am I supposed to say to him?"

"You can tell him I advised you to get another thoracic surgeon if you like. I won't deny it."

"Boy, you don't pussyfoot around."

"I'd prefer to avoid confronting him just yet, but if I have to to keep you off his table, I will."

Sam sighed deeply, face flushed, and said, "Give me a little time to think."

"Fair enough," I said. "I hate to put you in the middle. But ultimately, you have to be there."

"You're damned right about putting me in the middle," Sam grunted.

I walked out of the room down to the nurses' station and looked at his chart. There was the usual one-page surgical intern's note saying that Sam had been admitted for an aortic valve replacement, and not much more.

I wrote a one-pager myself, saying Sam was not medically cleared for surgery, pending some blood sugar results. It wasn't the most convincing note I'd ever put in a chart, but it would have to do.

The next morning, I was seeing my first patient at the office when Mrs. Bromley stuck her head in my office door.

201

"Sorry to interrupt," she said, "but there's a phone call from St. George's Hospital I think you had better take now."

She said that with enough gravity to dry my mouth and to alarm the patient sitting across the desk from me sufficiently so that she stood up, eyes wide, and backed out of the room murmuring something about letting me have some privacy. I reached for the phone.

It was the surgical intern on Seven South.

"You're Mr. Sawyer's medical attending, aren't you?" he said.

I said I was. He told me that the surgical interns and residents were making Rounds on Sam when they made the astute observation that he couldn't utter a complete, comprehensible sentence. They thought he was aphasic and wanted to know if I would have a neurologist see him, for presumed stroke. I told the intern I'd be right over, hung up, swept past several very disgruntled patients in my waiting room, told Mrs. Bromley to make my apologies, and flew out the door.

Sam was talking by the time I arrived.

"Damndest thing, Ben," he said. "Couldn't say more than two or three words. Thought I was having a stroke. Now, I'm fine."

"You were having something like a stroke, called a transient ischemic attack, Sam. It might be from your heart valve. Little pieces can break off and go to the brain. I'm having Nancy Colleo come up with her ECHO machine to take a look, but you'll probably need surgery within an hour."

"Boy, you don't pull punches."

"Have you thought about who you want to do the surgery?"

"That's *all* I've been thinking about. But who can you get? Dr. McIlheny told me he was going to be giving a conference this morning over at NIH. I'm not sure he'd even be around if I wanted him."

"Ann Payson just finished a case in the operating room. They're getting the room ready. You can go in twenty minutes."

"She's willing and available?"

"I've just talked to her. She'll be up," I said.

Ann arrived with Nancy Colleo and she watched Nancy's fabu-

202

lous ECHO machine demonstrate the self-demolition of Sam's valve.

"We'd better get you a new valve," said Ann.

"Let's go," said Sam.

Ann and I walked out into the hall, where Ryan was waiting for us. He had heard all the stat pages to Seven South and had run up to investigate.

"Actually, this works out very nicely," Ryan said. "Abe gets the surgeon of his choice, and McIlheny doesn't have any basis for complaint. Can't say Ann stole the patient."

"As long as we call him and leave word," I said.

"I'm not sure that's a good idea," said Ann, chewing her lip.

"Why not?"

"If I just run Sam down to the OR, I can always say things were happening so fast I just didn't have time to call. If I page him, and he breaks away from his conference or arrives before I'm through, there's no telling."

"Ann," I said, "if you play it aboveboard, act open and innocent, you're safe. Call his office. Leave word with his secretary. You don't have to stat page him. You can say you called. The secretary didn't understand the urgency."

"I don't like it," said Ann, looking unsure.

"Like it," said Ryan. "I'm the legal scholar here. Just cover your ass and call, then do the case before he even knows you've got him."

Ann shook her head, turned to the wall phone, and called McIlheny's office while Ryan and I hovered.

The secretary obviously asked if she wanted McIlheny paged.

"Just leave the message that I wanted to let him know about Mr. Sawyer," said Ann. "He'll get back to me."

"Nicely done," said Ryan as she hung up.

Ann smiled and waved and trotted off to the elevator to the OR.

Ryan looked after her.

"I hope we're not getting her in hot water," he said. "Her career means a lot to her."

I looked at him trying to understand that understatement.

203

Ryan looked flustered by my look. "I mean, she doesn't have kids, or a hobby that I know of. It'd be tough for her if McIlheny decided to get annoyed."

"You're the guy who's been putting her on the spot about trying to bring him down."

"Well, yeah, but I didn't mean to make her the cutting edge, you know. I thought we'd do the tough stuff, and she'd supply some inside help."

"Nothing's going to happen," I said. "Except Sam's going to get his valve fixed by the best thoracic surgeon around."

CHAPTER

40

I walked back into Sam's room and watched the surgical intern start an IV. The nurse injected him with some kind of preoperative medication, and Sam's eyes filled with panic.

"You're going to be there, aren't you?" he asked me when the room had cleared of nurses and interns and orderlies for a moment.

"I'm not much with scalpels, Sam. I'd just get in the way."

"Oh," he said, and I knew I was hooked again. I'd have to call Mrs. Bromley to cancel out the rest of the day's patients.

"I'll come in and watch, Sam."

He smiled and said, "Thanks."

We waited for escort to come. Escort was a black orderly who transferred Sam to a gurney with bored efficiency, rolling him off his bed onto a rubber sheet, which he hoisted up into a stretcher frame.

I followed along as the orderly wheeled him to an elevator, and we all jostled in, IV bags swinging, and Sam, frightened, looking up at the ceiling of the elevator, getting the patient's-eye view of the world on the way to the OR.

When we got to the OR suite, I told Sam I'd have to go change. I peeled off for the locker room, where I plucked scrubs from the neat pile by the hamper, stripped and dressed, pulled on booties and tucked in the nonconductive straps, pulled on a scrub hat, tied up a scrub mask, and looked at myself in the mirror, checking myself as carefully as if Tom McIlheny himself were about to inspect me.

But it wasn't going to be Tom McIlheny this time. It was going to be Ann Payson. And I didn't think she'd throw me out of the OR for having my hat on crooked.

In the OR they had Sam on the table, and the anesthesiologist was slipping the endotracheal tube into place. The anesthesiologist was José Cruz. He did his job smoothly and quickly, attaching the black rubber bag to the tube and squeezing it to breathe for Sam. A nurse anesthetist took over squeezing the bag while José took Sam's blood pressure. The nurses swirled around, and surgical residents set up the cloth and paper drapes.

A nurse shaved Sam's chest with broad, clean strokes, making quick work of it. One of the residents prepped Sam's chest by painting concentric circles with Betadine from the center to the far reaches of the shoulders and diaphragm and then laying down a clear plastic material through which Ann would make her incision. Over this went a green cloth with a large square cut out of its center, making Sam's chest a kind of giant bull's-eye.

The heart-lung pump team was there, checking out the units of blood they'd need for their pump, and as I watched, the circulating nurse came over, looked me straight in the eye from an inch away, and asked who I was.

She was an older nurse, the only one who wore a nameplate on her scrub dress: Mrs. Wilson. She seemed only minimally placated when I told her who I was.

"I'm here at Dr. Payson's invitation," I said finally, to shoo her away.

"Do you know how to avoid breaking field?" she asked. She had an old woman's voice, sour and dyspeptic.

"I'm not doing the surgery," I told her, trying to sound even and unbothered. "If I get within two yards of the field, you can holler."

"You can be sure I will," she said, and scuttled off.

The scrub nurse was a young nurse named Donna Green, who had come to see me about a nodule in her thyroid some months before. She was standing on the elevated platform the scrub nurses use that makes them look like the umpires at a tennis match. She was smiling behind her scrub mask—I could see it in her eyes. She said, "Hi, Dr. Abrams!" and she waved like a little kid. "This one of yours?"

"A very special one of mine," I said, folding my arms to avoid touching and contaminating anything and incurring the wrath of Mrs. Wilson, the circulating nurse.

"We'll be real sweet to him," said Donna Green.

CHAPTER

41

Ann stepped into the OR from the scrub room holding her hands up, arms bent at the elbows, fingers pointing toward the ceiling. She was followed by three residents holding their hands in the same pre-op salute. The old sour circulating nurse slapped a blue scrub towel in the hand of each, as per scrub ritual. Surgeons are very ritualistic. Do things the same way every time, and the patients don't get infected. Put your left shoe on first, and the patient gets infected. Don't ask why. Just go with the winning ritual.

The nurse helped each into a scrub gown and finally went to each with rubber gloves. Everyone's hands were thrust deep into the gloves in the prescribed manner.

Ann took her station and when everyone was in place asked for the scalpel and cut Sam right down the middle of the sternum, through the plastic covering. The operation was under way. Ann ran a relaxed but serious OR. The assistant circulating nurse turned on a portable radio and set it to the light rock station. They were playing Leo Sayer's "When I Need You You're Only a Heartbeat Away." Everyone laughed at that line—except Mrs. Wilson and Ann, who was absorbed in her work.

"They're playing your song, Dr. Payson," said one of the masked residents.

"Hmm?" said Ann, who in her concentration hadn't heard a thing. She was down to the pericardium.

I was standing on a stool about six feet behind Ann's back. I had a pretty clear view and was able to watch without much more than the usual excitement, even though it was Sam's chest she was working in. Everything was so covered and controlled it seemed totally disembodied. That wasn't Sam Sawyer, old friend and teacher. It was a chest, a heart, and a pair of lungs.

I felt someone at my side. It was Mrs. Wilson, whispering in a breathy hush, "There's an amphitheater here, you know. You'd be better off up there." She pointed to a little window on the wall across from the operating table. "There's an entrance from the hall," said Mrs. Wilson.

I found the entrance and took the chair in the observation booth. It was a very Spartan and diminutive version of the sort of booths you see at sports arenas, but it gave a bird's-eye view of the surgery. The main advantage, aside from the view, was the chair —you could watch the surgery while sitting down. There was a vent so I could hear everything; it was, in fact, the best seat in the house.

Ann got to the heart with astonishing quickness. She looked around for the prosthetic valve she would implant. The circulating nurse brought it over to a tray near her and laid it out in sterile fashion. Ann poked it, inspected it, and decided it would fit. Then she went after the valve in Sam's chest.

She was working on getting that one out when a tall, rangy figure entered the OR from the scrub room entrance. He was masked and wore a scrub hat, but he would have been identifiable from his long-legged gait alone. It was Thomas McIlheny. He stalked up behind Ann and looked over her shoulder. The back is considered unsterile, so it would be breaking scrub for Ann to turn around to see who was there, and I'm not sure she sensed him, she was concentrating so intensely, but I could hear McIlheny's voice, low and threatening, like firing along the battle line.

"I came as soon as I could," said McIlheny.

"Good," said Ann distantly. She asked the scrub nurse for another instrument and kept on working.

"Just hold up and I'll scrub in," said McIlheny.

The resident straightened up, and all eyes swiveled to McIlheny. Ann kept right on working. She asked for another instrument.

"This is not really an opportune time," she said. "Just let me get the valve seated."

McIlheny tensed, then looked over her shoulder again, like an umpire, and straightened up again.

"Nonsense," he said. "I'll scrub in now."

There was an instant of silence thick enough to slice, when even the whir of the heart-lung machine seemed to pause to catch its breath.

Ann asked for another instrument. The scrub nurse slapped it in her palm with a certain flourish, I thought, as if to affirm her own agreement with Ann's determination.

The circulating nurse was standing next to McIlheny now, holding an operating gown for him, although I couldn't see any sign that he had scrubbed his hands.

"I think you had better step aside," said McIlheny, low and ominous.

"This isn't the safest time to change horses," said Ann, not looking up, working systematically. She asked for another instrument. The scrub nurse slapped that one in just the same way.

Ann had the old valve out and was fitting in the new one.

The residents decided to keep their chins down and stare at what Ann was doing in the wound.

"I am asking you again to stand aside," said McIlheny, very slowly, enunciating very clearly, squeezing off each word like a gunshot.

Ann continued sewing in the valve, using the long silver needle holder with short, sure strokes, handing each placed suture to the resident as she worked her way around the valve. She had not looked up the entire time McIlheny was in the room.

McIlheny looked around the room, scrutinizing each person. The only person to meet his glare was the old circulating nurse, Mrs. Wilson, who was still holding the gown open in front of him. When he caught José Cruz's eye, José quickly looked down to his clipboard.

Finally, McIlheny turned on his heels and stalked out the OR door.

CHAPTER

42

Sam did very well postoperatively. His temperature went up just past one hundred, but otherwise he sailed through.

The prosthetic valve Ann had excised had been removed not a moment too soon—pieces of cholesterol plaque were crumbling off it. One of those pieces had undoubtedly been what caused his transient ischemic attack. And there was a great crack running halfway around the valve's equator. That valve wouldn't have lasted much longer and, when it went, so would Sam.

The surgeon, on the other hand, was not faring as well as the patient she had saved.

Ann sat stone-faced in her living room and spoke tonelessly. "He said I was suspended immediately, operating room privileges and academic duties and he said that he was recommending that my appointment to the faculty be terminated."

Ann was curled up in her chintz-covered Queen Anne chair, with a sweater wrapped around her shoulders, looking chilled and jolted. Her face was a pale gray, so different from her usual pink glow. There was a lot of movement around her mouth, as if it were in conflict with her mind about what to say.

I tried to look relaxed, stretched my legs out in front of me, and leaned back in her couch.

"I don't see how he can get away with it," I said. "Sam was my patient. He can't accuse you of stealing a patient he doesn't own."

"He admitted Sam Sawyer," snapped Ann. "He is the attending of record. His name is all over the chart."

Ryan's voice came from a dark corner where he nursed a Southern Comfort, "Kicking you off the faculty would be his biggest mistake. If he does that formally, you can file a grievance. There'll have to be a hearing."

"He told me I'm off the faculty," said Ann hoarsely.

"Then you can file the petition. I'll talk to Bill O'Donnell. He's the faculty rep. You'll call him, too."

"So what does that get me?" said Ann. "I'm out. No hospital in town will touch me if I'm dismissed from staff. No hospital anywhere will."

"This won't stick," said Ryan. "It's too ridiculous."

"It's anything but ridiculous," said Ann. "I never thought he'd go this far. I thought he might be angry, but to kick me off staff. . . ."

She shook her head. Her shoulders, normally so erect and high, were rounding, and she seemed a long way down in her chair.

"It's just a slap on the wrist," said Ryan. "He's insecure. He thinks he's got a rebellion on his hands, so he's trying to make an example of you so everyone else will keep his head down."

"He's doing a good job of it," said Ann.

"He knows you'll file a grievance and he'll lose and have to reinstate you. He just wants to save face."

"Well, he's sure fooled me, then," she said with an edge. "I feel as if I've been run over by a truck and I wasn't even in the road."

"You were in the road all right," I said. "You jumped in with both feet."

"Sam would have been a dead man if you hadn't," said Ryan.

"So say Dr. Ryan and Dr. Abrams, two most unbiased and unqualified sources."

"You don't have to prove McIlheny is the Boston Strangler," I said. "All you have to do is say that you were wrapped up in what you were doing and didn't feel you could step aside. He overreacted. End of case."

"That's the ticket," said Ryan. "Unfortunate major misunderstanding. Besides, it was your first offense. You don't execute people for their first offense."

"That's what it feels like," said Ann. "An execution. Yesterday I was Ann Payson, associate professor of surgery. Today I'm unemployed. A highly educated bum. I couldn't get a license to drive a cab in this town."

"You won't need one," said Ryan.

"What do I have to do to file this grievance?"

"Just call Bill O'Donnell. If McIlheny wants to really get cute and pursue it, they'll have to hold a hearing. You can even hire a lawyer—actually, the faculty association will pay for it. But you won't want to do that."

"Why won't I want to do that?"

"Because the review panel is made up of docs," said Ryan. "You bring a lawyer in there, you've got two strikes against you before anyone opens his mouth."

"So I plead my own case?"

"Basically. You let someone stand up for you—me or Abe— just to set the stage for what you're going to say in your own defense. Or you can sit back and say nothing, and let Abe ask everyone who was in the OR what they thought happened. That's the best part of this whole thing. Lots of witnesses. By the time they all testify, everyone's so confused they let you off and say it was all a big misunderstanding."

"You sound like you've seen this all before," said Ann. "I've never even heard of these hearings."

"I've seen one. They tried to bounce Bob Deaver from GI last year. He won his appeal. Had to reinstate him. Now he's just about untouchable."

214

"I never even heard about that," said Ann.

"They don't call in the papers. It's all pretty hush-hush."

"So I'm supposed to let you and Abe sing my praises and get me off the hook?"

"Sure. Sit back, relax."

"I'll do my own talking," said Ann. She was smiling, but she was serious.

Ryan shot me a look. It was a what-do-we-say-now look.

"Why don't you start by going back to see McIlheny when he's cooled off?" I said. "Defuse him."

"He's cool," said Ann. "He's cold as ice. I'll try, but I'm not counting on it. No, I'm going to have to get organized here."

That, at least, sounded more like the Ann we knew.

"You're right, though," said Ann. "I jumped into this with both feet."

She caught me in a blue-eyed vise. "Nobody pushed me. You kept pushing that kid in the SICU at me. Brother, you don't know the half of it. Nobody pushed me into anything. What I did had to be done."

"Ann," said Ryan, "don't go in headfirst. You can break a neck that way. All you have to do is show that the punishment exceeded all bounds of proportion."

"He'll say I was leading a mutiny. He's paranoid enough to believe it."

"Look, we ought to sit down, calmly, rationally, and discuss and analyze this. Plan strategy. You don't want to run into this thing unprepared."

"I thought you two were doing that all along. Compiling the statistics on the chief. Planning, preparing to bring him down. Well, now I'm your lightning rod."

"But you don't have to show you were right in trying to divert patients from McIlheny. That would be a tall order. Just get yourself off the hook. We'll get McIlheny."

"I'll do what's necessary," said Ann.

Ryan rolled his eyes and spoke to the ceiling. "Oh, here we go—bombs away. Push the button. The guy fires a few shots, and she's going to push the button. All-out war." Then he looked to me. "Abe, she listens to you. Talk sense to her."

"Ann, he's right. This is a game. You can't let him get you hot. You play to win, not to score points."

Ann looked from Ryan to me and back to Ryan again. "That's the strategy? I say, 'No offense intended,' and he has to say, 'Okay, all is forgiven'?"

"You got it," said Ryan. "Of course, he won't have to forgive you. This holy panel says your sins are atoned for. Praise Jesus."

"It's a Catholic institution," said Ann. "They don't say 'Praise Jesus.'" Then she added, "But, I swear, if there's going to be blood on the tracks, it won't be only mine."

Ryan stood up saying he had to go home to think. "This is going to require organization," he said. "We have to interview all the potential witnesses, find out who's for us, who's against us. Organization will be key." Then he looked at me and said, "Pack her in ice. We've got to stay cool. Right is might."

I walked out the front door of Ann's house with Ryan, and we stood on the porch and looked out toward the river, just visible through the trees across Canal Road, as if there were some answers out there.

"What do you think's going to happen?" I asked. "I mean what do you *really* think?"

"He might be able to make the faculty thing stick. But I doubt it, for something as stupid as this. If Ann promises not to sue, he might be willing to write her a letter so she can get on staff at some other hospital. So she'll still be able to go into private practice."

"I don't read McIlheny that way," I said. "He's out to crucify her."

"Then she's in trouble."

"And we put her there," I said.

"She didn't do this for us," said Ryan.

"And who convinced her McIlheny was so dangerous?"

Ryan shrugged. "You heard the lady," he said. "She knew what

216

she was doing and why. Sounds like she knows more about McIl-heny and his fuck-ups than she's been willing to say."

From what Ann had said, Ryan was right. She held cards she wasn't showing. She'd seen things. The kid in the SICU was just the last straw for her.

"Trouble is," said Ryan, "this isn't like you or me being bounced. We'd give McIlheny the finger, go hiking around the Himalayas for a year, and take root in some quiet place and be just as happy. Not Ann. She lives and breathes this stuff. You heard her. She's an associate professor. A Harvard grad. She's worked up to this, and none of it was handed to her. She would not be happy in private practice in Paramus."

"We'll make a list of things to do, people to talk to," I said. "But you might start in Chicago. Find out what you can about McIl-heny and why he left and what they really thought of him there. Any dirt. Find out if we should go there in person to talk to people."

"Think we can get a look at the letters the people at Chicago wrote for him?"

"Forget the letters," I said. "They never say anything."

"Sometimes they damn with faint praise," said Ryan. "You can figure out who you ought to take out for a drink and really talk to about the guy."

"How do we get the letters?" I said.

"Any letters of recommendation written on his behalf have to be in the search committee's file. Your buddy Dennis Rallston was on the search committee."

"Consider it done. I'll get you the letters. You'll check out Chicago?"

"Just get me the letters," said Ryan, counting on his fingers the things we had to do. "You'll talk to Sawyer?" he asked. "They'll interview him."

"Who will?"

"The board of inquiry."

"Board of inquiry?"

217

"I told you. There'll be a hearing."

"Board of inquiry sounds so formal."

"They are very formal about these things, big boy. We're talking careers, livelihoods, and all those things."

"You made it sound so casual to Ann. So easy."

"Ann's depressed enough right now; I didn't want to get into the grimy details."

"And who's on the board?"

"McIlheny will propose a list. Ann will get to propose a list. Each side can select one person from the other guy's list. The school of medicine, that is, the dean, will have a selection. That's three. The dean will run the thing, like a judge."

"Sounds like they're serious about this."

"They'll go through the motions, call witnesses, and all that. But nothing'll happen to Ann."

"Sure," I said. "Like the nothing that's already happened."

"She'll have to bow and scrape a little and say, 'A thousand pardons, no mean to offend great chief of surgery,' and she'll get off with a reprimand."

"Fine. She deserves a medal and she gets a letter in her file."

"There's no percentage in tilting at windmills."

I caught Ryan's eye. Fine time to say that. "How's our McIl-heinous chart?"

"Done. I've got it in the car. Want to look?"

"Just tell me about it."

"Looks bad for his side."

"We may need it."

"If we need it, if we wind up having to go after McIlheny as a crackpot," said Ryan, catching my eye with a smile that chilled me, "Ann's really in trouble."

Ryan looked at me and smiled, a tough guy with a child's face who'd seen all this before somewhere, I don't know where.

218

CHAPTER
43

The next morning I was parked in Dennis Rallston's plush waiting room when he arrived.

"Well, well, well," he said, grinning. "Do we have a man who's finally come to his senses?"

"Would I be here at eight-thirty in the morning if I had any sense?" I said.

"Then you'll take the job?" he said, offering me a meaty paw.

"Sorry, Dennis, that's not why I'm here."

His face clouded. "Then you're here with trouble. Nobody's ever here first thing in the morning, unless it's trouble."

"You're not chief for nothing," I said. "You pick right up on things."

I told him what happened as briefly as I could, still giving him the appropriate flavor.

"But this is a fight within the department of surgery," he said. "I mean, it's between McIlheny and Ann Payson."

"It's between the forces of light and the forces of darkness," I said, straightfaced.

"That's what you're going to have to convince this kangaroo court," said Dennis. "But what can I do? I'm new here myself. I can't go after Tom McIlheny even if I wanted to. Even if I knew all the things you say about him are true, which I don't know."

"You should want to know if it's true."

"Let that pass for a moment," said Dennis. "What could I do?"

"You can provide some ammunition," I said. "For starters, we need to see the letters of recommendation on McIlheny sent by the people in Chicago. We need to talk to some of those people."

"I can arrange for the letters."

"You can call in all the medical subdivisions. The GI guys, the cardiologists, the pulmonary guys—they all send patients McIlheny's way. Ryan and I couldn't be the only people to notice what's happening."

"I could do that," said Dennis. "But I won't."

"Why not?"

"Because I'm not in business to get Tom McIlheny. If people bring me problems from these other divisions, okay, I listen. But you're asking me to set up an inquiry all on my own. What're you getting hip-deep in all this shit for, Abe? These things get settled by who knows who and who backs who. You should be devoting your energy to shaping up Endocrine. That's what I need you knocking yourself out for. Not this."

"Ann Payson needs your help."

"I'd like to help her, but she went off the deep end, sounds to me. And what good's all this going to do Ann? So some of McIlheny's cases haven't done well. He's chief. He takes on the tough ones. You're not going to win by trying to knock pieces off Mount Rushmore."

"Thanks," I said, "for straightening me out." I stood up and walked out of his office, sinking into the deep carpet the whole way.

In the hallway I passed one of the residents Ann and I had eaten pizza with the other night.

"You hear about Ann Payson?" I asked him.

220

From the look in his eyes you'd think I'd just asked him if he'd seen Blackbeard the pirate stalking the halls with his saber drawn. "Yes," he said. "I was sorry to hear it."

"There's probably going to be a hearing about all this," I said. "We may need some character witnesses."

He didn't say anything.

"You think you could say something about what a great surgeon she is, if we need you?"

He hesitated, and I saw his sharp intake of breath; then he collected his thoughts and said very carefully, "I think Dr. Payson is a fine surgeon. But I think it would mean more for one of the attendings to say that. After all, I'm still in training. What's it going to mean, coming from me?"

"You could say what a good teacher she is."

"Well, even that. It'd probably be more convincing coming from another faculty member." He was having a hard time looking me in the eye.

"Thanks," I said, as neutrally as I could. I could see his position—no matter what happened, McIlheny would still be his boss.

I wandered down to the SICU. José Cruz was eating a doughnut and drinking coffee. I walked up and put my arm around his shoulders. He looked about as happy to have my arm around his shoulders as a draftee in the vaccination line.

"I need to talk to you, José," I said. "You know about what."

"Sure, sure," said José, beads of perspiration popping out all over his forehead. "Only I got a case in a moment."

"Won't take but a minute."

I dragged him outside the SICU door.

"You heard what happened. McIlheny dismissed Ann from the staff."

"Ho, yes. I heard."

"We're going to need you to testify, José," I said.

"Me?" said José, face glistening. "Why me?"

"Because you were there."

"But I didn't see nothing!"

221

"Then say that. There was no cause for McIlheny to blow up. Ann was just too busy to deal with him. Right?"

"Who's gonna make me testify?"

"The dean of the school of medicine."

"The dean?"

"He's running the hearing."

"But I didn't see nothing!"

"José, you were the guy who told me how dangerous McIlheny was. You remember. You wanted me to do something."

"I? I say that?"

I suddenly felt very depressed and turned away. I walked down the hall to the stairwell, took the stairs to the first floor, and got out of St. George's Hospital as fast as my legs would carry me.

CHAPTER
44

Ann, Ryan, and I met every evening prior to the trial, or "hearing," as the dean of the school of medicine insisted on calling it.

We divided up the tasks. Ryan was in charge of background on McIlheny. Dennis Rallston had supplied the letters, and Ryan, who knew how to read between the lines on those letters, identified McIlheny's potential detractors. I was in charge of evaluating the people who had been in the OR that day, interviewing them, identifying friend and foe, preparing our friends to say what needed to be said the way we wanted it said.

Ann's job was most important of all: jury selection.

The dean had called Ann in and spelled out all the rules and regulations of the game.

"He sounded about as open-minded and nonjudgmental as a cop reading some gangster his rights," Ann said.

"Don't worry about him," said Ryan. "He's a nonentity. It's the judges we've got to think about."

The first order of business was selecting jurors, or "panelists," as the dean called them. Neither Ryan nor I knew any of the names on McIlheny's list of proposed judges. Ann knew two, and she didn't like either particularly. Ryan and I split the list of five names and requested the curriculum vitae of each so we could check it over to be sure the guy hadn't trained with McIlheny at some point in his career, to be sure he wasn't some old crony.

Ann finally decided to agree on a surgeon at Bethesda Naval Hospital who had no apparent connections with McIlheny and whom she had once met.

"He didn't strike me as the brightest guy in the world," said Ann. "But we were on a grant review committee together a couple of years ago, and he seemed fair-minded at least. He listened to all the evidence before he made up his mind."

"You two get along all right on the committee?" I asked.

"You don't get to know anybody all that well. You're out at NIH all day in some conference room. They order sandwiches for lunch. That kind of thing."

The admiral was on Ryan's list of people to check.

"He went to NYU," said Ryan, looking at his notes. "Did his training at Bellevue and Boston City. Joined up during the big one and stayed in. Admiral. Still does a full operating room load. Residents say he's careful, workmanlike, no star, but solid. Nurses say he's a straight shooter."

"I can bet you checked the Navy nurses out," said Ann. "How'd you get into Navy Med to do that?"

"Charm and determination," said Ryan. "Maureen had a friend, a Navy Med recovery room nurse. Took her out for a drink at the officers' club."

Ann laughed. She hadn't done a lot of laughing lately. I'd never seen her so tight. She could laugh and chat all the way through a lung resection, keeping everybody in the OR loose and easy. But this trial had settled in her joints and steam-pressed her face.

"She said this admiral's a Reagan conservative," said Ryan. "All business. Doesn't joke around a lot. He'd probably lean toward McIlheny just because they're about the same age, and you know McIlheny's going to say all the right things about how important

224

discipline is in any organization, the danger of tolerating even the first signs of mutiny. The admiral will understand all about undermining authority and he'll identify with the chief of staff."

"He still seems the best of the lot," said Ann. "We've got a guy who trained at Mass General when McIlheny was chief resident, and they're probably old buddies—a guy who edited a book he asked McIlheny to write a chapter for, and it goes downhill from there. The admiral wins by default."

"We ought to ask for a new list," I said. "The rules were that you were to choose people you respected with whom you had no personal connections."

"Surgery's a small world," said Ann. "And McIlheny's been around a long time and knows everyone. The admiral's as good as we're likely to get."

McIlheny had already accepted one of Ann's choices, a Hopkins professor who had approved a grant for her five years before. McIlheny obviously hadn't done his homework. The Hopkins guy had written a pretty glowing review, not just of the grant application, but of Ann as a surgeon, physician, and human being. We were happy with that judge.

As the day of the hearing drew closer, the number of details to check seemed to multiply faster than mosquitos. And as the hearing work piled up, my least favorite patients seemed to sense my preoccupation. We got more and more telephone calls at the office, the kind of calls I especially love—people with sore throats who just had to have fifteen minutes of my time but who could not possibly schedule an appointment. The telephone message book grew thicker, and Mrs. Bromley grew more indignant.

"McIlheny is hiring these people to call in an attempt to distract you," she said. "Some of these people we have not heard from for ages. And most of them we have not been paid by in eons."

The meetings at Ann's house went later and later. Ryan had word from Chicago about McIlheny.

"Seems that at least half the department up there couldn't have been happier to see their old chief pack up his bags and move down here," he said. "'Good with a pen but less agile with a knife' was the bottom-line comment."

"Who said that?" asked Ann. She was smiling again.

"Everyone, in one way or another. The actual quote is from a guy named Wayne Sever. Know him?"

"No."

"Of course, nobody would speak for the record. Nobody volunteered to come down here and testify."

"We couldn't use it anyway," I said. "McIlheny's not on trial. You know his lawyer's not going to let us put him on trial."

"There's no way to save my skin without burning his," Ann said.

Ryan rolled his head back on his shoulders and groaned. "I get chest pain every time you start talking like that."

"It's going to come to that," said Ann. "We're going to say all the proper things. I'm going to be little Miss Wide-eyed Innocence and, 'Oh, but I didn't mean a thing,' and no surgeon on that panel's going to believe a single word of it."

"Try them," said Ryan. "Give them the chance to let you off the hook."

"Look," I said. "They'll know. McIlheny will know. The fucking dean will know what happened. But you can't say that. You say he misunderstood when you threw him out on his ass. Then everyone can smile and say, 'Kiss and make up,' and you're off the hook."

"But that doesn't solve the problem."

"Jesus H.," roared Ryan. "It solves the problem. Saving your skin is the problem here, lady. Don't you forget it."

"You're never going to sink his ship," I said. "Not in this forum. The school of medicine, the dean, the department of surgery, all a bunch of vested interests. They might be willing to admit McIlheny overreacted. That's no great stain on the institution. But try dragging the soiled linen out for view, and they're going to throw you out."

"Then why keep the data? Why review all the McIlheinous charts? What was that all about?" said Ann. Her voice had a

226

tremor. Her eyes were glistening. "Just to make you guys feel virtuous?"

"We can go after McIlheny," said Ryan. "But quietly. Let his three-year review come up. The dean will have our data under his hat. He can ask the right questions and can him quietly. But in a hearing like this? No way."

Ann looked to me. "You buy this?"

"All I know is people will always take the easy way out," I said. "Right now the easiest thing to do is to let McIlheny's decision on you stand. The next easiest thing to do is to say, 'Okay, she was a bad girl, but give her another chance.' That they might do, especially if we make it look easy. The hardest thing to get them to say is: 'McIlheny, you're a piss-poor surgeon, and Ann Payson had to save that patient from you.' You give them that choice, they'll run for cover."

Ann looked from me to Ryan and back to me again. "Some swell spot, guys."

CHAPTER

45

Ann was sitting cross-legged in her Queen Anne chair, wearing sweat pants and a rag sweater, looking tired. Ryan had left. I sat on her couch, watching her. We were working our way through a bottle of wine.

"You sure you don't want to hand this thing to a lawyer?" I said. "This is possibly going to get a little more complicated than we expected."

"I've given that considerable thought," said Ann, smiling. "It's possibly going to be a little awkward for you. You're both a witness and my spokesman, as we've set things up. But I think Ryan was right about how it would look if I got a lawyer."

"But McIlheny's got a lawyer for the department."

"That's a mistake, I hope," said Ann. Then she looked more closely at me. "Or are you having second thoughts yourself?"

"Hell, no. I'm raring to have at those bastards."

"Then it's settled," she said. She uncurled herself, walked across, sat on my lap, and kissed me.

"I do something right?"

"You do everything right," she said. "And you've been a prince to stick by me. You've knocked yourself out this past week. You and Ryan."

"We felt we got you into it."

"Don't," she said, and her eyes carried the message of how much she meant it. "Don't ever think you led me into doing something I had to do. I couldn't have lived with myself if I hadn't done something."

"You're not still thinking of trying to burn McIlheny?"

"I'll toe the line." Ann laughed. "As long as it looks like it'll work."

"Funny thing about all this," I said. "I had the feeling McIlheny really liked you. Kind of treated you like a daughter."

"I kind of liked him," said Ann, looking away. "Outside the OR, away from surgery. He's really a very smart man. First-rate mind, really."

"Better with the pen than with the knife, Ryan said."

"It's hard to believe that. You listen to him talk about techniques and cases. You really cannot believe this is the same guy connected to the patients you see in the SICU."

"So you had been seeing his cases all along? You knew we were on to something?"

"Everyone in the department knew. Why do you think McIlheny's trying to blow me away? Ryan was right. He's trying to make an example of me."

"It'd be a wonder if they didn't know. You've seen the McIlheinous chart," I said.

Ryan's compendium, McIlheinous Horrificus, a complete breakdown of the fate of every patient operated on by Thomas McIlheny since his arrival at St. George's. A document that told a very dismal story.

"I think there are some who still don't know," said Ann. "You come in and do your work and leave. The private docs have no idea. Even some of the faculty. They just do their work. They're not looking over anyone else's shoulder."

229

Ann ran her fingers through her hair and let out a lungful of air. Then she said, "How's Lydell Brown?"

"He called me the other day. He's walking around with just a cane. He's happy to be alive. I don't know if he owes McIlheny his life or his stroke."

"Neither do I."

"That's what makes it tough, the doubts."

"There aren't any, really," said Ann. "That's what I get for not minding my own business. At this point, there's really no doubt in my mind."

Her eyes held me. For the past few days she hadn't been looking anyone in the eye very often or for very long, but now she held me. "That's why McIlheny's doing this. He knows I haven't got any doubts about him anymore."

CHAPTER
46

The night before the hearing, Ryan snapped shut his briefcase, fat with papers on Ann's defense, and said, "That's it, folks. If we're not ready now..."

Ann kissed him on the cheek and patted his head. "You're a real stand-up guy, Ryan."

"Get some sleep, you two," said Ryan, and he left.

"Sleep," Ann laughed.

Ryan had commented on the darkening circles under her eyes, the obvious weight loss.

The last few nights she hadn't wanted to be alone, and I had camped out in her bed. That wasn't as exciting as it might sound —she spent most of the night sitting in a chair in her bedroom, looking out the window. Some mornings I'd find her crumpled on the couch, asleep in the living room, the reports Ryan had written for her scattered on the floor.

Now she said, "Let's go for a walk."

She pulled on a thick sweater, and we walked out into the chill night air. It was early November; the sky was full of stars, and the moon was nearly full. We walked along Reservoir Road, past the fenced-off reservoir, across from the fire station, past the German embassy, and toward St. George's.

Ann put her hand in mine once or twice and pecked my cheek, but we said nothing. The road noises and the sounds from planes swelled up periodically, but there were intervals of silence that neither of us broke. We just kept walking along the concrete sidewalk in the dark, toward the hospital.

We stopped to look into the stillness of Glover Park, which ran right up to the sidewalk.

"Funny how I've stopped seeing things," said Ann. "Before I was defrocked, I'd walk by this park and notice the trees, the birds —there was an enormous redheaded woodpecker—the squirrels getting fat for winter. This is a lovely time in Washington. But I can't see it at all now. All I can think about is Thomas McIlheny, the dean, and those judges."

"Ann, if they cave in to McIlheny and politics, we'll go hiking in the Himalayas or something. It'll be their loss. Screw 'em."

"It would be pretty to think it," said Ann. "But it wouldn't be like that."

"You're worth ten of them. There'd be a hundred places that would love to have you."

"I know, I know."

"That's right."

"Easier said than done," said Ann, turning to rivet me with her shining night eyes. "I can't go out to the boonies and cut out tonsils. What I do, you do at places like St. George's."

"It's not that small a world," I said. "There're plenty of places like St. George's that'd be overjoyed to land you."

We walked on. Above us loomed St. George's, set on the plateau like some medieval castle: lights winking; nurses and staff pushing in and out of doors, walking in pairs to the parking lots. A city that never sleeps. We watched it from below.

"That's where I want to be tonight," said Ann. "I can't get it out of my mind. I can't go hiking anywhere. I can't even walk by the river without being up there."

232

"There's more to life than ORs and intensive care units," I said.
She didn't appear to hear.

"Two weeks ago, I felt so lucky to be able to get away from the OR for a weekend, for a walk along M Street. Now I can't even walk in the front door. I'd give my eyeteeth to spend all night in the OR tonight."

"You could walk right up to the OR, right now, they'd throw you a party."

"No," she said. "I can't even go in the hospital. I'd feel like they all knew I'd been suspended. I couldn't look anybody in the eye."

"It's McIlheny who can't look anyone in the eye. You finally did something."

"Yeah," said Ann, "I did something all right."

CHAPTER

47

The lawyer for the department of surgery was a very smooth citizen indeed. I sat there in the wood-paneled library that served as the hearing room, thinking how lovely he looked in this setting of polished oak tables, bound volumes on the shelves, and Persian carpets on hardwood floors. He was seated now as the dean of the school of medicine droned on about the format for the hearing, but he would be well over six feet standing.

The dean was saying that this was an internal proceeding of the school of medicine, not a courtroom, that witnesses would not be sworn in, and that rules of evidence would not apply. He said he hoped everyone would respect the delicate nature of this hearing and the "unnecessary" damage it could do to personal reputations and to the morale of the school of medicine, and he hoped that everyone would be sensitive to this and would conduct himself accordingly.

The dean was obviously speaking to me when he said all this. No need to warn the lawyer about how to conduct himself in a gentlemanly fashion—looking at the lawyer that much was obvi-

ous. The dean outlined the format for the hearing and said that
Dr. Payson and the department of surgery (by which he meant Dr.
Thomas McIlheny, who was the department of surgery as far as the
dean was concerned, I supposed) each had been allowed a repre-
sentative and that Dr. Payson had chosen Dr. Abrams and that the
department would be represented by Mr. Sean Herlihy. Mr. Sean
Herlihy was obviously the fair-haired boy I was looking over. His
hair was white and spotless and swept back from his temples majes-
tically; skin fresh, pink, and well scrubbed; nails manicured; teeth
white and straight; his eyes the color of a cloudless Aspen sky. He
wore a gray vested pin-striped suit. He was clearly a litigation
lawyer, and he would have been a Sigma Chi, probably, at some
place like Boston College or—knowing McIlheny's preference for
old school ties—at Cornell or Dartmouth or some other Ivy
League place. He would have spent his college career majoring in
Budweiser and coeds, and he would have pulled all-nighters before
his finals, and would have done well enough at gut courses to get
into Columbia Law, once his Law Boards got figured in. He
showed just a little paunch above the belt from too many three-
martini lunches, and he could charm the socks off any jury in the
land.

As I looked at him my heart sank. Looking at all those arrayed
against us facing us across that no-man's-land of hardwood floor,
my heart sank. There was McIlheny, looking just as crisp and
pressed as ever in his snow-white coat with his name embroidered
in bright blue letters over his breast pocket, not a hair out of place,
gaunt and ascetic-looking, but ruddy, with alert ice-blue eyes.
Next to him was his secretary taking notes. Even she looked immaculate, precise, as if she'd never made an error in her life, not
even at a hundred words a minute on her IBM self-correcting.

The only hope was the jury—or the panel, as the dean called
them, to emphasize the fact that this was not a trial. All three of
them were lined up like a mini–supreme court, and I eyed each in
turn. There was the guy from Bethesda Naval, in his black winter
uniform festooned with a garden of ribbons on his chest, his white
hat on the glistening table in front of him. He looked like an old

235

salt, a no-nonsense surgeon, with thick skin around his eyes and neck.

Ann's choice, the Hopkins surgeon, sat next to him. He was a round little man with intelligent eyes that managed a lively expression without really having any expression at all. The dean's choice sat on the other side of him. A gray man. All gray—hair, eyebrows, irises, suit, and tie. Only the whites of his eyes and his white shirt for contrast. He could have been a ghost, but he coughed occasionally, so I knew he was breathing.

The dean sat at the judges' table, which formed the bridge linking the long tables facing each other, with McIlheny on one side and Ann on the other. At our table was Ryan, who acted as our secretary but didn't look at all interested in his notepad, and between him and me, Ann.

Ann looked tense, sitting bolt upright, hands folded in her lap, head turned to the dean. I wished she could relax a little. I had the feeling it was not going to be over quickly, and I didn't think she could last long sitting like a cadet. I hoped she'd taken a few extra units of insulin that morning to cover her stress hormones, which had to be sky-high. Her face and neck were bright red.

The tables for the judges, the defense, and the prosecution formed a U, and in the open space at the mouth of this configuration sat a stenographer. Next to her was a chair for witnesses. Ann and McIlheny would testify from where they sat, but the others would be brought in one at a time and would sit on the hot seat.

CHAPTER
48

The dean finished his little speech by saying that we were all here to hear the grievance of Dr. Ann Payson, who contended that she was dismissed from the department of surgery without due cause. He turned to McIlheny's table, where McIlheny looked as if he had swallowed a rotten pickle whole, and asked for the department of surgery's statement outlining the grounds for the dismissal of Dr. Payson.

Herlihy, the lawyer, smiled and said, "If it pleases the dean and panel, I think we can get the facts out most expeditiously if I ask Dr. McIlheny a few questions."

For a moment I felt a whiff of relief. Herlihy had sounded just like a lawyer, and if there's one thing it pays not to sound like in front of a panel of three surgeons, it's got to be a lawyer. I thought I detected a little shifting among the judges' panel. The admiral leaned forward on his elbows, and the corners of his mouth bent down.

The lawyer asked McIlheny to describe the events of October twenty-first.

237

McIlheny cleared his throat and you could tell if you'd heard him speak before that he was trying very hard to speak slowly and deliberately and to sound very much in control.

"I was called to the operating room by stat page by a very upset nurse in the OR suite," said McIlheny.

"Why was she upset?" asked the lawyer.

"She said that Dr. Payson was in the operating room with my patient and was in the process of operating on him."

"The patient was Mr. Samuel Sawyer?"

McIlheny said yes. He said that he rushed up to the OR as fast as he could and when he arrived the place was in a state of turmoil.

"Like Tehran the day after the revolution," McIlheny said.

"By which you mean," asked the lawyer, "nobody seemed to know who was in charge?"

"Well, not exactly. They knew who was in charge. They were just not sure they liked it."

I stood up a little to get the dean's attention. "I wonder if I might be allowed to interrupt for a moment to clarify something?"

The dean nodded.

"I believe we are going to hear from some of the people who were in the OR at the time, and we'll get their state of mind and their reactions directly. I wonder if I might ask Dr. McIlheny to keep his account of the events confined to what was said by himself and by others and to his own reactions and allow the rest of us to draw our own conclusions about the attitudes of the nurses and doctors in the OR."

The dean said he thought that was a reasonable point.

The lawyer looked over at me and smiled. "We'll try to refrain from hearsay evidence," he said and winked at me.

I sat down.

McIlheny said that he had scrubbed and gowned as quickly as he could. He had asked the circulating nurse what was happening, and she had told him that Dr. Payson had stormed into the OR with the patient, unannounced, and that they hardly had time to get the patient on the table and prepped when she had opened his chest and

238

started replacing the aortic valve. McIlheny said he walked over to the surgical field, looked into the wound, and could see that Ann—he called her Dr. Payson—was well into the removal of the valve and had not yet begun to insert the replacement valve.

"I then asked Dr. Payson to step aside so that I might complete the procedure," said McIlheny.

Herlihy's voice became very ominous, and he asked: "And what did Dr. Payson reply?" He was getting a little too theatrical for my taste, but the judges were all leaning forward.

"She refused to allow me to take over the case. She asked me to leave the OR."

The lawyer looked up at the panel, then looked over to Ann, and then back to McIlheny.

"She refused to allow you to operate on your own patient?" asked Herlihy, incredulous, as if he were hearing this for the very first time.

I figured it was time to deflect the dramatic reading a little. I stood up. "May I ask," I said, "what exactly were her words?"

"Well, I'm not sure I can remember them exactly, word for word."

"That's all right," I said, "we'll hear them from Dr. Payson herself later. But as closely as you can remember them."

"Well." McIlheny shifted a little in his chair and shrugged his lab coat off his neck. "She mumbled something about not wanting to stop operating."

"Do you remember her saying that she felt she was at a critical point in the operation and did not feel that she could safely step out at that moment?"

"Well, she might have had some excuse. But I was standing right there; I could see where she was in the procedure. She hadn't even got the valve out."

"But in her judgment, she could not safely turn the patient over. She did say that, did she not? Her reply was that she was concerned for the patient's safety, was it not?"

"She was claiming superior judgment to that of Dr. McIlheny?" asked the lawyer again with that phony incredulity.

239

"Every surgeon has to make critical judgments while operating," I said. "Dr. Payson will explain why she felt she was in a better position and had more information at that moment."

"Well, let's not get into her testimony now," said the lawyer. "Allow us to get Dr. McIlheny's statement."

McIlheny said he had tried repeatedly to take over, but Ann had refused and finally ordered him out of the OR in as humiliating a fashion as she could.

"She was establishing who was in command," he said. "And of course she was playing to her audience."

McIlheny said he was concerned that they not argue over a patient with an aortic valve half out and so had left the OR.

"Well, that must have been a very dramatic moment," said the lawyer. "Have you ever seen anything like it before?"

"Never."

"You must have been stunned."

"I was speechless."

"Why did you leave?"

"Well, as I said, I was most concerned for the patient. It would only invite disaster for me to stand there and argue with her. I was more concerned with the patient's welfare than with my personal feelings right at that moment."

"Did you draw any conclusions about why Dr. Payson would act in such an extraordinary fashion?" asked the lawyer.

I admired the way he asked that question. It didn't call for McIlheny to say why Ann did what she did, which would have had me on my feet again. He was just asking what McIlheny concluded about her motivations.

"Well, at first I thought that Dr. Payson's blood sugar might have fallen to the point where she was irritable. She's an insulin-requiring diabetic, you know."

That had me up again. "Are you telling us that you walked out of the OR thinking that Dr. Payson was hypoglycemic, that her brain was so deprived of sugar that she was acting irrationally? And in the same breath you say you were concerned only for the welfare of the patient?"

"Well, no. I didn't really think . . ."

"Or are you simply trying to let the judges, the panel, know that Dr. Payson is a diabetic?" I said.

"Well, any number of thoughts crossed my mind."

"Evidently," I said.

"Well, since you force me to say it, I'll get into it," said McIlheny. "But it requires some background. Dr. Payson was one of the holdovers on the staff from the prior chief of surgery. As commonly happens, especially when the program has been loosely and permissively run, some people resent the new chief. This happened here, and the resentment was especially strong since the program had been so lax for so long that those people felt especially bitter when I tightened things up. Dr. Payson was something of a ringleader through all this. I can't say I was especially surprised that when the revolt came, she was at the cutting edge, if you'll excuse the pun."

The Hopkins surgeon chuckled. No one else in the room even smiled.

"But you just told us how astonished you were," I said.

"Well, I was stunned by the rashness of her act, by the willfulness of it, and by the public way she chose. But I was not surprised that it was her."

"Then you had warned Dr. Payson before that you were not satisfied with her performance?" I asked.

"I had pointed out some ways she might tighten up her practice. There were a lot of sloppy habits in place. She and her coterie resented the new rigor I tried to establish."

I picked up a manila folder from my table. "I have here Dr. Payson's department file. There is an evaluation signed by you, dated July eighteenth. Her rating was in the first category. There is no mention of reprimand."

McIlheny shifted in his seat, and looked down at his hands. "Well," he said to his hands, "I don't use a doctor's record as a tool for personal retribution. Dr. Payson was technically a decent surgeon. I was talking about her attitude and her ability to function as part of a team."

241

I continued, "Now, you stated that Dr. Payson operated on your patient, Mr. Sawyer. Is that correct?"

"Yes."

"Did you discover that Mr. Sawyer had ball variance and needed his valve replaced?"

"No. You did."

"Then he was my patient. You were acting as a surgical consultant?"

I was being careful not to say I'd referred Sawyer to him because, in fact, I hadn't.

"Yes, of course. I don't see what you are driving at."

"Did I ever ask you to do surgery on the patient?"

"You cooperated in his care in clearing him for surgery while he was on the surgical service."

"But did I ever ask you to do that surgery and did I ever clear him for you to do surgery on him?"

"Well, I don't see the point in these technicalities. You knew he was there. We discussed the surgery in his room together in front of him."

"Did you inquire about the nature of the emergency that precipitated the mad dash to the OR, as you describe it, before you dismissed Dr. Payson from the staff?"

I could feel Ann shift in her chair next to me. It pricked her every time that bald statement reared its head. Dismissed from the staff. But that's what had happened.

"Of course."

"And what did you learn?"

"Well, the patient had a little trouble speaking, and it was felt that he might have suffered a small TIA."

"Is that all you learned?"

"Well, there was some kind of a study done that suggested the valve was deteriorating."

"Some kind of study? An ECHO showed the valve was disintegrating. Are you suggesting now that there was no particular rush to get the patient to the OR? Are you suggesting that Dr. Payson fabricated an emergency so as to set you up for a public humiliation?"

"Well, I was certainly set up. But I don't disagree that there was a certain amount of urgency."

"Do you agree that the proper procedure was done?"

"He needed his valve replaced. As I had planned to do."

"And you agree that the patient did well?"

"Well, there were some postoperative complications, but by that time I was firmly in control of his case."

"Postoperative complications? What complications?"

McIlheny's eyes wandered around the room looking for a neutral corner. "The patient had a postoperative fever." He said this clearing his throat, so it was hardly audible.

I had him repeat this and then repeated it for him. "A fever, you say. A fever." I let that roll around the room again like distant thunder. Now, you have to understand, a post-op fever is so routine most surgeons don't even consider it a complication. I was trying to establish that this was a man who made mountains out of molehills, a man who exaggerated. A man who might take a diplomatic rebuff as a full-scale insurrection. There was some impatient shifting in chairs among the judges.

"Would it be fair to say that the main transgression here, in your eyes, was the fact that Dr. Payson behaved disrespectfully when you attempted to intervene?"

"Intervene? I did not intervene. She intervened!"

"When you attempted to take over the surgery."

"The main transgression, as you call it, was that a patient's life was endangered by Dr. Payson in her attempt to grandstand and to create an explosive scene in which she could order me out of the OR."

"She had her hand on the throttle, and you were trying to wrest control. Who was endangering whom?"

Herlihy jumped up at that. "You are hardly in a position to judge who was endangering the patient!"

McIlheny was half out of his seat. "Cases are handed back and

243

forth regularly in the OR. That was a lame excuse, and everyone from scrub nurse to surgeon knew it. She was ordering me out of the OR. She wanted to show me who was boss and she didn't care who she had to trample on to do it!"

He had me there. It was the point I hoped to bury, but he was too smart to let it go. Cases are handed back and forth all the time, and every surgeon sitting on that tribunal knew it. If Ann had wanted to, she could have stepped aside.

I sat down and let the debris settle, and they called the first witness.

José Cruz looked fat and sweaty sitting in the wooden chair in no-man's-land. He was twisting a scrub mask in his hands as if he were wringing out a wet towel. Herlihy asked him to recount the events, and he gave a squeaky but neutral account, saying that Dr. Payson was up to the point of removing the valve when Dr. McIlheny arrived, that Dr. McIlheny asked to be allowed to take over, that Dr. Payson said she didn't think it was the right time, and that Dr. McIlheny left. He made it sound like a disagreement about who would go to lunch first, and I felt better. The dramatic scene, the open rebellion and public humiliation, was nowhere to be found in José Cruz's picture.

Then Herlihy went to work on him.

"Dr. Cruz," he said in that unctuous, friendly manner that was supposed to warm everyone's heart, lull you half to sleep, and make you speak McIlheny's version of the truth, "You've told us that Dr. McIlheny asked to take over and that Dr. Payson refused. Was this a common occurrence in the ORs at St. George's?"

José shrugged and pursed his lips, not sure what everyone wanted to hear. He smiled and looked at McIlheny, and the smile evaporated and came back with a couple of corners badly bent. "I don't know. I mean, I never seen anything like it myself."

Herlihy grinned. "And you've been around a long time. Did anyone else talk while Dr. McIlheny and Dr. Payson were arguing?"

I stood up. "I'm not sure we have heard Dr. Cruz describe an argument."

244

Herlihy grinned at me. "While they discussed who would do the case?"

"No," said José. "Everyone was very quiet."

"Were you made uncomfortable by this . . . discussion?"

"Who, me? Well, I wasn't doing anything. I was at the head of the patient."

"But I mean, were you made to feel uneasy by this event?"

José now looked as if he understood and said, "Oh, yes, uncomfortable. Yes, it was very uncomfortable." And he smiled like a good boy who had got the answer right.

Herlihy sat down and I popped up. I asked José what he thought of McIlheny. He acted as if he didn't quite understand the question and said Dr. McIlheny had very good credentials and a good reputation. I asked him whether or not he was afraid to bring complications to Dr. McIlheny's attention, whether Dr. McIlheny acted as if anything that went wrong with a patient in the SICU was José's fault and not his own. José shot a sidelong look in McIlheny's direction and looked back to me like a drowning man looking for a life preserver.

Finally he said, "Dr. McIlheny is a very precise man. He demands the best for his patients. Sometimes he gets a little mad when things don't go right."

"'But there's a difference between being demanding and throwing tantrums like a baby.' Those were your words describing McIlheny to me, were they not?"

"Who, me?" said José, shaking his head, convincing himself he had never said any such thing or thought it. "No, not me."

"Would you say that Dr. McIlheny is the kind of man who might overreact to a rebuff? A man who might find insult where none was intended?"

José again acted as if he needed a translation. He had a convenient habit of not understanding when things got sticky. "I think Dr. McIlheny is a man of great pride" was all he finally said.

I gave up and they let him go. I was just as glad as he was to see the door close behind him.

245

CHAPTER
49

They called Mrs. Wilson, the circulating nurse, next. She was a sixtyish, plumpish lady with bifocals and a superficial pleasantness covering a lot of hostility. At least, that's the way I saw her. McIlheny probably saw a proper nurse, the kind he'd like to keep on and promote. Herlihy asked her what happened that day, and she opened slowly enough, but gave Ann both barrels. Dr. McIlheny had been the soul of tact and gentility, and everyone in the OR from pump technician to nurse heard Dr. Payson impudently order him from the room.

"What, specifically, did Dr. Payson say that struck you as impudent?" I asked.

"Well, it wasn't so much what she said as the way she said it. She was like, well, you know, like a little . . ." She started to say "girl" but thought better of it and didn't finish.

"Like a what?" I asked.

"Like she didn't respect Dr. McIlheny."

"How old would you say Dr. Payson is, Mrs. Wilson?"

"I don't know. About thirty."

are you?"

is Dr. McIlheny?"
hat all this . . . I don't know. About sixty, maybe

n OR nurse for how many years?"

Dr. Payson was born?"
ıt that doesn't mean . . ."
ıany women surgeons have you seen at St.

ever have been many."
You can give us a guess."
"She's the only one."
"You don't like Dr. Payson, do you?"
"She's a nice enough person."
"But she shouldn't be a surgeon, is that what you mean?"
"Well, I know she's qualified, she's passed all her tests and every-
thing."
"Is passing tests all it takes to be a surgeon? Would you want her
operating on you or on your children?"
"No."
"Why not?"
"I don't think she has enough self-control."
"Why is that, Mrs. Wilson? Are women likely to fall apart
under pressure? Break down and cry? Is that what you think Dr.
Ann Payson did that day?"
"She acted like a stubborn child. That's the way I saw it."
Herlihy had no more questions for Mrs. Wilson, and they let her
go.
Ann leaned over and whispered, "What a nice lady. Did you
hear? She thought I was just thirty."
She was smiling. The masklike quality her face had had earlier
was gone. She looked more like herself.
"Not a bad job on old Mrs. Wilson, counselor," Ann said.
Next was the scrub nurse, Donna Green. She looked more

247

comfortable than the prior witnesses and she told the story pretty much the way José had. Herlihy asked her if she was shocked by the dispute that day.

"Well, no, not really. I guess you could say I could see it coming for a long time."

Herlihy's eyebrows drifted up; he was working hard to keep his tone curious, a little bored. "Oh, how's that? Had there been friction between Dr. Payson and Dr. McIlheny before?"

"There was friction between Dr. McIlheny and just about everyone before."

"Why was that?"

Donna started to speak, stopped, reworked her answer, and came out with it carefully. "Dr. McIlheny had quite a temper. He had chewed out quite a few people. I'd never seen him get on Dr. Payson, but he wouldn't have won any popularity contests, and he'd come down on enough of the staff that you knew sometime he was going to see some of that coming back at him."

Herlihy played with a paper in front of him on the desk, not looking up. He asked, "Coming back at him? You mean, Dr. Payson was giving him what he had coming?"

"Well, I'm not sure what you mean."

"Oh." Herlihy looked up, with a come-on-now grin. "Of course you do."

"Well, he was awfully high-handed. He'd throw things around the OR, throw scrub nurses out, throw residents out. He—"

"Did he ever throw you out?"

"No. Not me personally."

"So you weren't unhappy to see Dr. Payson stand up to him?"

I stood up, but Donna said, "Not at all," before I could object. I sat back down.

The dean looked at his watch and called it a day.

248

CHAPTER
50

We went to Ryan's office. Ann sat on his stuffed chair, Ryan sat behind his desk with his feet up, and I paced.

"A regular Perry Mason," Ryan said, pouring cups of coffee from a thermos and handing them across the desk. "Abrams, you chose the wrong calling. You made Herlihy look sick."

Ann sipped hers. The high color had drained from her face, and her skin had a sick, granular look.

"You probably ought to eat something," I told her.

"Yeah, I might get hypoglycemic and throw you out of the room."

"That just bought him trouble," said Ryan.

"But he got in the diabetes," said Ann. "I might not be stable and fit."

"That's not what he's charging. They're building the case that there was an insurrection brewing, that you were the ringleader, and that you chose to stage the coup over the gaping chest of Samuel Sawyer."

"They haven't proved shit," said Ryan.

"Oh, yes, they have," said Ann. "They've shown that there was a scene. Abe neutralized them on Mrs. Wilson, but it all fell apart with Donna."

"She was trying to help," said Ryan.

"I know," said Ann. "But she played right into their hands. I was the agent of revenge. I led the coup openly, it was humiliating to McIlheny, and he had a perfect right to keep order in his house and bounce me off the staff."

Ryan swirled the coffee around the cup, then swallowed. "So where do we go from here?"

"Our case is fairly straightforward," I said. "Ann would have yielded up the case if McIlheny hadn't blown up. If he had waited. But she was right in the middle of lifting the valve out, and he flew off the handle. He acted like it was his patient, but in fact Sawyer was *my* patient, and I asked Ann, not him, to do the case. Ann was just doing what Sawyer's attending physician asked her to do. McIlheny was the interloper, not her."

"I don't like it," said Ann, draining her cup. "Hit me again," she said, holding the cup out. "Every one of those guys, those judges, knows I could have asked McIlheny to stay, and he could have scrubbed in and stayed for the valve."

"But is that really true?" asked Ryan, leaning forward. "Wasn't that a moment not to switch horses midstream?"

"No, there aren't really any such moments. Oh, maybe if I had been at the point where I had the new valve in place with all the sutures lined up—but that's not the point. Every one of those judges knows what happens in ORs. They all know if they had walked in they would have expected me to say, 'Wait a minute,' not 'I don't think it's safe for you to take over at this time.'"

"Well, what can we do?" I said. "You've got to say you were preoccupied and he burst in on you."

"It won't wash," said Ann. "I'll try it, but I don't think it'll work."

"It'll work," I said.

"If it doesn't work, brother," Ann said, eyes hard, "then we will do things my way."

CHAPTER
51

Everyone looked a little less tense the next morning. Maybe we were all just a little more tired. Herlihy had on an even more expensive-looking suit this day. It was a blue vested number with which he wore a light blue shirt and a wine-and-maroon-striped tie. He looked like an expensive lawyer and even more confident and relaxed than he had the day before.

He called Sam Sawyer as his first witness.

Sam flicked me a glance, nothing anyone else would pick up.

Herlihy asked him how he was feeling and a few other innocent-sounding questions meant to show what a nice guy Herlihy could be, giving him an opportunity to establish how very much he cared that Sawyer had done well and had fully recovered from surgery. Herlihy's heart was definitely in the right place.

Then he asked Sawyer about the moment he was told Ann would do the surgery. That's the way Herlihy put it, "the moment." I had to hand it to Herlihy, he could be subtle—the moment, as if there had been some dramatic scene when Sam Sawyer

251

found himself confronted with the ultimatum, the moment of the crime.

"Well, it wasn't quite like that," said Sam. "It wasn't so much a moment as a whole sequence of events."

I liked the way he put that. He couldn't have put it better for my side if he'd been coached—which, of course, he had. I wondered how soon Herlihy would pick up on that.

"You have to remember," Sam said, "I had had something pretty scary happen. I couldn't talk for about half an hour that morning. Abe, Dr. Abrams, showed up and told me it was a ministroke from a piece of the valve breaking off. A piece had gone to the speech center in my brain. The valve was beginning to break apart."

"You must have been in a state of shock," said Herlihy. "I would expect it would have been a difficult position to make a decision. How was your state of mind?"

That tactic must work very well on juries when they aren't made up of surgeons. You gave them your permission, sure, but you were so terrified you would have done anything those doctors told you to do. Herlihy was building the usual case—patient as helpless victim, in crisis, confronted with doctors who gave lip service to free choice but railroad the patient into doing what they want him to do for their own self-serving reasons. It was a tactic Herlihy must have used so often he couldn't get out of the habit, like putting top spin on his serve. It usually worked for him. But he was forgetting who was listening.

Sam answered, "Well, no, I was clearheaded, if that's what you mean. Dr. Abrams explained that I needed surgery without delay. And I could believe him after what I'd just experienced."

Herlihy didn't like that so much.

"You must have been pretty stunned by the rapid turn of events," said Herlihy. "I mean, you were admitted by Dr. McIlheny and suddenly you're being rushed off to the OR to be operated upon by a surgeon you'd never met."

"Well, it was exciting," said Sawyer. That was the first time there was any real laughter. The surgeons on the panel actually looked like human beings for a few seconds. The only person not laughing was McIlheny.

"But I had met Dr. Payson before," Sam continued, "and I had been very impressed with her, so I felt quite happy to have her doing the surgery."

"I see," said Herlihy, but he wasn't sure he did see. He decided he didn't like the drift and said he had no more questions.

I stood up and asked Sam if I had ever recommended Dr. McIlheny to him. "Well, no. You recommended Dr. Payson. I had heard of Dr. McIlheny and read about him and I consulted him more or less on my own and wound up asking him to do the surgery."

"On your own?"

"Yes, I suppose so."

"And when I recommended Dr. Payson on that morning, did you suggest that we delay and await the arrival of Dr. McIlheny?"

"Hell, no. What did I know? I hadn't been able to talk for half an hour. Couldn't find my words. A ministroke. From that valve breaking up into little pieces. I was impressed that something had to be done and I put myself in your hands. You said you wanted Dr. Payson to do the surgery and Dr. McIlheny wasn't around. I said, 'Go.'"

Herlihy had been doodling on notepaper during this last exchange, but now he raised his eyes as if he'd just awakened, as if all the testimony up to this point didn't mean a thing, but now he'd heard something that did and he said, "You say Dr. McIlheny wasn't around, so you went with Dr. Payson. If Dr. McIlheny had been around, whom would you have chosen?"

Sam flicked a look at McIlheny, a little apprehensively, I thought. He still liked and respected McIlheny, but he didn't want to sink Ann and me. He drew in a breath. "Well, that's kind of a moot point, since Dr. Payson was there and Dr. McIlheny wasn't."

"I understand," said Herlihy. "But just as a hypothetical. If Dr. McIlheny had been called, and if he had been there."

"Dr. McIlheny had been called," I said.

253

Herlihy didn't move his head in my direction, he just shifted his eyes toward me, keeping his face to Sam, and he said, "That remains to be established." Then to Sam, "If you had both surgeons standing in front of you?"

"Well, I do have both in front of me now," said Sam. "And I can't say I have much basis for choice. They are both excellent surgeons, I'm sure. But how does a layman know? I went with Ben Abrams's advice at the time. I meant no disrespect to Dr. McIlheny. And I certainly am happy with the care I got from Dr. Payson."

I stood up. "I was running the show, as far as you were concerned?"

"Absolutely," said Sam. "And I'm alive to tell the tale, so I guess I'm glad you were."

That got a chuckle from the panel of judges, which Herlihy didn't like at all. He tried to retake control with a quick question, more to cut off the judges' reaction and to redirect their attention than to make any point.

"Now," Herlihy said. "Now, well. You did say your choice had been Dr. McIlheny over Dr. Payson?"

"I wouldn't say I chose anyone over anyone else. I just decided to go with the older, more experienced man. But I was very happy with Dr. Payson, as things evolved."

Herlihy sat down. I said I had no more questions and sat down. Herlihy said he had no more questions. I figured I had a draw: Herlihy had shown that Sam had not lost faith in McIlheny. He had also set up the scene of a patient admitted by McIlheny being whisked off to surgery by Ann. But he hadn't shown Ann twisting anybody's arm. And I had established that I, not Ann, had been the main factor in changing Sam's mind, and that would be crucial to our case. Whatever else they might argue, they weren't going to be able to picture Ann as a hungry surgeon stealing patients behind McIlheny's back.

Sam got to his feet, and I asked one more question as he turned to go.

"Do you remember having any postoperative complications?"

254

"None. I was up and gone, seemed to me, before I could develop a five o'clock shadow."

No complications. I let that sink in. Perhaps McIlheny was prone to overreact.

"Thank you, Mr. Sawyer," I said. And I meant it.

Herlihy watched Sam walk out and looked across to me with something like a smile. I think that was a lawyer's nod. I had put one by him. His eyelids were a little droopy, but I had his attention now. He looked at me from under them. I thought I saw just a little apprehension there.

CHAPTER

52

Before I asked Ann to testify I summarized the facts of the case as they had been presented. There were certain things about which there was no dispute: Ann had done the surgery, and the patient had done very well. The chief of surgery had demanded to be allowed to take over the case, Ann had replied, and he had left the operating room. What was in dispute was whether or not what she had said represented the first salvo of an insurrection. Had Ann been insubordinate, or simply misunderstood?

"Surely, if no one else in that operating room had perceived an insult other than Dr. McIlheny, we would all agree that Dr. McIlheny took offense where none was intended and acted inappropriately to dismiss Dr. Payson from his staff," I said. "But we have heard testimony that some people perceived what Dr. Payson said as a rebuff. I believe each person in that OR heard her words differently, with his or her own bias. Dr. Payson can now say what she actually said and how she meant it."

Ann spoke clearly and steadily. She looked as if she was under a pretty substantial strain, but she looked like a woman who could function under strain.

Ann said that I had asked her to do Sam's surgery under emergency circumstances. She had just finished another open-heart case, so she was in the OR, and her whole team and the pump team were there and ready to go, she was available, and the case was clearly urgent. She emphasized that she evaluated the data I gave her and independently came to the conclusion that Sam's surgery could not safely be delayed.

The touchy part was her rendition of the OR scene with Dr. McIlheny. We had worked on this from a lot of angles.

"Did you attempt to reach Dr. McIlheny to tell him of your intention to operate on Mr. Sawyer?" I asked.

"I called his office. His secretary said he was not in. I explained that I was about to take the patient to surgery, and she said she would page him."

I turned to Herlihy. He was leaning back in his chair with his hands clasped on his belly, with the tolerant smile of a small-town Southern judge who had already made up his mind.

I said, "Is there any question that Dr. Payson made that call?"

Herlihy just shook his head and kept on smiling.

I turned back to Ann and asked, "At what point in the procedure were you when Dr. McIlheny arrived in the OR?"

"I was completing the extirpation of the prosthetic valve," said Ann.

"Did it show signs of damage?"

"It showed significant damage. There was clear ball variance, with adherent clots, presumably the source of the embolic event described earlier."

"At what point in the procedure did you become aware of Dr. McIlheny's presence in the room?"

"I was completing the removal of the prosthetic valve."

"What did he say? And what did you say?"

"Dr. McIlheny said that he wanted me to step aside so that he could take over surgery."

"And you replied?"

"I said I thought this was an inopportune moment."

"And what did he say?"

"Nonsense."

"Nonsense? He said 'Nonsense'?"

"Yes."

"And you said?"

"I said I did not think it would be safe to have him take over right then, and I kept working as I spoke."

"Did he accept this explanation?"

"No. He once again asked me to step aside. I continued working and I believe he left the operating room. At any rate, he was gone next time I had an opportunity to look up."

There was a silence then. Herlihy said nothing. McIlheny sat motionless. The judges didn't move. Nobody moved. Herlihy then started to rise. He worked up his best face of the morning. It was a wonderful look, really. It was a mixture of incredulity, confusion, incomprehension, and near-laughter, as if he had just heard Ann say the earth was flat and she could prove it.

He said, "Dr. McIlheny said that cases can be handed over at almost any point during surgery. Cases are passed back and forth between cooperating surgeons constantly. Are you telling these learned surgeons that you could not have handed Dr. McIlheny control of this case? What was so special about this case?"

Ann drew in her breath. "What I am saying is that in the operating room, with the anesthesiologist, nurses, and pump-room techs listening, I gave what I believed to be a reasonable-sounding explanation for why I should continue operating. I hoped it would sound reasonable to Dr. McIlheny."

Herlihy waited for her to continue, but she said nothing more. The judges waited, brows furrowed. Ann sat quite erect, staring across the room into Herlihy's eyes.

"Am I understanding you to say that you, in fact, did not feel it was unsafe to hand the case over at that moment? That you had no intention of handing the case over no matter what part of the procedure Dr. McIlheny arrived for? You were simply making an

258

excuse? You knew full well that Dr. McIlheny could see that you were lying, but what you said was only for the benefit of the other people in the room?"

Ann answered quickly, "I was trying to avoid a scene. I was trying to complete the procedure."

"The procedure on Dr. McIlheny's patient. The procedure Dr. McIlheny had come to the operating room to do."

Ann said, "I thought the question here was whether or not I was being insubordinate. I am trying to say that I was careful about what I said in the operating room, to avoid being insubordinate. I was trying to be anything but insubordinate. I was trying to leave Dr. McIlheny an avenue by which he could gracefully leave. And, in fact, he did leave."

"Oh, no, Dr. Payson," said Herlihy. "You are confusing insubordination with insolence. You may have been trying to avoid insolence, but you were most definitely intent, by your own admission, on insubordination. And Dr. McIlheny dismissed you from the staff for insubordination."

Ann's face, already full of color, blotched deep red, and her neck blossomed with deep red patches. She looked to me. I couldn't think fast enough. Herlihy was going on.

Herlihy straightened up and put his hands in the pockets of his vest, arched his back, and intoned in his best Churchillian growl, "Insubordination is not a tone of voice. The most serious and damaging insubordination is committed by action, not words. And by refusing to hand over a case belonging to Dr. McIlheny, you were publicly and seriously insubordinate."

Herlihy turned to the judges, just to be sure they were with him on this point. He certainly had their attention. "You paint yourself as a woman who was just trying to avoid a fight. You were no insurrectionist. But if you'd really been so intent on avoiding scenes, why call Dr. McIlheny's office in the first place? If you just wanted to steal the case, why not just do it—sneak off into the OR with the patient and do the case, send your bill, and hope Dr. McIlheny never hears about it? Why lure the man to the OR only to confront him with some excuse, transparent to everyone, so that

259

he has no choice if he cares at all for the patient but to turn and leave?"

"I did not *lure* anyone to the OR."

"But you do steal cases. And you do face them down in the OR, don't you, Dr. Payson?"

"I was asked to do the case by Dr. Abrams and the patient. I did not steal the case."

"Oh, come on, Dr. Payson. Your being asked to do the case is like saying the government of Afghanistan invited those Soviet troops in. Dr. Abrams is your good friend. His 'asking' you is something that happened after Dr. McIlheny dismissed you. And the patient, who today says he was happy to have you, was at the time scared witless and would have taken help from Jack the Ripper if he'd shown up in a white coat. The patient consulted you originally and chose Dr. McIlheny instead. Is that what galled you? Was that Dr. McIlheny's offense, why you seduced him into a scene of such humiliation?"

Ann's eyes glazed over. She wasn't going to cry, but she wasn't capable of saying anything. She was like a fighter out on his feet, staggering around the ring.

I jumped up. "Your construction is a very neat one for your client, but it flies in the face of what we've heard Sam Sawyer tell us. Dr. Payson wasn't involved in convincing the patient to have emergency surgery, I was. He told you that. He didn't even see Dr. Payson until he was taken to the OR. He wasn't stolen; he was delivered."

"Quite so," roared Herlihy. "By her brother in arms and special friend, Dr. Abrams." The way he said 'special' admitted only one meaning.

I let that go.

I continued, "And as for luring Dr. McIlheny to the OR, what would you be saying now if Dr. Payson had not called? That she sneaked the patient off in the dead of the night? If she says nothing, you have her stealing patients. If she renders the standard courtesy, she's a seductress. You've really got her coming and going. Either she's a thief in the night or a revolutionary."

260

"Or both." Herlihy grinned. "I have no questions. I rest my case." He waved a hand, dismissing me, dismissing Ann, dismissing everybody. He thumped down disgustedly into his chair, folded his arms, and turned his face toward the wall, mind made up.

That left me standing there without much to say.

The dean cleared his throat through a silence so thick you could have sliced it with a scalpel and said, "Well, if that is all . . ."

"That's not all from our side," I said.

"We've spent the better part of two days going over this case," said the dean. "I only asked the doctors on the panel for two days of their time." You'd have thought we'd asked the dean to sit through the third showing of Aunt Minnie's slides of her trip to Yosemite.

"There are significant points that still need to be cleared up," I said.

"Well, how much more time will you need?"

"We will need an hour."

The dean looked at his watch and scowled at me. He wanted to put the hearing and all who had to endure it out of their misery. But I didn't like the looks on the faces of the judges after Herlihy had sat down. If the hearing ended at that point, I was sure Ann was cooked.

"It's getting late, and I have appointments this afternoon. Can you gentlemen take another morning for this?"

I didn't see the nods, but they must have made some move because the dean craned his neck in his stiff white collar and said, "All right, then, we'll meet again tomorrow at eight. For one hour."

CHAPTER

53

Ryan, Ann, and I walked to the elevator in silence, like a bunch of pallbearers. I pushed the button. A year passed. The elevator came. We all got on and looked at the numbers light up as the floors passed so we wouldn't have to look at each other.

We got off on Ryan's floor and walked down to his office. I watched him fumble with the keys, trying to steady his hands enough to get them in the lock. Ann took them from him and unlocked the door.

We took our usual places—Ann on the couch, Ryan in his chair behind his desk, and me on the corner of his desk. Ryan reached into his desk drawer, pulled out the bottle of rye and three tumblers, and poured out three drinks. He held one up silently to Ann, who was staring at a spot about two feet above his head. She made no move to take the glass, and Ryan shrugged his shoulders and belted the drink down. Then he held a glass out to me, and I shook him off, and he belted that one down, too. Then he went to work on the drink he'd poured for himself.

"I stand corrected," said Ann suddenly. Ryan didn't fall out of his chair, and I only jumped a foot. We stared at her washed-out, white face. She looked as if she'd been through two periods with the Philadelphia Flyers, and they'd done all the scoring, and she'd done all the bleeding. "Yesterday I said it couldn't look much worse. Today I stand corrected."

"That's what a good lawyer can do," I said.

"He had me convinced you were insubordinate," said Ryan, shaking his head. "Everything we tried to set up, he blew away. Even calling McIlheny to let him know you were taking Sam to the OR—which you didn't even want to do at the time—even that made things worse. It made it look like you intentionally set him up."

"I felt like such a damn fool," said Ann, face red. "I mean, I'm trying to play semantics and sounding more and more guilty. 'Did you intend to give up that case or did you not intend to give up that case?' He had me because he was right. He actually succeeded in bringing out the truth."

"You didn't intend to humiliate McIlheny. That's not the truth."

"The truth is that given the choice between humiliating him and giving Sam to him, I chose to save Sam," said Ann. "But that wasn't clear to the panelists because they don't know I thought I was saving Sam from a guy who couldn't cut his way out of a paper bag. Our grand strategy didn't tell them that. We didn't trust them, so now they all think I was trying to embarrass McIlheny and I got what was coming."

Ryan shook his head and grunted. He looked up, eyes glistening. "Sorry, Ann."

I couldn't look her in the eye.

Ann's crystalline voice came through the fog surrounding my brain. "Hey, guys, don't give up and bury me yet."

Ryan and I looked up from our stupor.

"We played it safe," said Ann. "And it burned us every time: calling McIlheny to tell him I was going to do Sawyer, trying to build the case on how hard I tried to avoid being insubordinate. We tried to play the lawyers' game. And they blew us away." She shrugged. "But Abe got us tomorrow. Tomorrow I'm going to play the game my way. No more trying to show Dr. Ann didn't violate some definition of insubordination," Ann said. "It won't wash with this jury. That's the big mistake we made today. We've got three surgeons sitting at that table, and we tried to play lawyer. You can't beat lawyers at courtroom theatrics. No more lawyers' games."

"What's the game tomorrow?" asked Ryan.

"Tomorrow we go back to basics," Ann said. "Tomorrow we tell the truth."

CHAPTER
54

The judges were all in place behind their table at eight the next morning, with a shared look of distaste on their faces and grim, hard mouths. They looked as happy to be there as a bunch of rabbis at a pork feast. The dean was there, too, with a Styrofoam cup of coffee steaming on the tabletop in front of him. He was trying to look relaxed, or at least less tense than the hanging judges. Herlihy was there in a brown suit, looking at his Rolex watch every few minutes as if this case were over and he had other, more important places to be, bigger battles to win.

Ann and Ryan were in their places. Ann looked as grim as anyone, but her skin looked better, and her pupils were big as saucers, making the whites look startlingly white. She wore a gray suit and a snow-white shirt. She looked both delicate and durable, and not yet ready to stay in her corner with her head down.

McIlheny was the only one missing at five after eight. By then everyone in the room had looked at his watch five times, and we were looking to the dean to call things to order. Then McIlheny arrived in his long white coat, pressed and spotless as ever. He avoided looking in our direction and took his seat exchanging smiles with Herlihy.

The dean looked to me and said, "Dr. Abrams, why don't you proceed?"

I turned to Ann and said, "In your statement yesterday you said that during your confrontation with Dr. McIlheny in the operating room you were trying to remain respectful and you were trying to avoid confrontation. Why, then, did you summon him to the OR? Perhaps you could have avoided any confrontation at all had you simply done the surgery and said nothing."

"I was unsure of what to do," said Ann, in a voice as clear as spring water and as unhurried as advancing glaciers. "On the one hand, I didn't want to do the surgery behind Dr. McIlheny's back. On the other hand, I hoped to avoid a scene in the OR. I guess I hoped if I was straightforward and aboveboard Dr. McIlheny might react by simply coming to the OR, asking me if I had the situation in hand, and then simply leaving."

Herlihy didn't rise from his chair. He just rolled his head in a weary slide, eyes half-closed, and asked, "Why did you expect he wouldn't want to do his own case?"

"I wasn't sure when he would be able to make it to the OR. He might not have made it until I had the valve replaced. Then everyone would have been happy."

I picked up before Herlihy could follow up. "But if Dr. McIlheny had arrived quickly you had no intention of stepping aside?"

"That's correct. I was convinced I ought to do the case from start to finish. I was hopeful that I could do this without provoking a hostile reaction from Dr. McIlheny, but things obviously didn't work out that way."

Herlihy was on his feet, leaning forward with his knuckles on the table. "This is a startling admission. You've just impeached your own testimony. Yesterday you said you intended no insubordination. Now you admit you had no intention of allowing Dr. McIlheny to assume command of his own case. Now it turns out mutiny was in your heart all along, you just preferred to avoid the appearance of mutiny."

266

Ann swung her eyes to meet Herlihy's. Her eyes glinted. "I said I showed no hostility toward Dr. McIlheny. I was respectful. But I knew what I had to do and I was intent upon doing it. That much must be clear by now."

"And why," I asked, "did you intend to do the case yourself?"

"For two reasons: First, because you, as the patient's attending physician, asked me to do the case and not allow Dr. McIlheny to do it. Second, because I was convinced that your reasons for not wanting Dr. McIlheny to do the case were sound."

Ann looked directly at me when she said that. Then she looked across the room at Tom McIlheny with a look like a blow. She looked directly into the eyes of the three surgeon judges, who leaned forward, awake and interested again. She had all their attention now.

"And what convinced you that I was correct to refuse to allow my patient to be operated on by Dr. McIlheny?"

"You had previously shown me a table of Dr. McIlheny's operative statistics that you had compiled. This coincided with other information I already had to raise doubts in my mind about his ability to perform this procedure safely."

"Now just a moment," roared Herlihy, surging out of his chair like a geyser. "Dr. McIlheny is not on trial here. We aren't interested in the basis of Dr. Payson's misconceptions and professional jealousy."

But Herlihy was wrong there. The judges were very interested. It was written all over their faces.

Herlihy was on his feet now, arms pointing, face red, inflamed with the wrath of the righteous cause. "This whole line of inquiry is irrelevant, immaterial, and has to stop right here. You can't win your case by smearing Dr. McIlheny."

I looked to the dean, holding the stack of McIlheinous charts in my hand, ready for distribution. "Dr. Payson's defense rests on two points. The first is that she didn't go looking for this fight, she was forced into a corner and had to come out swinging. And the reason she felt cornered I hold here in my hand. She had a chief who was a demonstrably inadequate surgeon. She couldn't let him handle Sam Sawyer's case if she cared anything about the risk to Sawyer's life."

Herlihy was howling now, a Doberman straining at the leash. "Don't think you're immune from having to answer a charge of slander. There's a record of this. We may be an internal hearing, but we are still not immune from the law."

"I have in my hand a compilation of one hundred cases done by Dr. McIlheny since his arrival here last January. It's broken down by type of case, mortality, morbidity, and infection rate. Dr. Payson was shown this. She did not seek out this information, but once presented with it, she could not ignore it."

Herlihy said, "Let me see that. We are at least owed the courtesy of being allowed to examine it before it's introduced into evidence."

"The rules of evidence don't apply in a hearing like this," I said. "In the interest of time, I would like to distribute this now."

I handed it to Ryan, who then dropped a copy in front of each judge, the dean, Herlihy, and McIlheny before Herlihy could get around the table to stop him. Herlihy was erupting now, trying to wedge his voice between the judges and the papers they were studying. They weren't listening to him.

"Now, if you look at the column for valve replacements, broken down to aortic and mitral, you'll note that Dr. McIlheny has attempted eleven aortic valves since his arrival here. You'll note that six had to be redone; three for infection, three for unseating, with two sudden postoperative deaths. Only three were uncomplicated by reoperation or death."

Herlihy still hadn't picked up his paper to read it. He was still trying to get somebody to agree that it wasn't fair to look at the chart. McIlheny, at his elbow, was staring in a kind of doped stillness at the chart. Herlihy was saying something about how outrageous this all was, how nobody had presented any evidence to certify these numbers as correct.

I described how the numbers were collected and why. I told the story just as it happened. The nurses coming to Ryan. Ryan coming to me. The record room research. Our attempts to get Ann to do something. Her reluctance.

McIlheny listened to all this placidly, watching me with eyes so blank they could have been buttons, and when I finished he said, "Well, now you've had your say. Perhaps I will be allowed to respond."

"You don't have to," said Herlihy. "They've sunk their own boat. It's all out in the open now."

"I'm not sure about the numbers listed here. I haven't had time to compile them, since I've been here only a little over nine months and I've had my hands full trying to whip the department into shape. I wouldn't be surprised if there were something like eleven aortic valves, maybe double that if you count the easy cases I gave away to the house staff. That has to do with my commitment to teaching. I don't keep the easy ones to make my numbers look better. I take the tough ones, and naturally, that skews the numbers."

"Any case you scrubbed in on is listed here," I said. "There were only eleven cases of aortic valve replacement you scrubbed in on. Of those, two died post-op, and six required a second thoracotomy for unseating valves. That's greater than seventy percent morbidity, almost twenty percent mortality."

"As I said," McIlheny replied calmly enough to unnerve me. "I haven't been here that long. I'm sure with time the numbers will look more appealing, as you have more than eleven cases to look at. I've been operating for twenty years. Eleven cases is the wink of an eye."

"Eleven cases of aortic valves," I said. "One hundred cases in all. The morbidity and mortality is more or less the same in other categories."

"I'm not interested in your fabrications," he said. "I can get you my own numbers, and I assure you they'll look a lot better than anything you're likely to come up with." His voice was rising through the octaves, and his words came galloping along, falling all over themselves. "The only thing this whole thing proves is that I was right all along—there was a scheme to get to me. You can see the main plotters right in front of you. Abrams, Ryan, and Payson. Well, I can't touch those two, but they miscalculated when it came to Payson. I could clean house in my own department and I started with her. You can't run a department, tighten up a sloppy organization, without making enemies. I'm sorry in some ways it had to be Dr. Payson. In many ways I thought she had the most potential to be a good surgeon. But I had to clean up the department and step on toes. And evidently it earned me some enemies."

He finished his speech and caught his breath. I turned to Ann, who in contrast to McIlheny looked quite calm. I asked, "Were you surprised by the numbers on this chart? Was your mind poisoned by a bunch of numerical accusations?"

Ann spoke clearly. "The numbers on this chart only confirmed what I had been seeing in the surgical intensive care unit every day. Numbers can't tell the whole story. Numbers can be arranged and rearranged and sometimes come out with different meanings. But the numbers in your case kept adding up to the same thing. No, I wasn't surprised. I would have been surprised if the numbers were any different."

I looked at the judges, who were looking now at Thomas McIlheny with faces that demanded a response.

Before McIlheny could collect himself I asked, as innocently as I could, hoping he'd answer, "Do you remember a patient named Marcocello?"

McIlheny's eyes narrowed. I don't think he recognized the name at first. "Mr. Marcocello," I said. "You did a bypass on him. Or, that is, you started to do a bypass on him, but then the anesthesiologist told you about his blood pressure."

"Oh, certainly, Mr. Marcocello," he said, smiling at being able to recall the patient. Then a guarded look descended over his eyes. He was looking for the curve ball I was surely going to serve up.

"You did not complete that bypass, did you?"

"No."

"Would you mind telling us about that case? Why did you not do the bypass?"

McIlheny shifted in his chair, then smiled a smug satisfied smile. "Because you told me not to."

"Did I?"

"Yes. We had split the sternum when José—Dr. Cruz—told us about the blood pressure, which was very high."

"Two-twenty over one-twenty," I said.

"If you say so. And I terminated the procedure. You came into the operating room and suggested we work him up for pheochromocytoma."

"The memory does do interesting things, doesn't it, Dr. McIlheny?" I said. I let him chew on that for a moment.

"Do you want to think about it? I have the chart here, if you want to refresh your memory."

"I remember that case quite clearly. It happened as I said it."

"There were some omissions of import," I said. "For example, when the anesthesiologist told you of the blood pressure, you did terminate the bypass procedure, but you immediately called for another tray to begin a new one. Is it coming back now?"

"I might have."

"You had, in fact, made an abdominal incision before I even stepped into the operating room, had you not?"

It had grown very quiet in the room. The judges were leaning forward to hear because McIlheny's voice kept dropping. The loudest noises were his breathing, which had become somewhat noisy and fast, and the shifting and rustling of papers by Herlihy, who looked as if he didn't know whether to raise his hand or just bellow. He had no idea what we were talking about or why any of this might be important.

"I have two surgical residents sitting outside I can call in to refresh your memory," I said. "If you'd like."

"No, I remember now. I suppose I had begun an abdominal exploration."

"For what purpose?"

271

"The patient was in hypertensive crisis. There was the clear possibility of a pheochromocytoma, and I had the anesthesiologist cover us with some nitroprusside."

"Cover you?"

"Yes. There was a study from the Cleveland clinic showing you can safely operate on pheos with nitroprusside alone."

"You had a similar case, if I remember. When you were at Mass General."

McIlheny's shoulders relaxed just a bit. He couldn't see my angle now, but that triumph from the General was a port in the storm.

"Well, yes. We wrote it up, actually. I was chief resident. We were doing a splenectomy, and the case was very similar to this one. The patient's blood pressure went through the roof, and I explored the left adrenal under nitroprusside coverage and successfully removed a seven-centimeter pheo. I reported that in *JAMA*. It was the first pheo removed under nitroprusside. The Cleveland clinic had the first series, almost twenty years later."

"There were some important points of difference between these two cases, wouldn't you agree?" I asked. "In the first you were only inches away from the adrenal gland to begin with and already in the abdomen. You rather stumbled on it. In this case you stopped chest surgery and went to open the abdomen. Is that the way you ordinarily pursue the diagnosis of pheo, Dr. McIlheny? Exploratory laparotomy for the diagnosis of pheochromocytoma?"

I said that not so much to McIlheny as to the judges. They were a group of knitted brows and hard looks. They looked like a group of tax auditors picking up a scent.

"Of course, if you have the luxury of time. But this was an emergency situation."

"Oh, yes. You said. Hypertensive crisis. Tell me, had you looked in the patient's fundi? You know that diagnosis—"

McIlheny cut me off; he was straining to smooth things over the way a man combs hair over a bald spot. "You weren't there. I had no time for fundoscopy. I had a man with a blood pressure going

272

out of control. I had an emergency situation that you just walked into. I was in a better position to judge."

"This sounds strangely familiar. You had been in the operating room with the case from the beginning, and that gave you a certain advantage in judging the situation? Isn't that your argument? Isn't that the same argument you dismissed out of hand when Ann Payson used it?"

"Those were entirely different circumstances!"

"Yes, you were about to explore a man's adrenals for a blood pressure of two-twenty over one-twenty, and only after I was dragged into the OR by a very distraught surgical resident and confronted you did you relent. I'd say they were different circumstances."

Herlihy lurched to his feet. He looked as if he'd taken a few left jabs and maybe a hook to the temple and his eyes were out of focus, but he could see me now. "Just a minute, Dr. Abrams. Do you have your boards in thoracic surgery?"

It was a favorite courtroom tactic. Impugn the qualifications of your adversary. It worked for juries, who didn't have a prayer knowing who was really right when the technical terms started flying, just as Herlihy had no idea who was scoring points, me or McIlheny, except from what he could see in McIlheny's posture—the chest caving in, the shoulders hunched, the voice trembling.

I looked sidelong at the judges and caught their looks. "No," I said, "I do not."

Herlihy was trying to find his rhythm. "Well, are you board-certified in general surgery?"

There was some impatient rustling among the judges.

"No," I said patiently.

"Then how do you presume to tell Dr. McIlheny how to handle a surgical emergency in his own operating room?"

"I would not expect you to know that answer," I said. "I would expect Dr. McIlheny to know it. I am sure the members of the panel know."

Herlihy looked from me to McIlheny, who was trying to hoist up

273

a smile. He thought it was a smile, but it was as false as a paper flower and twice as dead.

After a silence that couldn't have lasted more than a week the dean drew in a breath, and everyone looked over to him. He pulled the starched white collar away from his neck and brought his voice up from somewhere forgotten and said, "If that is all, I think we better call a close to this hearing. The panel members have been very generous in giving their time for an extra morning. Thank you."

With that he adjourned the meeting as if he were presiding over nothing more important than a Cub Scout den meeting.

CHAPTER
55

It was over. There was nothing more to do. Ann, Ryan, and I sat at our side of the table and watched Herlihy stand up and shake McIlheny's hand. Herlihy was smiling, talking. McIlheny was not. They left together, neither looking back in our direction.

I looked over to the judges' table and was surprised to find it empty. We were alone in the room.

One of the odd things about dealing with something as consuming as a trial is that sudden feeling of emptiness when it's all over, and you realize that life around you has been going on, that everything else hasn't stopped as your life has.

"Well," said Ryan, "what now?"

"I'll take you home," I told Ann.

"Home?" she said, detached as an echo. She shook herself from wherever she had been, far away, to the present time and place and said, "Don't you have patients today?"

"That's right," I said. "I was supposed to call in. I promised Mrs. Bromley."

I left Ann with Ryan and walked toward the door. Ann pulled

out a handkerchief and dabbed her eyes. Ryan put his hand on her shoulder. It was the first time I'd ever seen Ryan look his age.

"How did it go?" asked Mrs. Bromley. "Just tell me—up or down? You will give me a full report later."

"I'd bet even money," I said. "After this morning. Up until this morning, I would have given better odds to a three-legged horse in the Kentucky Derby."

"Oh, dear."

Mrs. Bromley told me she had held off my patients as long as she could and said I absolutely had to come in and see the teeming masses in my waiting room, or Western civilization was apt to collapse before evening, and it wouldn't matter who won the trial.

Then she said, "How's Dr. Payson?"

"Oh, you know. Grace under fire."

Mrs. Bromley said, "Tell Ann," and she stopped, gathering her words. "Tell her she did the right thing. And when you do the right thing everything turns out for the best no matter how it looks at the time."

"I'll tell her."

I walked back to Ann and Ryan. She was smiling now. Her eyes were red but dry, and she looked better.

"I'll give you a lift home," I told her. "But you were right, I've got to get back to the office."

"Poor baby," said Ann. "You don't have to. I can walk."

"Oh, don't be like that," I said. "You can at least let me give you a ride."

We drove home. Ann was silent, looking out her window. I told her what Mrs. Bromley had said. Ann didn't say anything. I wasn't sure she had heard. She seemed to be absorbed, looking out at the ornate gates in front of the French consulate.

Several blocks later she said, "That's so much like Mrs. Bromley."

She wouldn't let me out of the car even to walk her to her door. We sat in the car in front of her house.

"Go save lives," she said.

"What will you do today?" I asked.

"Haven't thought yet," she said, smiling. She looked restless, and the smile looked pasted on. "You go ahead."

"Come on back to the office with me," I said. "Don't be alone. See a few patients. Mrs. Bromley says we've got plenty to spare."

"I am not currently allowed to engage in patient care," she said with that same smile hanging around her lips, getting no help from her eyes.

"You can see patients anywhere but St. George's," I said. "Don't confuse that place with the real world."

"That place is my world," she said. Now her face wasn't playing games anymore.

"Ann, you heard what Mrs. Bromley said about doing the right thing."

"Oh, yes. Everything will turn out right."

"Trust Mrs. Bromley."

"Oh, yes."

"Come to the office. You can have tea with her."

"No, I'm going for a walk by the river."

"The river?"

"Clear my head," she said. "Don't worry. I'm just going to walk by it. I won't throw myself in."

"That a promise?"

"Absolutely." She laughed. "I'm safe until the verdict comes out."

CHAPTER
56

I saw ten patients that afternoon, setting a new office record and greatly relieving Mrs. Bromley, who had pretty much exhausted her repertoire of excuses while I had been sequestered with Ryan and Ann.

After the last patient had left, I walked back to the lab and started loading the centrifuge with the Vacutainer tubes of blood I had drawn on the patients. Mrs. Bromley slipped in and watched me balance the machine.

"You'll be in bright and early in the morning?" she asked. "We're quite booked to the hilt again tomorrow."

"Yes, I'm a doctor again. I've had my fill of playing lawyer."

"Now I want my report," she said. "Minute by minute. Leave nothing out. You are being debriefed."

I told it just as it happened, leaving nothing out except the part about Ann crying after it was all over. I worked as I talked, unloading spun-down bloods and pouring off the sera into the little plastic vials we sent off to the lab. Mrs. Bromley attached the labels and popped the vials into the plastic bag as she listened. I finished recounting as we were finishing the samples.

Mrs. Bromley said, "It must be very difficult for her."

"Oh, it's difficult all right," I said.

"When do they hand down the verdict?"

"I don't know. Could be a day. Could be a week."

"My word, it's the way they do executions. They never tell you exactly when. You're just hauled up before the wall."

"An invidious comparison, Mrs. Bromley."

"I do hope she'll be all right."

We closed up the office, and Mrs. Bromley carried all the plastic lab bags out to the insulated aluminum box on the office door and locked them in for the lab courier who would come after we'd gone.

"Tell Ann we shall all have a glass of Dom Pérignon when the verdict's in."

Ann looked refreshed and better. She was wearing a plum-colored knit shirt and green slacks. She kissed my cheek at the door and handed me a drink.

We sat on her couch, alone together, drinking Irish Mist. Her blood sugar had been running high for the days of the trial, but now that it was all over, it had come crashing down along with her stress-hormone levels, and she had to eat and drink to keep up with her insulin.

"What do I do if they back McIlheny?" Ann asked me. Her eyes held mine tightly

"If they can't take a joke," I said.

She shook her head, and her eyes started to well up and look red.

"Seriously," I said. "We'll move to some small town in New England, buy a Volvo . . ."

"And every state licensing board and every malpractice policy application asks whether you've ever been dismissed from a hospital staff."

"So you say yes and explain."

"And never practice again," said Ann heavily. "And do what? Be a housewife? Sell real estate?"

"You think every doc ever dismissed from a staff is denied a license?"

"I don't know," said Ann. "I just know I don't want to find out what happens. What do they do, put you on probation in your new place? Somebody has to operate with you every case, to watch you, to be sure you're safe? God, how humiliating."

"I goaded you into this," I said.

"Oh, don't do that," said Ann. "Don't play the role of the guy who made me do the right thing."

"You would have done what you did if I hadn't brought you all the cases McIlheny botched? If I hadn't begged you about Sam?"

"Is that what's been behind your devotion?" said Ann, really angry. "Guilt? The thought that you got me into all this, despite all I've said?" She smiled and kissed my head. "I'm sorry," she said. "I'm just not myself right now."

I asked her what she felt like doing.

"Don't know. Nothing, really."

"Dinner?"

"Where?"

"Adams-Morgan? La Plaza?"

"Not tonight."

"Georgetown?"

"No."

"Drink? Holihan's?"

"Don't think so. No."

"Ride? We could go out MacArthur Boulevard to Great Falls."

"No. Let's just go to bed," she said.

We slept in her big bed with the green down comforter and held each other at first, but later she rolled away. I awoke a few times during the night. She wasn't in bed. I walked to the bedroom door and stood so I could see her, sitting cross-legged on the couch, reading a thick book—a textbook, I thought, from the size of it. I went back to bed wondering why she would be doing that.

280

CHAPTER
57

The next morning, I left Ann drinking coffee in her kitchen, pretending to read the paper. She was staring at the front page, but her eyes weren't moving. Her mind was elsewhere, with the judges. I said good-bye, she looked up and smiled, and I drove to the office.

The first patient of the morning was Lydell Brown. He walked into my office without crutches, limp barely noticeable, and shook my hand. His wife was with him and she was smiling.

"You look great," I told him, and I wasn't lying. He looked like an almost-normal human being. It was wonderful to see, of course, but also vaguely disconcerting—Thomas McIlheny had got him to this day. That valve I listened to, clicking away happily, functioning normally, was working just fine, and it had been sewn in place by Thomas McIlheny's hand. Looking at the happy faces of Lydell Brown and his wife, I felt a wave of premonition sweep over me about the verdict on Ann.

McIlheny had done a lot of right things in his career. Every surgeon on that tribunal had had disasters. But you add up the pluses as well as the minuses. To clear Ann they'd have to, in effect, call McIlheny a net minus.

"We'll be going back to see Dr. McIlheny this afternoon," said Mrs. Brown. "You think he'll want to continue seeing Lydell? Or will you be the doctor?"

I told her I would see Lydell monthly, and he could see Dr. McIlheny as the need arose. The need would never arise, of course, no matter what happened to the valve. Lydell would never need the ministrations of Dr. McIlheny again, as far as I was concerned. He might need the services of Dr. Payson, wherever she might be, or of some other thoracic surgeon, but he would not be needing Dr. McIlheny. I said, "We'll see how things go."

I watched them walk out together, leaned back in my desk chair, and propped my feet up on the desk. I had promised myself to not call Ryan about what he might have heard. Ryan couldn't know anything about what the judges were thinking. But he might have heard if the verdict was in. I wasn't sure Ann would tell me if it was bad. She might just pack up and slip out of town. She might just walk into the Potomac River.

I looked at my schedule—four more patients. I was ten minutes late for the next one. He could wait. I knew Ryan's office number by heart and punched it in. He answered on the first ring.

"Heard anything?" he asked when he heard my voice.

"No. I was calling to ask you."

"That's bad," said Ryan.

My mouth turned dry. I had trouble forming my word, "Why?"

"The verdict should be out today."

"How do you know?"

"I hear things. If my sources are right, it should be out this morning. This afternoon at the latest."

"What do your sources tell you about the verdict?"

"Nothing."

"How do they do it? Reconvene the court, or what?"

"No," said Ryan. I didn't like how gloomy his voice sounded. "Just a phone call, usually. Ann hasn't called you?"

"No."

"That doesn't sound good."

I hung up and buzzed Mrs. Bromley on the intercom. "Has Dr. Payson called this morning?"

"You've got to be kidding," said Mrs. Bromley. "You know I've been on pins and needles. I'd put her right through. Shall I call her?"

"No," I said. "How many more patients?"

"Mr. Larson is here. Three more after him. None arrived."

"I'll see Mr. Larson. Call the others and reschedule them."

"For when?"

"Tomorrow, next week, whenever. Just clear out the rest of the morning."

I have no idea what Mr. Larson wanted and heard not a single word he said, but I spent twenty foggy minutes with him and then ran out the door with Mrs. Bromley's voice at my back: "Call me if you hear anything."

Driving to Ann's place was a mighty effort of self-restraint, trying to keep my foot from mashing the accelerator, trying to do less than sixty down Foxhall Road, a bona fide speed trap any day of the week.

Ann answered the door with nothing but surprise in her face.

"I thought you had patients this morning," she said. Then suddenly, "Have you heard something?"

"No, I thought you might have."

"No, I haven't heard anything. Why did you come back? You heard something."

"No, I called Ryan. He said he thought we might hear today."

"I was just going to call Ryan. It's amazing. I never thought to ask him how they do it."

"Telephone call. I just asked him."

"And he thought today?"

"What does Ryan know?"

"You wouldn't be here if you didn't think it was coming this morning. You know what it is. You'd have told me if it was good."

283

Ann suddenly looked as sad as I'd ever seen her look. Sadder than when her favorite fish turned belly up unexpectedly one morning. Not quite as bad as she looked in the SICU standing next to the little kid with the mediastinitis after McIlheny did his patent ductus, but very sad.

"I don't know anything. I just heard it might come today."

"I'm not sure I want you here when it comes."

"Oh, well. I can leave."

"What did you think? That I'd throw myself out a third-story window?"

"Your house only has two floors above ground."

"Second, then."

"No, I just wanted to be here."

"I'd have called you either way."

"Let's have a drink."

"No," said Ann. "I don't want to do it that way. Besides, if Ryan's wrong, and the call doesn't come until Friday, we could be very drunk by then."

"That might not be such a bad idea."

We sat around looking at, not reading, newspapers, not saying much. Around eleven o'clock the phone rang. Ann looked at me and it rang again. She stood up very quickly and walked into the kitchen to take it there. I could see her full-length through the doorway from my seat on the couch in the living room. I could just hear her.

She said, "Hello?"

Then, "Ryan! You dirtball. Abe's over here. . . . No, we haven't heard a thing. You've got us all worked up. . . . Yes, of course. 'Bye."

She looked at me from her spot near the phone after she'd slammed down the receiver. "This is going to be quite a morning," she said. "If the phone rings much more, I may die of a heart attack before I ever hear from the dean."

The phone rang again. She looked at me, alarmed.

"Probably just Ryan again, or Mrs. Bromley," I said.

She picked it up. Her face changed.

"Yes?" she said. She turned away from me and looked down, but I could still hear her. She was waiting for someone to come on the line after his secretary had got Ann on the line. I knew who that someone had to be.

"Yes," she said, with no expression at all. "Yes, I understand." Still no expression. Just a dead, dull voice. I stood up, but she waved me off.

"I see," she said. "Yes, I understand. Yes, I think I will do that. Thank you."

She hung up. There was not a trace of fear or happiness or anger or elation or sadness on her face as she turned. It was expressionless, reeling from a blow, simply stunned before the reaction.

"Was that the dean?" I asked.

"Yes," she answered, deadpan.

And then, all at once, she bounded across the room, jumping up and catching me with her legs and arms and kissing me.

And she cried.

Tears of joy.

"Full reinstatement," she said, laughing.

"Full reinstatement?" I echoed.

"No probation. No nothing. Just back on staff. Effective immediately."

"What?"

"The dean thinks, however, that I might be well advised to take a vacation for a couple of weeks. 'Just to let things cool off.' Besides, he said, I must be somewhat fatigued from all the strain. Can you believe that ass?"

It took a while to sink in past the buzzing in my head. I had to sit down. I was reacting to Ann now. She was filling the room. She was dancing around it, swirling, a ballerina, kicking and pirouetting.

"You won?" I said.

"We won, good doctor," she said, swirling over and kissing me again, then orbiting away from me. "*We.* The dean said, 'The panel found in your favor and has recommended acting favorably on my petition.'"

"But what did they say? I mean, do we get a report, or what?"

"The man's telling me I'm back on staff. I'm not asking for a notarized letter by certified mail. It was definitely the dean. I'd know that voice anywhere."

"We've got to call Ryan. And Mrs. Bromley," I said.

Ryan's victory howl could be heard coming across the kitchen phone from my post in the living room. Ann held the phone away from her and pointed it at me.

"Right is might!" I could hear him crow when we finally stopped hooting.

We arranged to meet for drinks at Mai's restaurant that evening. Ryan wanted to invite the nurses Maureen and Kathy. "After all, they did the chart with us."

"I think I'd rather go by and thank them myself," said Ann. She didn't want the celebration taking on the cast of a victory party.

I called Mrs. Bromley with the news and invited her to the restaurant.

"I never had any doubt," she said. "Well, maybe just for a moment."

I called Ryan back. "Don't we get a letter of explanation or anything?" I asked.

"All Ann's entitled to is a letter saying she's been reinstated, as far as I know." He had calmed down a little, but his voice was still hoarse. "But Ipse res loquitur—the fact speaks for itself. They bought our defense."

"And what was our defense?" I asked.

"That McIlheny's a for-shit surgeon."

Ann was listening from her other phone. "We don't know what they concluded," she cut in. "They might have thought that I got led down the garden path by you two scoundrels, led into thinking ill of a good surgeon, Tom McIlheny, but that I shouldn't be kicked out for that."

286

"I'd really like to have been a fly on the wall in that jury room," I said.

Ryan and Ann both agreed with that.

We all hung up.

Ann said, "I need some air."

We walked out of her house into the bright morning sun, down the steep steps to Reservoir Road, and turned toward the hospital. Ann drew the collar of her tweed jacket up against the chill November wind. Her face looked pink and healthier than it had for weeks.

"I feel alive," she said. "The way those guys on death row must feel when the governor grants them a new trial. I can walk over to the hospital now and walk right on to the SICU or into the OR suite and look everyone in the eye and smile. I feel like I could do twenty cases today and never break for coffee."

"You could look people in the eye before the verdict," I said. "You're no better a surgeon today than you were yesterday. And if those birds had come down on McIlheny's side, you would have been no worse a surgeon."

"But today everyone knows it. I'm endorsed."

I shook my head. It didn't seem worth pushing the point. I said, "What does McIlheny do now? Shake your hand and say it was a great fight?"

"He's not drafting a letter of resignation. I can tell you that."

"But how does he act? What does he do when he sees you in the OR suite?"

"He'll nod hello. He'll behave himself. He'll survive."

"And so will you," I said. "You'd have survived even if the verdict went the other way. Watching you lately, I think you'd survive anything save thermonuclear war. Maybe even that."

"It's been nice to have friends."

"Clumsy and bumbling though they may be."

"You were certainly neither of those. I thought you were very fine friends to have. Eloquent even, on occasion."

"Eloquent occasionally. Wrong often."

287

"In the end, it doesn't matter how often you are wrong," Ann said. "What matters is how often you are right."

"That's a funny thing for a surgeon to say."

"Well, I wasn't speaking as a surgeon. Of course, it matters how often a surgeon goes wrong. I was speaking apart from surgery."

"You mean there's life after surgery?"

"There is life apart from surgery," said Ann. "You're right about that. Losing hospital privileges shouldn't be the end of the world."

I laughed. "Come off it. As soon as you get back in the OR, you're going to send down roots. We'll need a bulldozer to dig you out of there."

"No," Ann said, unsmiling.

We had followed the road past Glover Park and were in sight of the hospital. It loomed ahead of us now, up on its hill looking massive and medieval in the gray sky.

"Then you wouldn't have jumped out the window if things had gone the wrong way?"

"I like to think not. I've decided I've become too narrow, too single-minded. I'm expanding my portfolio."

"And how are you going to do that?"

"I am going to start spending more nights with you."

"A pretty thought," I said, and meant it, even if she didn't.

EPILOGUE

Ann embarked on the vacation the dean ordered. She invited me to come with her, but I was still catching up at the office with weeks of all those sore throats and sick thyroids and I'm-sure-I've-got-hypoglycemias that Mrs. Bromley had put off. So Ann flew down to Club Med, Cancún, without me. She went alone, she said. I have a fertile enough imagination to picture her not remaining alone for long down there among all the tanned instructors, but she came back two days early, skin brown, but bored. She just couldn't stay away. Snorkeling, great food, sun and wine hazes, and males with gold chains and perfect bodies just could not compare with the operating room for fun.

"Oh, you're really expanding your portfolio," I told her. "You've discovered life on the outside of the operating room—all five days of it."

"But that's a start." She laughed. "Oh, I'm much more balanced now."

"And you never once thought about Bard-Parker scalpels or anything surgical."

"Well, maybe at night," she said, "when they set out all those stainless-steel knives and utensils for dinner. But it was just too indolent most of the time. And I missed you."

"You missed the operating theater is what you missed."

"And you." She smiled. "I told you, I am much broader now. My life is more balanced."

More balance meant she showed up at my door four nights a week, and I got invited over to her place the other nights.

After some weeks of this she said, "I'm spending too much time driving out here. Why don't you move in some things and spare me the trip?"

I did that, and after several more weeks she said, "This place is small for us. Maybe we should buy a Volvo and move to the suburbs."

"I've already got a house in the suburbs."

"Too small. We need more room."

I was too happy to press her about what all this might mean. Ann never liked to discuss implications. It was enough for me that we spent together whatever time she had.

Since her reinstatement she had become even more sought out at the hospital—no one had to worry about offending McIlheny. She had been stamped as a protected item. She had so little spare time I worried I might be crowding her.

"But I like being with you," she said. "By five o'clock, I miss you."

"You're just infatuated. You were dazzled by my courtroom theatrics."

"I was touched," she said. "You were a rock. You were tough enough to be a surgeon."

I'd heard that line before.

Not long after, we started looking at Volvos. Ann wanted a station wagon.

"That's really doing the whole route," I said. "All we'd need is the dog and three kids."

"Well," she said. "I don't know about the dog. But you know

how kids happen, and we've been doing what it takes often enough lately."

Ann had been the one to take precautions against parenthood. I wasn't sure what I was being told, but I decided not to ask. She always told me when she was ready to tell me things.

Of course, I was high as the proverbial kite on the Fourth of July.

We continued to speculate about the contents of the judges' report to the dean, but as Ryan had predicted, we never came any closer than speculation. Whatever it said, McIlheny stayed on as chief of surgery for another year. He still operated most days, but then they made him a provost of the university and gave him some post in the medical school and he had less and less time for surgery and more and more committee meetings to attend.

I never heard Ann say a bad word about McIlheny. She never brought up his name, but she didn't change the subject or leave the table, either, if someone else did. And one morning I noticed a thick blue textbook on a shelf in her living room. It caught my attention because it looked like a textbook and she kept her textbooks at her office in the hospital. It was the same book I had seen her reading that night after the trial when we still hadn't heard the verdict. I drew it out and dusted it off. It was Thomas McIlheny's textbook of surgery.

I propped myself up on the green couch and read the chapter he wrote himself on wound healing.

Ann was on the phone, talking to someone at the hospital about a patient who needed his chest opened with some urgency.

She hung up and told me I could drive her to the hospital. She had some surgery to do.

Then she noticed what I was reading.

"What do you think?" she asked.

We got up to go to the hospital.

"It's a very nice chapter," I said.

"Oh, it's the best textbook of surgery there is," she said.

We ran down the steps to my car and roared off toward the hospital, down Reservoir Road, past the German embassy and Glover Park.

"It's nice," she said, "to be going in to do surgery."

I pulled into the emergency room entrance and stopped the car, and she leaned over and kissed me and said, "Don't wait up. I'll just crawl in next to you if I get home before morning."

She straightened up and waved. Behind her rose the massive walls of St. George's, parted by glass doors and buzzing with activity, uniformed staff moving in and out, ambulances parked in front of the emergency room entrance, unloading patients on stretchers, people in wheelchairs, the usual swirl and bedlam surrounding a busy institution.

I watched her run down the driveway and disappear into the hospital.